For Jane

PROLOGUE

In the fabled, glittering world that was St Petersburg before the First World War there lived, in an ice-blue palace overlooking the river Neva, a family on whom the gods seemed to have lavished their gifts with an almost comical abundance.

Count and Countess Grazinsky possessed – in addition to the eighty-roomed palace on the Admiralty Quay with its Tintorettos and Titians, its Scythian gold under glass in the library, its ballroom illuminated by a hundred Bohemian chandeliers – an estate in the Crimea, another on the Don and a hunting lodge in Poland which the countess, who was not of an enquiring turn of mind, had never even seen. The count, who was aide de camp to the tsar, also owned a paper mill in Finland, a coal mine in the Urals and an oil refinery in Sarkahan. His wife, a reluctant lady of the bedchamber to the tsarina, whom she detested, could count among her jewels the diamond and sapphire pendant which Potemkin had designed for Catherine the

1

Great and had inherited, in her own right, shares in the Trans-Siberian Railway and a block of offices in Kiev. The countess's dresses were made in Paris, her shoes in London and though she *could* presumably have put on her own stockings, she had never in her life been called upon to do so.

But the real treasure of the Grazinsky household with its winter garden rampant with hibiscus and passion flowers, its liveried footmen and scurrying maids, was a tiny, dark-haired, bird-thin little girl, their daughter, Anna. On this button-sized countess, with her dusky, duckling-feather hair, her look of being about to devour life in all its glory like a ravenous fledgling, her adoring father showered the diminutives which come so readily to Russian lips: 'Little Soul', of course, '*Doushenka*', loveliest of endearments but, more often, 'Little Candle' or 'Little Star', paying tribute to a strange, incandescent quality in this child who so totally lacked her mother's blonde, voluptuous beauty and her father's traditional good looks.

Like most members of the St Petersburg nobility, the Grazinskys were cultured, cosmopolitan and multilingual. The count and countess spoke French to each other. Russian was for servants, children and the act of love; English and German they used only when it was unavoidable. By the time she was five years old, Anna had had three governesses: Madame Leblanc, who combined the face of a Notre Dame gargoyle with a most beautiful speaking voice, Fräulein Schneider, a devout and placid Lutheran from Hamburg – and Miss Winifred Pinfold from Putney, London.

It was the last of these, a gaunt and angular spinster with whose nose one could have cut cheese, that Anna inexplicably chose to worship, enduring at the hands of the Englishwoman not only the cold baths and scrubbings with Pears soap and the wrenching open of the sealed bedroom windows, but that ultimate martyrdom, the afternoon walk.

'Very bracing,' Miss Pinfold would comment, steering the tiny, fur-trussed countess, rigid in her three layers of cashmere, her padded capok lining, her sable coat and felt *valenki* along the icy quays and gigantic squares of the city which Peter the Great had chosen to raise from the salt marshes and swamp-infested islands of the Gulf of Finland in the worst climate in the world.

'Not at all like the dear Thames,' Miss Pinfold would remark, watching a party of Lapps encamped on the solid white wastes of the Neva – and receiving, on the scimitar of her crimsoned nose, a shower of snow from an overhanging caryatid.

It was during these Siberian walks that Anna would meet other children who shared her exalted martyrdom: pint-sized princelings, diminutive countesses, muffled bankers' daughters clinging like clumps of moss to the granite boulders of their English governesses. Her adored Cousin Sergei, for example, three years older than Anna, his face between the earmuffs of his *shapka*, pale with impending frostbite and outraged manhood as he trudged behind his intrepid Miss King along the interminable, blood-red facade of the Winter Palace; or the blue-eyed, dimpled Kira Satayev, hardly bigger than the ermine muff in which she tried to warm her puff-ball of a nose.

Yet it was during those arctic afternoon excursions that Anna, piecing together the few remarks that the wind-buffeted Miss Pinfold allowed herself, became possessed of a country of little, sun-lit fields and parks that were for ever green. A patchwork country, flower-filled and gentle, in which a smiling queen stood on street corners bestowing roses which miraculously grew on pins upon a grateful populace . . . A country without winter or anarchists whose name was England.

Anna grew and nothing was too good for her. When she was seven her father gave her, on her nameday, a white and golden boat with a tasselled crimson canopy in which four liveried oarsmen rowed her on picnics to the islands. Each Christmas, one of Fabergé's crafts-men fashioned for her an exquisite beast so small that she could palm it in her muff: a springing leopard of lapis lazuli, a jade gazelle with shining ruby eyes . . . To draw her sledge through the park of Grazbaya, their estate on the Don, the count conjured up two silken-haired Siberian yaks.

'You spoil her,' said Miss Pinfold, worrying, to the count.

'I may spoil her,' the tall, blond-bearded count would reply, 'but is she spoilt?'

And the strange thing was that Anna wasn't. The little girl, wobbling on a pile of cushions on the fully-extended piano stool to practise her *études*, gyrating obediently with her Cousin Sergei to the beat of a polonaise at dancing class or reciting *Les Malheurs de Sophy* to Mademoiselle Leblanc, showed no sign whatsoever of selfishness or pride. It was as though her mother's cosseting, the fussing of the servants, her father's limitless adoration, produced in her only a kind of surprised humility. Miss Pinfold, watching her charge hawk-eyed, had to admit herself defeated. If ever there was such a thing as natural goodness it existed in this child.

When Anna was eight years old, the gods tilted their cornucopia over the Grazinskys once again and, in the spring of 1907, the countess gave birth to a son whom they christened Peter. The baby was enchanting: blue-eyed, blond as butter, firmly and delectably fat. The count and countess, who had longed for a son, were ecstatic, friends and relations flocked to congratulate and Old Niannka, the ferocious Georgian wet nurse with her leather pouch containing the mummified index finger of St Nino, filled the house with her mumbling jubilation.

Seeing this, Miss Pinfold moved closer to the Countess Anna, as did Mademoiselle Leblanc and Fräulein Schneider and the phalanx of tutors and grooms and servants who surrounded the little girl, waiting for jealousy and tantrums.

They waited in vain. To Anna, the baby was a miracle of which she never tired. She had to be plucked from his side at bedtime and would be found in her nightdress at dawn, kneeling beside the cot and telling the baby long and complex stories to which he listened eagerly, his head pressed against the wooden bars.

Love begets love. As he grew, Petya followed his sister everywhere and his cry of: 'Wait for me, Annoushka!' in lisping Russian, entreating English or fragmented French echoed through the birch forests round Grazbaya, along the tamarisk-fringed beaches of the Crimea, through the rich, dark rooms of the palace in Petersburg. And Anna *did* wait for him. She was to do so always.

As she moved from the idyll of her childhood into adolescence, Anna, still looking like an incandescent fledgling, only ran harder at the glory that was life. She fell in love with her handsome Cousin Sergei, with the blind piano tuner who tended the count's Bechsteins, with Chaliapin who came to sing gypsy songs in his dark and smoky voice after the opera. She became a Tolstoyan, renouncing meat, finery and the anticipated pleasures of the flesh. It was a bad time for the Grazinskys, as Anna hobbled round the palace in brown worsted and a pair of unspeakable birch bark shoes said to have been made by the Great Man himself in the year before he died. Fortunately, before her feet sustained permanent damage, Diaghilev brought his dancers back from their triumphant tour of Europe and Anna, who for years had hung out of her parents' blue and silver box at the Maryinsky *being* the doomed Swan Queen or mad Giselle, now took up with passion the cause of the rogue impresario and the dazzling, modern ballets which stuffy St Petersburg had condemned out of hand.

'Oh, how beautiful it is! *Chto za krassota!*' was Anna's cry during these years: of the glistening dome of St Isaacs soaring above the mist, of a Raphael Madonna in the Hermitage, a cobweb, a remarkably improper négligé in a shop window on the Nevsky Prospekt.

There seemed no reason why this fabled life should ever end. In 1913 Russia was prosperous and busy with the celebrations to mark three hundred years of Romanov rule. In the spring of that year, Anna, holding down her wriggling brother Petya, attended a Thanksgiving Service in Kazan Cathedral in the presence of the tsar and tsarina, the pretty grand duchesses and the frail little tsarevitch, miraculously recovered from a serious illness. A few days later, she helped her mother dress for the great costume ball in the *Salles de la Noblesse* . . .

'It'll be your turn soon, *mylenka*,' said the pleasure-loving countess as she fastened the famous Grazinsky emeralds over her old *boyar* dress of wine-dark velvet and set the sun-shaped, golden *kokoshnik* on her abundant hair. For, of course, she had planned Anna's debut for years, knew to the last hair of their well-born heads the young men she would permit to address, and ultimately espouse, her daughter.

There was just one more year of picnics in the birch forests round Grazbaya, of skating parties and theatricals with Sergei, now in his last year at the exclusive *Corps des Pages*, and pretty, frivolous Kira and a host of friends.

And then the archduke with the face of an ill-tempered bullfrog and the charming wife who had so dearly and unaccountably loved him, were assassinated at Sarajevo. To the Russians, accustomed to losing tsars and grand dukes time and time again in this way, it seemed just another in an endless succession of political murders. But this time the glittering toy that was the talk of war slipped from the hands of the politicians . . . and a world ended.

Overnight, meek, devoted Fräulein Schneider became 'the enemy' and had to be escorted to the Warsaw Station under guard. Mademoiselle Leblanc, who had aged parents, also left to return to France. Miss Pinfold stayed.

'God keep you safe, my Little Star,' the count whispered to Anna, holding her close. 'Look after your mother and your brother,' – and rode away down the Nevsky, looking unutterably splendid in his uniform of the Chevalier Guards. Three months later, he lay dead in a swamp-infested Prussian forest, and the flame that had burned in his daughter since her birth, flickered and died.

*

They carried on. The countess, aged by ten years, organized soup kitchens and equipped a fleet of ambulances at her own expense. Although Anna was too young to enrol officially as a nurse, she spent each day at the Georguievski Hospital, rolling bandages and making dressings. As the shortages and hardship grew worse, Miss Pinfold increasingly took over the housekeeping, organizing the queues for bread, the foraging for fuel.

When the revolution came and the Bolsheviks seized power from the moderates, the Grazinskys fared badly. They had been too close to the court and, with no one to advise them, they tarried too long in the two rooms of their looted palace which the authorities allowed them to use. It was only when Petya was stoned on the way home from school that they finally acted and joined the stream of refugees fleeing northwards through Finland, east to Vladivostock, south to the Black Sea and Turkey.

The Grazinskys went south. They had entrusted the bulk of their jewels to Niannka, the count's Georgian wet nurse, who was sent ahead with a king's ransom in pearls, emeralds and rubies hidden in her shabby luggage.

The old woman never arrived at their rendezvous. They waited as long as they dared, unable to believe that she had betrayed them, but were eventually compelled to travel wearily on. In March 1919 they reached Sebastapol, where Miss Pinfold retired behind a palm tree to fish, from the pocket of her green chilprufe knickers, their last remaining jewel, the Orlov diamond, and persuaded the captain of a Greek trawler to take them to Constantinople.

A month later, they reached England.

'You *cannot* be a housemaid, Anna,' said Miss Pinfold firmly. 'It is quite absurd. It is out of the question.'

'Yes I can. Pinny. I *must*. It is the only job they had vacant at the registry office. Mersham is a very beautiful house, the lady told me, and it is in the *country* so it will be healthy, with fresh air!'

Anna's long-lashed Byzantine eyes glowed with fervour, her expressive narrow hands sketched a gesture indicative of the Great Outdoors. Miss Pinfold put down the countess's last pair of silk stockings, which she had been mending, and pushed her pince-nez on to her forehead.

'Look, dear, English households are not free and easy like Russian ones. There's a great hierarchy below stairs: upper servants, lower servants, everything just so. And they can be very cruel to an outsider.'

'Pinny, I *cannot* remain here, living on your hospitality. It is monstrous!' Anna's 'r's were beginning to roll badly, always a sign of deep emotion. 'Of course I

11

would *rather* be a taxi driver like Prince Sokharin or Colonel Terek. Or a doorman at the Ritz like Uncle Kolya. *Much* rather. But I don't think they will let women—'

'No, I don't think they will either, dear,' said Pinny hastily, trying to divert Anna from one of her recurrent grievances. 'And as for living on my hospitality, I've never heard such nonsense. If you and your mother stayed here all your lives, I could never repay the kindness your family has shown to me.'

They were sitting in the tiny parlour of the mews house in Paddington which Pinny, by sending home her savings, had managed to purchase for her old age. Pinny's sister, who had been living there, had tactfully gone to stay with a cousin. Even so, the little house was undeniably crowded.

'It's all right for Mama, Pinny. She isn't well and she's no longer young. But I . . . Pinny, I need to work.'

'Yes, Anna, I understand that. But *not* as a housemaid. There must be something else.'

But in the summer of 1919 there wasn't. Soldiers back from the war, women discharged from the armament factories and work on the land – all haunted the employment agencies seeking jobs. For a young girl, untrained and foreign, the chances were bleak indeed.

The Grazinskys had arrived in London two months earlier. Virtually penniless, their first thought had been for Petya. The countess had caught typhus in the squalor of the transit camp in Constantinople and was too weak to do anything but rest, so it was Anna who had braved the Grand Duchess Xenia at court and extracted from that old friend of her father's the offer of Petya's school fees at a famous and liberal public school in Yorkshire.

But for herself Anna would take nothing.

'You will see, Pinny, it will be all right. Already I have found a most *beautiful* book in your sister's room. It is called *The Domestic Servant's Compendium* by Selina Strickland, and it has two thousand and three pages and in it I shall find out *everything*!'

Miss Pinfold tried to smile. Anna had always been in possession of 'a most beautiful book': a volume of Lermontov from her father's library, a Dickens novel read during the white nights of summer when she should have been asleep.

'If you would just be patient, Anna. If you would only wait.'

Anna came over and knelt by Pinny's chair. 'For what, Pinny?' she said gently. 'For a millionaire to ride past on a dapple-grey horse and marry me? For a crock of gold?'

Pinny sighed and her sister's budgerigar took advantage of the ensuing silence to inform anyone who cared to listen that his name was Dickie.

'All the same, you cannot be a housemaid,' said Pinny, returning to the attack. 'Your mother would never permit it.'

'I shan't tell my mother. I'll say I've been invited down as a guest. The job is not permanent; they're taking on extra staff to get the house ready for the new earl. I shall be back before Petya comes home from school. Mama won't notice, you know how she is nowadays.'

Pinny nodded, her face sombre. The last year had aged and confused the countess, who now spent her days at the Russian Club playing bezique and exchanging devastating ideas on how to economize with the other emigrés. Her latest suggestion, attributed to Sergei's mother, the Princess Chirkovsky – that they should buy chocolate cake from Fullers in *bulk* because of the discount, had given Anna and Pinny a sleepless night the week before.

'You'd better keep it from Petya too,' said Pinny drily, 'or he'll leave school at once and become an errand boy. He only agreed to go because he expects to support you in luxury the day he passes his school certificate.'

'No, I certainly shan't tell Petya,' said Anna, her face tender as always when she spoke of her brother. Then she cast a sidelong look at her governess, seeing if she could press her advantage still further. 'I think perhaps it would be sensible for me to cut off my hair. Short hair will be easier under a cap and Kira writes that it is becoming *very* chic.'

Kira, whose family had fled to Paris, now had a job as a beautician and Anna regarded her as the ultimate arbiter in matters of taste.

But Pinny had had enough. The comical dusky down that had covered Anna's head in early childhood had become a waist-length mantle, its rich darkness shot through like watered silk with chestnut, indigo and bronze.

'Over my dead body will you cut your hair,' said Winifred Pinfold.

Three days later, carrying a borrowed cardboard suitcase, Anna trudged up the famous avenue of double limes towards the west facade of Mersham, still hidden from her by a fold of the gentle Wiltshire hills.

The day was hot and the suitcase heavy, containing as it did not only Anna's meagre stock of clothing, but all two thousand and three pages of Selina Strickland's *Domestic Compendium*. What the Torah was to the dispersed and homesick Jews and the Koran to the followers of Mahommet, Mrs Strickland's three-volume tome, which clocked in at three and a half kilos, was to Anna, setting off on her new career in service.

'"Blacking for grates may be prepared by mixing asphaltum with linseed oil and turpentine,"' she quoted now, and looked with pleasure at the rolling parkland, the freshly sheared sheep cropping the grass, the ancient oaks making pools of foliage in the rich meadows. Even the slight air of neglect, the Queen Anne's lace frothing the once-trim verges, the ivy tumbling from the gatehouse wall, only made the environs of Mersham more beautiful.

'I shall curtsy to the butler,' decided Anna, picking up an earthworm which had set off on a suicidal path across the dryness of the gravel. 'And the housekeeper. Definitely I shall curtsy to the housekeeper!'

She put down her case for a moment and watched a peacock flutter by, displaying his slightly *passé* tail to her. There was no doubt about it, she was growing *very* nervous.

'"The tops of old cotton stockings boiled in a mixture of new milk and hartshorn powder make excellent plate rags,"' repeated Anna, who had found that quotations from The Source helped to quieten the butterflies in her stomach. '"A housemaid should never wear creaking boots and—"' She broke off. '*Chort!*'

The avenue had been curving steadily to the right. Suddenly Anna had come upon the house as abruptly as William Kent, the genius who had landscaped the grounds, intended her to do.

Mersham was honey-coloured, graceful, light. There was a central block, pillared and porticoed like a golden temple plucked from some halcyon landscape and set down in a hollow of the Wiltshire hills. Wide steps ran up from either side to the great front door, their balustrades flanked by urns and calm-faced phoenixes. From this centre, two low wings, exquisite and identical, stretched north and south, their long windows giving out on to a terrace upon which fountains played. Built for James Frayne, the first Earl of Westerholme, by some favourite of the gods with that innate sense of balance which characterized the Palladian age, it exuded welcome and an incorrigible sense of rightness. Anna, who had gazed unmoved on Rastrelli's gigantic, ornate palaces, looked on, marvelled and smiled.

The next moment, blending with the pale stone, the blond sweep of gravel, a huge, lion-coloured dog tore down the steps and bounded towards her, barking ferociously. An English mastiff with a black dewlap like sea coal and bloodshot eyes, defending his master's hearth.

'Oh, hush,' said Anna, standing her ground and speaking softly in her native tongue. 'Calm yourself. Surely you can see that I am not a burglar?'

Her voice, the strange, low words with their caressing rhythms, got through to the dog, who braked suddenly and while continuing to growl at one end, set up with the other a faintly placating movement of the tail. Slowly, Anna put up a hand to his muzzle and began to scratch that spot behind the ear where large dogs keep their souls.

For a while, Anna scratched on and Baskerville, shaking off five years of loneliness while his master was at war, moaned with pleasure. When she picked up her case again he followed her, butting her skirt lovingly with his great head. Only when he saw that, unbelievably, she had turned from the front of the house and was making her way through the archway which led towards the servants' quarters did he stop with a howl of disbelief. There were places where, as the earl's dog, it was simply not possible for him to go.

'Snob!' said Anna, leaving him with regret.

She crossed the grassy courtyard and found a flight of stairs which seemed to lead towards the kitchens.

'I shall curtsy to *everybody*,' decided Anna and went bravely forward to meet her fate.

*

17

Waiting to see what the London agency had sent them this time, were Mrs Bassenthwaite, the housekeeper, and the butler, Mr Proom.

Their expectations were low. They had already received, from the same source, an under-gardener who had fallen dead drunk into a cucumber frame on his first day and a footman who had attempted to hand a dish of mutton cutlets gloveless and from the *right*. But then, having to recruit servants from an agency was in every way against the traditions of Mersham and just another unpleasantness resulting from the dreadful war.

Mrs Bassenthwaite was a frail, white-haired woman who should have retired years earlier but had stayed on to oblige the Dowager Countess of Westerholme, shattered by the loss, within a year, of her adored husband and handsome eldest son. She was a relic of the splendid days of Mersham when a bevy of stillroom maids and laundry maids, of sewing girls and house-maids had scurried at her lightest command. Once she had prowled the great rooms, eagle-eyed for a speck of dust or an unplumped cushion, and had conducted inquests and vendettas from which ashen-faced under-lings fled weeping to their attics.

But now she was old. The austerities of war, the informality of modern life, its motors and telephones confused her and she increasingly left the running of Mersham to the butler, Mr Proom.

There could have been nobody more worthy. Cyril Proom was in his fifties, a bald, egg-headed man, whose blue eyes behind gold spectacles gazed at the world with a formidable intelligence. An avid reader of encyclopaedias and other improving literature, Proom, like Mrs Bassenthwaite, had once been head of a great line of perfectly drilled retainers: under-butlers and footmen, lamp boys and odd men, stretching away from him in increasing obsequiousness and unimportance.

To this epoch, the war had put an end. More than most great houses, Mersham had given its life's blood to the Kaiser's war. Upstairs it had taken Lord George, the heir, who fell at Ypres six months after his father, the sixth earl, succumbed to a second heart attack. Below stairs it had drained away almost every able-bodied man and few of those who left were destined to return. A groom had fallen on the Somme, an under-gardener was drowned at Jutland; the hall boy, who had lied about his age, was blown up at Verdun a week before his eighteenth birthday. And if the men left to fight, the maids left to work in munitions factories, in offices or on the land; creating, as they departed, a greater and greater burden for the servants who remained.

It was during those years that Proom, sacrificing the status it had taken a lifetime to acquire, had rolled up his sleeves and worked side by side with the meanest of his minions. With the rigid protocol of the servants' hall abandoned, Jean Park, the soft-spoken head kitchen maid, was even persuaded to step into the shoes of Signor Manotti, the chef, who returned to his native land.

Lady Westerholme had done what she could to ease the pressure on her depleted staff. She shut up the main body of the house and retired, with the earl's ancient uncle, Mr Sebastien Frayne, into the east wing, trying, amid a welter of planchettes and ouija boards, to follow her loved ones into their twilit world. Inevitably, her sadness and seclusion and the economies forced upon her by two lots of death duties took their toll. The shrouded rooms through which only the dog, Baskerville, now roamed, grew dusty and cold; in the once trim flowerbeds, wild grasses waved their blond and feathery heads; the proud peacocks of the topiary grew bedraggled for want of trimming. Finally, when the armistice was declared the servants, waiting anxiously for news, wondered if Mersham was to share the fate of so many great houses and go up for sale.

For the whole hope of the House of Frayne now lay in the one surviving son, Lord George's younger brother, Rupert. The new earl had spent four years in the Royal Flying Corps, his life so perilous that even his mother had not dared to hope he might be spared. But though his plane had been shot down, though he'd been gravely wounded, Rupert was alive. He was about to be discharged from hospital. He was coming home.

But for good? Or only long enough to put his home on the market? Remembering the quiet, unassuming boy, so different from his handsome, careless elder brother, the servants could only wonder and wait. Nor were there any clues in the instructions the new earl had sent from his hospital bed: the state rooms were to be re-opened, everything that needed to be done to bring Mersham up to its old standard was to be done – but any new staff engaged to make this possible were to be strictly temporary.

And hence this agency, which up to now had spelled nothing but disaster and whose latest offering had just been admitted to the housekeeper's room.

Anna had curtsied – she had curtsied *deeply* – and now stood before them with clasped hands, awaiting her fate. And as they studied her, the butler and the house-keeper sighed.

Neither of them would have found it easy to describe the characteristics of a housemaid, but they knew instinctively that despite her navy coat and skirt, her high-necked blouse and drab straw boater, this girl had none of them.

The entry on 'Slavonic Painting' in his *Encyclopaedia of World Art* gave Proom a head start on Mrs Bassenthwaite in accounting for the long, lustrous eyes framed in thick lashes the colour of sunflower seeds. It threw light, too, on the suppliant pose of the narrow, supple hands, the air of having simultaneously swallowed the sins of the world and a lighted candle which emanated from the new housemaid. The saints on Russian icons, Proom knew, were apt to carry on like that. There, however, the religious motif suddenly came to an end. Though Anna had attempted to skewer her hair back into a demure knot, glossy tendrils had escaped from behind her strangulated ears, and the bridge of her attenuated Tartar nose was disconcert-ingly dusted with freckles.

'Your name is Anna Grazinsky?' said Proom, consult-ing the paper from the agency, already aware that he was playing for time. 'And you are of Russian nationality?'

'Yes, sir.'

'I see here that you have no previous experience of housework?'

'No, sir. But I will work very hard and I will *learn*.'

Proom sighed and glanced at Mrs Bassenthwaite, who lightly shook her head. For the girl's accent, with its rolling 'r's and lilting intensity, quite failed to dis-guise her educated voice, as did the shabby coat and skirt the grace of her movements. 'Inexperienced' was bad; 'foreign' was worse . . . but a *lady*! This time the agency had gone too far.

'I'm afraid you may not understand how hard you would be expected to work,' said Proom, still somehow hoping to avoid his fate. 'We are taking on temporary staff for a period of intense cleaning and refurbishment prior to the Earl of Westerholme's return. During this time no formal training would be given and you would be expected to make yourself useful anywhere: in the kitchens, the scullery, even outside.'

'Like a tweeny?' enquired Anna, gazing at him out of rapt, tea-coloured eyes.

Tweenies had loomed large in the English novels of her childhood: romantic, oppressed figures second only to Charles Kingsley's little chimney sweeps in their power to evoke sympathy and tears.

Proom and Mrs Bassenthwaite exchanged glances. Neither of them felt equal to explaining to Anna that nothing so mundane as a tweeny would have been allowed within miles of Mersham, these unfortunates being confined to lowly middle class households employing only a housemaid and cook.

'I really think, Miss Grazinsky,' said Mrs Bassenthwaite, leaning forward, 'that you would do better to look for a different type of employment. A governess, perhaps.'

Anna stood before them, silent. It was not, however, a passive silence, reminding Proom inexorably of a puppy he had once owned *not* asking to be taken for a walk.

'I *promise* I will work,' she said at last. 'Most truly, I promise it.'

The butler and the housekeeper held steady. If there is one thing dreaded by all experienced servants, it is a gently bred female below stairs.

Then Anna Grazinsky produced a single word. 'Please?' she said.

Mrs Bassenthwaite looked at Proom. After all, they were only taking her on as a temporary measure. She nodded and Proom said, 'Very well. You can have a month's trial. Your salary will be twelve and six a week – and *there's no need to keep on curtsying!*'

Anna had been dreading a dormitory shared with the other maids, who would despise her, but she was assigned a little attic tucked under the domes and urns and chimneys that adorned Mersham's roof. It was stuffy with its one small window, but scrupulously clean, containing an iron bed, a chair, a deal chest and a rag rug on the floor. A brown print dress and two starched aprons were laid out for her with a white mob cap. Another uniform, black alpaca with a frilled muslin cap and apron, hung behind the door for 'best'.

She unpacked quickly, placing Selina Strickland's tome on the chair beside her bed. It was very hot there, under the roof, and very silent. And suddenly, standing in the tiny room, sealed off from the body of the house and the world she had once known, she felt so bereft and homesick that tears sprang to her eyes.

Her father's well-remembered voice came to save her. 'When you're sad, my Little Star, go out of doors. It's always better underneath the open sky.'

She went over to the window and pushed it open. If she pulled herself up she could actually climb out on to the ledge that ran behind the balustrade . . .

A moment later she was standing there, one arm round a stone warrior and sure enough it was better, it was *good* . . . Mersham's roof, glistening in the sunshine, was a gay and insouciant world of its own with its copper domes and weathervanes, its sculptured knights at arms. The view was breathtaking. Facing her was the long avenue of limes, the gatehouse, and beyond it, the village with its simple, grey church and trim houses clustered round the green. On her left were the walled gardens and the topiary; to her right, if she craned round her warrior, she saw a landscape out of an Italian dream: a blue lake curving away behind the house, a grassy hill topped by a white temple, an obelisk floating above the trees . . . She could smell freshly cut grass, the blossoming limes, and hear, in the distance, a woman calling her chickens home.

One could be happy here, thought Anna. Standing there, on the roof of his house, watching the honey-hued stone change colour with the shadows of the clouds that raced across the high, light sky, Anna Grazinsky addressed the absent and unknown earl: 'I will make your house very beautiful for you,' she said. 'I promise. You will see!'

Then she climbed down into the room again and picked up the brown print dress. It was too large, but the apron would hold it in and she'd manage for now. The cap, though, was a problem. Whatever angle she put it on, it slipped drunkenly, if not unbecomingly, over her ears.

'But first I will go and wash,' decided Anna, for she had grown hot and grubby on the roof – and set off to search for a bathroom.

It was a foolish and unproductive quest. Since the lovely Palladian house had first been built, in 1712, there had been many improvements – but a bathroom on the servants' floor was not among them.

Rather more servants than usual had gathered in the kitchen for a quick cup of tea as Anna came down-stairs. For, of course, news of her foreignness, her general unsuitability, her gaffe about the 'tweeny' had spread like wildfire.

The kitchen at Mersham was a huge room, high and vaulted, with a battleship of a range, a gigantic dresser full of gleaming pewter and a wooden table large enough to be a skating rink. Standing at the table now, crumbling pastry like small rain through her deft, plump fingers was Mrs Park, the soft-voiced, gentle countrywoman who had replaced the chef, Signor Manotti. The fact that she was in every way unworthy to succeed so great a man was Mrs Park's continuing despair. No cook ever had less 'temperament' or more skill. Unable to pronounce the French names of the exquisite dishes she sent to the table, she could never believe she was not failing some culinary god with her Englishness, her simplicity, her female sex. Everyone loved her and she had made of the kitchen, so often a forbidden and defended fortress, the place where all the servants came to rest.

Beside Mrs Park sat the first footman, James, one of the few who had returned from the war. Under the guidance of Mr Proom, whom he revered, James had worked himself up from lamp boy to his present eminence. He had started life as a scrawny and undersized Cockney and it was Proom, seeing in the lad a real potential for self-development, who had brought him a pamphlet describing the body building exercises used by the current Mr Universe. Since then, James had never looked back. The state of his gastrocnemius and the progress of his wondrously swelling biceps were matters of continuing concern to the maids, who bore with fortitude the knowledge that the real glories – the fanning of his trapezius across the small of his back, the powerful arch of his gluteus maximus – were, for reasons of propriety, forever lost to them.

Next to James sat Louise, the head housemaid, and below her the under housemaids, buxom giggly Peggy and her younger sister, Pearl. Sid, the second footman, sat opposite James; Florence, the ancient scullery maid, was filling her bucket by the boiler; Win, the simple-minded kitchen girl, who nevertheless understood Mrs Park's lightest word, was perched humbly on a stool near the foot of the table. Even Proom, who habitually took tea in the housekeeper's room, had lingered by the dresser, busy with a list.

Light footsteps were heard coming down the flagged stone corridor and Anna appeared in the doorway.

Louise, the pert and acerbacious head housemaid, was the first to see her.

'Here comes the tweeny!' she said.

'Now, Louise,' admonished Mrs Park gently, removing her hands from the bowl of pastry. 'Come in, dear, and have a cup of tea.'

But Louise's gibe had in any case fallen flat. Anna smiled with pleasure, came forward to curtsy to Mrs Park and, when bidden to sit down, slipped into a place below Win's at the very foot of the table.

The servants exchanged glances. Whatever was

going to be wrong with the new housemaid, it had to be admitted that it wasn't snobbery or 'side'.

The next day Anna began to work. It was work such as she had not known existed: not as a nursing orderly in the hospital in Petersburg, not as a waitress in the transit camp in Constantinople. Between the myriad, airless, servants' attics tucked away beneath the balustrades and statuary, and the kitchens, pantries and cellars that ran like catacombs under the body of the house, was a world which knew nothing of either. Here were the great state rooms: the famous library, the picture gallery with its Van Dykes and Titians, the gold salon and the music room. It was to the spring cleaning of these rooms, shuttered and shrouded during the war, that Proom had assigned Anna.

'She won't last two days,' prophesied Louise, the ginger-haired and prickly head housemaid. 'You'll see, she'll be back in London with her tail between her legs before the week's out.'

But Peggy and her sister Pearl were not so sure. There'd been a sort of *look* about the Russian girl.

That first day Anna rose at five-thirty, snatched a piece of bread and jam in the servants' hall, and by six, clutching her housemaid's bag, had followed Louise, Peggy and James, loaded with buckets, stepladders, druggets and mops, up to the library.

Mersham's library was world-famous. Its satin-wood bookcases, its pedestal desk and writing tables were made by Chippendale and reckoned to be among his finest work. A sumptuous, moss green Aubusson

28

stretched to the windows of the south terrace and on the barrel-vaulted ceiling the Muses swam most decoratively.

'Oh, what a beautiful room!' exclaimed Anna, only to get a sour look from Louise, who was briskly pouring soda into a bucket.

''ere,' she said, handing Anna a bucket of steaming water and a cloth. 'Start on this geyser, and don't drip!'

'This geyser' was Milton in old age, whose marble head stared thoughtfully and somewhat snottily from a plinth between the windows. When Anna had rinsed and dried the poet's face, the convolutions of his wig and the lacework on his Puritan collar, she moved on to Hercules resting – unnecessarily, she could not help feeling – on a slain lion, whose mane had most horribly collected the dust. Next came the overmantel depicting scenes from Dante's *Inferno*.

'Better wring your cloth out harder for those,' advised Louise, looking with disgust at the tortured souls writhing in agony across the chimney breast. 'Bloomin' sculpture! I hate the stuff.'

By this time Anna's water was black with dirt and she had carefully to carry her bucket down a long parquet corridor, across the blue john and jasper tiles of the great hall, down the service stairs and through a green baize door into the scullery, where Florence, the ancient scullery maid, filled it for her. She was crossing the great hall again when Fate dealt her an undeserved blow in the form of Baskerville, who discovered her with yelps of joy in a place where it was meet and right for her to be and padded passionately after her into the library. Nor could James, trying to dismantle the chandeliers, or Louise, cleaning the windows, prevent him from lying like a felled ox across the foot of the stepladder on which Anna, scrubbing Plato, Aristotle and Cicero in a niche above the door, was precariously perched with her bucket.

By lunchtime Anna's back ached and her hands were sore but she persevered and she kept – though this was harder – silence. It was late in the afternoon when, moving a silver photograph frame to safety, she found herself staring for the first time at the long-awaited earl.

The photograph, taken just before the war, showed two young men standing on the steps that led to the front door. The older was strikingly handsome, with regular features, springing hair and an easy smile. The other, who was hardly more than a boy, was slighter, darker, and had turned half-away as though looking at a landscape visible to him alone.

'That's Lord George, the one that was killed,' said Peggy, coming over to her and pointing at the older of the two. 'He was a smasher! My, didn't we half have to run for it when he was around!'

'And this is the new earl?' queried Anna. 'His brother?'

'That's right. Mr Rupert, he was then. He's much quieter like. Got a lovely smile, though.'

'He looks nice, I think,' said Anna, and stepping

over the recumbent Baskerville, she began to scrub the cold and protuberent stomach of Frederick the Great.

Just before it was time to pack up for the day, Proom appeared silently as was his wont and took Louise aside.

'Any difficulties?' he asked, inclining his head towards Anna.

'Not really,' said Louise reluctantly. 'Except for that bloomin' dog following her about. She's as green as they come, of course, but she hasn't stopped, not for a minute. And I must say you don't have to tell her anything twice.'

On her third day at Mersham Anna discovered that the butler, so regal and authoritative in the servants' hall, suffered from a bedridden and deeply eccentric mother, with whom he shared a cottage in the stable block.

She had spent the whole day in the windowless scullery washing, piece by exquisite piece, the Meissen dinner service – a tedious and frighteningly responsible job with which Proom, rather to his own surprise, had entrusted her. Seeing her pallor and the circles under her eyes, Mrs Park had sent her out to the kitchen garden with a message for the under-gardener, Ted.

Anna was on her way back, crossing the stableyard, when a pot of geraniums flew out of an upstairs window and crashed into pieces at her feet. Retrieving the remains of the shattered pot and going to investigate, she found herself in the presence of an ancient, ferocious old lady, glaring like a beleagured ferret at the end of a high brass bed. Mrs Proom's appendix, removed ten years earlier in Maidens Over Cottage Hospital, stood in a glass jar on a shelf above her head; various lumps under the counterpane indicated that she had taken the silver to bed in case of burglars.

'Who are you? Why are you dressed like that? Where's Cyril? I want my tea!' she began.

'I am dressed like this because I am a housemaid. Mr Proom is decanting the claret and I will bring your tea if you permit,' Anna replied.

Half an hour later, Mr Proom, noticing with foreboding the remains of the broken flowerpot and wearily ascending the stairs to his mother's room, found her absorbed in a game of dominoes in which the new housemaid was cheating, with an expertise which shattered him, so as to let the old lady win.

'I'm sorry I'm late, Mother,' he began.

'Sh! Be quiet, Cyril. I don't need you,' said the old woman, gleefully moving a piece.

Only when Anna had left did she ask again: 'Who is that girl? Why is she dressed like that?'

'I've told you, she's the new housemaid, Mother.'

'Rubbish,' said Mrs Proom.

Anna had been at Mersham for a week before she met the first member of the family. In addition to the Lady Mary Westerholme, the dowager countess, Mersham had for many years provided sanctuary for the present earl's great uncle, the Honourable Mr Sebastien

32

Frayne. It being Louise's day off, Anna was instructed to take up his tea.

'You want to listen outside the door,' Peggy told Anna. 'There'll be some music playing on the gramophone. If it's that stuff all loud an' wailin' an' women shrieking and that, you want to watch out. Specially there's one called the Libby's Tott or something. If he's playing that you want to keep the tray between you an' him and put it down and run quick. But if it's that stuff that sounds like church, you know, all on the level and not much tune, then it's all right to have a chat. Not that it's ever more than a bit of a pinch and a grope, but you not being used to it like . . .'

It was with a sinking heart that Anna, pausing outside Mr Sebastien's door, heard the unmistakable sound of the *Liebestod* issuing forth. Isolde was dying and she was dying hard. Bravely, Anna knocked and entered.

Mr Sebastien Frayne was reclining on a large Chesterfield, his eyes closed in ecstasy, his hands folded over a large stomach. He was close on eighty and seldom left his room, which resembled the den of a musical badger, strewn with manuscript paper, ashtrays, music stands and books. There was egg on his dressing gown and his white hair was dotted with cigarette ash, but the eyes he turned to the door were the blue and candid eyes of a child.

'I have brought you your tea, sir,' said Anna, above the soaring voice of the soprano issuing from the huge horn.

Mr Sebastien's eyes gleamed. A new maid. At first sight unpromising in her absence of curves, but on closer inspection not unpromising at all. In fact intriguing. How did she manage to get a dimple in a face so thin?

'Put the tray down here,' said Mr Sebastien craftily, moving closer to the edge of the sofa and patting the low table beside him.

Anna advanced. Suddenly the music surged and gathered force, its *leitmotif* transfigured in one of Wagner's brilliant changes of key and, as the bereaved soprano prepared to fall ecstatically upon her lover's corpse, Anna gave a deep sigh and said, 'Oh, say what you will, but it is *beautiful*.'

Mr Sebastien looked at her sharply, his seduction campaign of tired lecheries momentarily forgotten.

Anna was standing in the middle of the room, the tea tray clasped to her breast, her huge, peat-coloured eyes shining. 'Who is it singing? Not Tettrazini, I think?'

'Johanna Gadski,' said Mr Sebastien. 'The best Isolde in the world, without a doubt.'

'My father didn't care for Wagner. He found it too excited.' The music had made Anna dangerously forget her status. 'He and Chaliapin used to argue and argue.'

'Come here,' said Mr Sebastien, his eyes razor-sharp under the bushy white brows.

She came forward and put down the tray. The music was mesmerizing her; she had turned to the gramophone like a plant turns to the light. Now she was right beside him. He could put an arm round her waist, pull her down on to the sofa, give her a kiss . . .

'Stay and listen,' said Mr Sebastien, not touching her, 'it's nearly over. Sit down.'

'I must not sit down,' said Anna. 'I am the maid.' Even Wagner could not efface the thought of Selina Strickland's views on a maid sitting down in the presence of her employers. But the music held her and, caught in its toll, she compromised and slipped to her knees beside the sofa, her elbows resting on the arm.

When it was over she sighed deeply and turned to him, her face mirroring the drowned look of someone returning from another world. 'It is kind of you to let me listen,' she said. 'It is hard to live without music.'

'There is no need at all for you to do so,' said Mr Sebastien. 'I have a good collection of records. I would be delighted to play you anything you choose.'

Anna shook her head. 'Were you a professional musician?' she asked.

'I wanted to be,' said Mr Sebastien. 'I played the piano and the cello and composed a bit. I think young Rupert gets his love of music from me. But they wouldn't let me. In those days, the aristocracy wouldn't let their sons do anything sensible and I was too feeble to rebel.'

'Oh, I know, it is monstrous!' said Anna. 'I also have suffered in this way. I wanted so *much* to be a ballet dancer and they would not let me. Although,' she went on, anxious to be fair, 'it would not have been possible in any case because my toes were not of equal length.'

'I have some ballet music also,' said Mr Sebastien craftily. '*Casse Noisette* . . . *The Sleeping Beauty* . . .'

'And Stravinsky, do you have? Is it recorded already? *The Rite of Spring*?'

'No, I do *not*,' said Mr Sebastien. 'In my opinion *The Rite of Spring* is a work totally lacking in melody or sense.'

'But *no*!' Anna's cry rent the air. For a moment it looked as though, Selina Strickland notwithstanding, she would stamp her foot. 'It is not *true*. One must be *modern*!'

'If to be modern is to be cacophonous, discordant and obscure,' began Mr Sebastien . . .

Battle, most enjoyable, was joined.

Anna, coming down half an hour later, fearful of a reprimand, was greeted by an interested cluster of faces. The Russian girl was flushed and she was muttering beneath her breath.

'He grabbed you, then,' said Peggy. 'Well, I warned you.'

'No, no, he did not touch me,' said Anna absently. Then the full impact of what she had just said hit her. 'It is because I am not pretty!' she said tragically.

And Mrs Park, who had taken less than twenty-four hours to forget that Anna was a foreigner and a lady, said, 'Now don't be foolish, dear. Just drink your tea.'

For the Dowager Countess of Westerholme, Proom, who had stood behind her chair as second footman when she came to Mersham as a bride, would probably have laid down his life. Nevertheless, when about ten days after Anna's arrival he was told by Alice, the dowager's maid, that someone was to go to the village and inform Mr Firkin, the sexton, that his deceased wife did not want him to give away his top hat, he was not pleased.

The dowager was a small, vague woman in her fifties with silver hair, wide grey eyes and a penchant for the kind of tea gowns and flowing chiffon scarves which so often seem to go with a belief in spiritualism. Though somewhat lacking in intellect, she was a deeply kind and compassionate person, who bore with fortitude the fact that none of the dauntingly trivial messages which she faithfully took down in automatic writing came either from her revered husband or adored eldest son. Of late, instead, her boudoir had turned into a kind of clearing house in which the Deceased, unable to bypass so willing a recipient, made their wishes clear to her. And as often as not, these involved posting off to the vicar or the grocer or the undertaker with letters marked URGENT in the dowager's sprawling hand.

'I can't spare any of the men today,' Proom told Alice. 'We've got all the pictures in the long gallery to re-hang and the music room's not started yet.'

'Well, someone's got to go,' said Alice.

'Why don't you send the tweeny,' said Louise, who was mixing furniture polish in the pantry opposite.

'She's nutty on fresh air and it'd get that dratted dog out of the house for a bit.'

Entering the dowager's drawing room half an hour later, Anna found herself in a familiar world. Her own mother's apartments had contained just such a clutter of occasional tables, potted plants, embroidered screens and piled-up magazines. Only the planchettes and astral charts were different.

'Come in, my dear. You're the Russian girl, aren't you? Now I want you to take a very important message. It's for Mr Firkin, the sexton. Can you find his house, do you think? It's just opposite the church with the walnut tree in the garden.'

'Yes, my lady, I'm sure I can.'

'Good. Now I want you to tell him that a message has just come through from his wife. At least I think it must be his wife. She said her name was Hilda and I'm sure Mr Firkin's wife was called Hilda. Yes, I know she was because . . .' She broke off and began to rummage in her *escritoire*. 'Now where was I?'

'You were going to give me a letter, my lady.'

'That's right; here it is. The poor woman really sounded desperately worried. For some reason she cannot bear the idea of him giving away his top hat. It's strange how these things seem to go on mattering, even on the Other Side.'

Anna took the letter and bent to pick up the scarf that had slipped from the dowager's shoulders. She was rewarded by a charming smile, which changed, suddenly, to a look of intense scrutiny.

'My goodness! Really that is *most* remarkable. Just stand over there, dear, where I can see you properly.'

Puzzled, Anna went to stand by the window.

'Most unusual, really, quite amazing. You can be very, very, proud.'

'Proud of what, my lady?'

'Your aura. It's one of the purest and most beautiful I've seen. Especially the orange. Only it isn't orange so much as *flame*. But a very gentle flame. Like candlelight. Like starlight, even.' She broke off. 'Oh dear! What *is* the matter? What have I said?'

'It's nothing,' said Anna, wiping away the sudden tears. 'I'm so sorry. It's something my father used to call me. I will go and find Mr Firkin straight away.'

Forgetting, for once in her life, to curtsy, Anna fled.

And so, day by day, Mersham yielded to the energy and attack of its staff and grew more beautiful. The shutters were thrown open to the light, Ted brought tubs of poinsettias and lilies into the house. The silver table pieces, burnished by James to unbelievable perfection, were returned to the state dining room, the freshly washed chandeliers sparkled in the sunlight. The men took their liveries out of mothballs; new aprons were assigned to the maids.

Till, on a hot night in mid-June, Anna, who had that day polished the one hundred and thirty-seven banister rails of the great staircase, crawled along the interminable parquet floor of the long gallery with her tin of beeswax and turpentine and beaten fifteen Persian rugs, opened her attic window, leant her weary head on her arms and said to the absent earl:

'It is ready now. You can come.'

And the next day, he came.

2

He came down by car, driving himself in the old black Daimler that had been his father's and as the familiar landmarks appeared, his apprehension increased.

Rupert had neither wanted nor expected to inherit Mersham or the burdens of the title. It was George who had had all the makings of a landowner and a country gentleman: outgoing, debonair George, whose bones now lay deep in the soil of Flanders. Rupert had seen his beautiful home as a place of refuge to which he might occasionally return, but his ambitions had lain elsewhere: in scholarship, in music – above all in travel. The high, wild and undiscovered places of the world had been the stuff of Rupert's dreams all through his childhood. That being so, it had been no hardship to grow up in his brother's shadow. Shadows are cool and peaceful places for those whose minds are overstocked with treasure.

Rupert's three years at Cambridge had seemed a glorious preparation for just such a life. He took a First in history and was invited by his tutor, a brilliant madman who specialized in North Asian Immortality Rites, to join him in a field trip to the Karakorum.

Instead, the autumn of 1914 saw Rupert in the Royal Flying Corps, one of a handful of young pilots who took off in dilapidated BE2s from airfields conjured up in a few hours out of fields of stubble, bivouacked between flights in haystacks and ditches. Two years later, when George was killed at Ypres, Rupert was in command of a squadron flying Camels and Berguets against Immelmann and the aces of the German Reich. The chance that he would survive to inherit Mersham seemed so remote that he scarcely thought of it.

Then, in the summer of 1918, returning alone from a reconnaissance, he was set upon by a flight of Fokkers, and though he managed to dispatch two of them, his own plane was hit. The resulting crash landed him in hospital, first in St Omer, then in London. Some time in the months of pain that followed they gave him the DFC for bringing his plane back across the lines in spite of his wounds, but his observer, a moon-faced kid called Johnny, died of his burns, and the manner of his dying was to stay with Rupert for the rest of his life.

And while he lay in hospital, tended by a series of devastating VADs, the war ended and Rupert found himself still alive.

Alive, and Seventh Earl of Westerholme, owner of Mersham with its forests and farms, its orchards and stables. Owner, too, of the crippling debts, the appalling running costs, the mortgage on the Home Farm.

It was only the memory of George on the last leave they'd spent together, that prevented Rupert from instructing his bailiff to sell then and there. George, his eyes glazed, his uniform unbuttoned after an evening of conventional debauchery at Maxim's, turning suddenly serious. 'If anything happens to me, Rupert, try and hang on to Mersham. Do your damndest.' And as Rupert remained silent, he had added a word he seldom used to his younger brother. 'Please.'

So Rupert had promised. Yet as he pored over the documents they brought to him in hospital he saw no way of bringing the estate, so hopelessly encumbered, back to solvency. And then, suddenly, this miracle . . . this undreamt of, unhoped-for chance to make Mersham once again what it had been and see that all the people in his care were safe.

Thinking with an upsurge of gratitude of the person who had made this possible, his apprehension lifted and, stepping on the accelerator, he turned in past the empty gatehouse, drew up on the wide sweep of gravel and braced himself against the onslaught of the lion-coloured shape now tearing down the steps towards the car.

He was home.

'Welcome home, my lord,' said Proom, coming forward to greet him. 'I trust you had a comfortable journey?'

'Very comfortable, thank you, Proom,' said Rupert. He broke off: 'Good heavens!'

Proom followed his master's gaze. On either side of the grand staircase with its Chinese carpet and crystal chandeliers, stretching upwards like ranking cherubim, were Rupert's footmen in livery, his housemaids in brown, his kitchen maids in blue, his scullery maids and hall boy and housekeeper and cook. Compared to pre-war days they were a mere handful, but to Rupert, accustomed now to the simplicities of wartime living, they seemed to reach to infinity.

'As you see, I've assembled the indoor staff, my lord,' said Proom somewhat unnecessarily. 'It was their wish to greet you personally after your ordeal.'

If Rupert's heart sank, there was nothing to be seen in his face except pleasure and interest. He went forward, his hand outstretched.

'Mrs Bassenthwaite! How well you look!'

'And you too, my lord,' lied the old housekeeper. They had read about him in the papers for, surprisingly, it was Rupert not George who had been twice mentioned in dispatches, had won the MC while still a subaltern and become – even before his final act of bravery – a legend to his own men. Now the old woman who had known him since his birth saw in the new lines round his eyes, the skin stretched tight across the cheekbones, the price paid by those who force themselves against their deepest nature to excel in war.

'And Mrs Park! Well, if you're still presiding over the kitchens it will be worth coming home.'

He walked on slowly, greeting all the old servants by name, cracking a joke with Louise, asking, with a grin, after James's pectoral muscles, enquiring if the second footman felt his wound.

He had reached the half-landing and Proom, very much the major domo, was at his side, introducing a new maid.

'This is Anna, my lord. She is from Russia and has joined us temporarily.'

Rupert only had time to register a pair of intense, dark eyes in a narrow, thoughtful face before the new girl curtsied.

All the girls had bobbed curtsies as he passed, but Rupert was about to encounter for the first time this weapon of social intercourse in Anna Grazinsky's hands. One arm flew gracefully outward and up like an ascending dove, her right foot, elegantly flexed, drew a wide arc on the rich carpet – and she sank slowly, deeply and *utterly* to the ground.

Panic gripped Rupert. Even Proom, immune as he was to the devastating effect of Anna's curtsies, stepped back a pace. For here was homage made flesh; here, between the bust of an obese Roman emperor and a small, potted palm, Rupert, Seventh Earl of Wester-holme, was being offered commitment, servitude, another human being's *all*.

Rupert instinctively looked round for the red roses that should have been raining down from the gallery, the bouquet which anyone not made of iron must surely bring in from the wings. For unlike Proom, who had merely suffered uncomprehendingly, Rupert recognized the origin of his new housemaid's curtsy. Thus had Karsavina sunk to the ground after her immortal rendering of *Giselle*; thus had Pavlova folded her wings after her *Dying Swan*.

'You have studied ballet, I see,' said Rupert gravely.

Anna, delighted to have her gifts appreciated, lifted her head, said, 'Yes, my lord,' and smiled.

For the new earl was nice. She had thought he might be from his photograph and his dog, and he was. An intelligent, sensitive face with wide grey eyes, a high and slightly bumpy forehead and unruly, leaf-brown hair. She liked the lines etched into his face to give it maturity and strength, the courtesy with which he spoke.

And so she smiled at him – into him, he could have said – managing to combine the look of a baby monkey rendered ecstatic by the unsolicited gift of a sudden nut, with that of a guardian angel receiving uplifting tidings about the Fate of Man. Fighting desperately to turn this routine encounter with a new domestic into normal channels, Rupert said, 'Your family all left Russia safely, I hope?'

'My mother and brother are well, thank you. My father died at Tannenberg.'

It was only when the light in her eyes was extinguished, at the mention of her father, that Rupert realized how brightly it had burned.

'I'm so sorry,' he said gently. 'It was a frightful battle, that. We were very slow, I'm afraid, in realizing

46

how horrific the Russian casualties were. But you are happy here, I hope?'

'Oh, yes, very,' she said, and catching Proom's eye added belatedly, 'my lord. Everybody is most kind to me. Only about the bathrooms am I not happy,' she said, her 'r's beginning to roll badly, as they always did when discussing this most vexed of topics.

'What is wrong with the bathrooms?' enquired Rupert, startled.

'What is wrong,' said the new housemaid very seriously, 'is that there are not any of them. Not anywhere in all the attics. Perhaps you did not know this?'

Rupert frowned. Had he known it? Had he ever *been* in the attics in which his servants slept? Well, this was just the sort of thing which, from next month on, would be most competently dealt with. And, remembering the good news he was bringing his mother, and resisting an urge to offer the new housemaid the use of his own bathroom in the master suite, Rupert moved on up the stairs.

'Oh, my dear, I'm so happy for you! So terribly, terribly happy!' The dowager's eyes were misty as she looked at Rupert. 'It was what I wanted for you so much, someone to share your life.'

Mrs Park, remembering Rupert's light appetite, had sent up a meal as exquisite as it was delicate: salmon in oyster sauce, croquettes of leveret with peas, and wild strawberries which Anna had found and picked in the woods behind the lake. With it they had drunk the

Leitenheimer 1904 which Proom had saved for just this day and now the family was alone, taking coffee and liqueurs in the library.

'I know.' Rupert smiled at his mother and tried for the fifth time to push Baskerville off his feet. 'And I know you'll like Muriel. I can't imagine a more suitable mistress for Mersham. Not that she will want to oust you.' He stretched a hand out to his mother. 'Mersham's big enough for both of you, heaven knows!'

'No, dear.' The dowager shook her head. 'There's no house big enough in the world for two women. But you know I've always meant to move into the village when either of . . . when you got married. Colonel Forster's promised to rent me the Mill House and I shall be very happy there. Now tell us about Muriel. Everything. Where did you meet her?'

'In the hospital. She was a VAD and truly, Mother, I think she saved my life. The other nurses were sweet but they all seemed to be straight out of finishing school.' Rupert grinned ruefully, remembering curly-headed Belinda Ponsonby, who had perched on his bed half the night smoking and sobbing about her boyfriends; Fiona Fitz-Herald, who had dropped a scalding hot water bottle on to his gauze dressing and tiny, tender-hearted Zoe van Meck, who had stuck a hypodermic halfway in his arm and fainted. 'Muriel was always so calm and efficient and in *control*. You've no idea what it meant to me.'

'I can imagine.'

'I didn't dream that she had come to care for me,'

he went on, and the dowager smiled, for Rupert had always been unaware of the charm he held for women. 'It wasn't just that I knew she was an heiress – you know how people gossip in a hospital – but she's also extremely beautiful. *And* an intellectual! She has this passionate interest in eugenics.'

'Fair or dark?' asked Uncle Sebastien, that life-long connoisseur of women.

'Fair. Truly golden-haired with deep blue eyes. I don't know if I'd ever have dared to propose with Mersham in the state it's in, but she made it so easy for me.' And Rupert frowned a little, trying to remember, for it had all been rather dream-like, his courtship of Muriel from his hospital bed. So much so that he couldn't actually recall how they had got engaged. He'd just woken from a disturbed and pain-filled sleep and she'd been there beside him, holding his hand, promising to care for him and make of his beautiful home a place of which he would be deeply proud. 'She's so generous, too. She wants to see to the indoor running costs straight away – not even wait for the wedding. That's why I asked you to engage only temporary staff.'

'It all sounds delightful,' said the dowager, 'and of course *completely* explains why the sexton's wife didn't want him to give away his top hat. Now tell me, dear, when's the wedding to be? And where? Because I must go at *once* and call on her parents.'

'Well, Mother, that's the point. You see, Muriel's an orphan.'

'Oh, my dear! The poor, poor girl.' Though genuinely

49

devastated, the dowager was not averse to the removal of so pushing a figure as the mother of the bride. 'How very sad for her! How dreadful!'

'Yes, she's had a very lonely life. But the thing is, mother – and *please* say if it's inconvenient or you aren't up to it – we wondered whether we could be married here. In the village church.'

The dowager's eyes glowed. 'But of course! How *lovely*! Oh, Rupert there's nothing in the world I'd love more. You can't imagine how pleased everyone will be. And the servants too; they've worked so hard.'

'You mustn't tire yourself, of course – I know Muriel means to spare you as much work as possible. But we both feel a quiet country wedding is what we want and very soon. There's so much to do here and nothing to wait for. In fact, we hoped we could call the banns next week and be married at the end of July.'

'As quickly as that?' The dowager was startled. 'Still, I don't see why not.'

'Muriel was wondering if she could come down almost straight away? If it's not correct for me to stay in the same house with her I could go over to Heslop and stay with Tom. I want him for my best man anyway.'

'Oh, I'm sure there's no need for that. Perhaps just the night before the wedding. Goodness, how exciting it all is! We must have an engagement party straight away so that she can meet her new neighbours. What about the bridesmaids, has she decided?'

'She was going to ask Lavinia Nettleford, I think. I believe she nursed with her. You know her, I expect?'

The dowager frowned, trying to distinguish Lavinia among the brood of girls that the Duke of Nettleford, much to his chagrin, had fathered in darkest Northumberland.

'Is she the eldest one?'

'I believe so. And there's a schoolfriend of Muriel's: Cynthia Smythe. But Muriel says she'd be very happy for us to choose another one – maybe a little girl to act as flower girl and carry her train.'

The dowager smiled. 'Well, we don't have to look very far there, do we?'

'Of course!' Rupert was delighted. '*Ollie!* Mother, you're a genius!'

It was close on eleven before the overjoyed dowager and Uncle Sebastien went up to bed.

'Come,' said Rupert, left alone with his dog, and Baskerville, still not quite believing that the bad times were over, loped after him through the French windows, his great muzzle glued to Rupert's side.

It was a night to dream about: windless, warm and scented, with a streak of gold and amethyst still lingering in the sky. Rupert's route took him down the terrace steps, across the lawns and through a wicket gate on to the mossy path which led around the lake. Here his ancestors had planted exotic, fabulous trees which nevertheless grew and flourished in this sheltered English valley: jacarandas and Lebanon cedars, maples and tulip trees, whose roots stretched to the edge of the now smooth and pearly water.

Baskerville left the path to chase rabbits, returned to make slobberingly certain that his master had not been spirited away again and raced back into the woods. Rupert passed the Temple of Flora, white in the gathering darkness, the gothic folly, said to be haunted by his guilty forebear, Sir Montague Frayne – and stopped dead.

He had come to a little grass-fringed bay, clear of the reeds which thronged the northern shore. A girl was standing by the edge of the lake, already up to her knees in water. She had her back to him and her dark hair fell in a loose mantle to her waist. As he watched, she bent to the water, dipped her arms in it and began a strange and curious ritual. With one arm she pulled back the mass of her hair, while with the other she rubbed her neck, her shoulders, her narrow back . . .

A goddess invoking in the darkness some magic rite? A gypsy girl up to some incomprehensible trick? Then, his eyes growing accustomed to the dusk, he saw in the girl's right hand a most prosaic and familiar object; at the same time a well-remembered and tranquil smell, faint as gossamer, soothing as nursery tea, stole towards him – the smell of Pears soap.

The girl in the lake was methodically and dedicatedly washing herself. And as soon as he realized this, he knew who she was.

Chivalry now dictated, unquestionably, that Rupert should turn and move silently away. Instead, he stepped back into the shelter of a copper beech and waited.

Anna had finished washing now and, putting down the soap, she twisted her hair into a knot high on her head and began to walk slowly into the water.

She might get into trouble, Rupert reasoned with himself, for there was a place where the tree roots went deep into the lake. I'd better stay.

But there was no question of her getting into trouble; he knew that perfectly well. She swam easily and somehow, across the silent water, he caught her delight, her oneness with the dark water and the night.

It was when she finally turned for the shore that Nemesis overtook her in the form of Baskerville, finished with his rabbit, bounding over to the water and barking for all he was worth.

'*Durak! Spakkoina! Sa diss!*' She began to berate the dog in her own language, her voice low and husky and a little bit afraid, while she endeavoured to wrap herself into her towel. Baskerville, suddenly recognizing her, made matters worse by leaping up and trying to lick her face.

Rupert's voice, curt and commanding, dissolved this tableau in an instant.

'Here!' he ordered. 'At once. And sit!'

Baskerville came, grovelled, and keeled over, doing his felled-ox-about-to-be-conveyed-to-the-slaughter-house routine, his legs in the air. Rupert left him, picked up the bundle of clothes she'd abandoned on a flat stone and walked over to the girl.

'You win,' he said. 'I'll build some bathrooms.'

She took them, still clutching her towel. 'Are you angry?' she asked. 'You should not be, because *nowhere* does it say in the book of Selina Strickland that one may not wash after working hours in the lake of one's employer.' And, as Rupert remained silent, she went on anxiously, 'You will not dismiss me?'

'No, I will not dismiss you. But get dressed quickly. It's getting cold. I'll turn round.'

It took her only a moment to slip into her brown housemaid's dress. Still barefoot, her wet hair tumbling round her shoulders, she looked, as she came towards him, like a woodcutter's daughter in a fairy tale. Rupert put out a hand and felt hers, work-roughened and icy. Then he took off his coat and draped it over her shoulders.

'No!' Anna was shocked. 'You must not do that. It is very kind but it is not *correct*,' she said, adding with devastating effect, 'my lord.'

A faint terror lest she should begin to curtsy took hold of Rupert.

'Do you often come out at night like this?' he asked.

Anna nodded. 'Housework is not uninteresting exactly, but it is very dirty. And I do not understand . . . I mean, in Russia my gover . . . in Russia we were always being bathed. Hot baths, cold baths and the English grocer in the Nevsky had *seven* kinds of soap. But here . . .'

So she had had a governess, his new housemaid. He

was not surprised. Suddenly he felt, rather than saw, a new and fiercer anxiety take hold of her.

'You have been here a long time?' she hazarded. 'You saw me . . . swimming?'

Rupert was silent, waiting for tears of indignation or the fury of modesty defiled.

Anna covered her face with her narrow, El Greco hands. Now her head came up and she peered at him through tragically splayed fingers.

'I am too thin?' she enquired.

And surprising himself by the fervour with which he lied, Rupert said, 'NO!'

News of Rupert's engagement, spreading to the servants' hall, the outdoor staff and so into the village, was received with universal delight. Miss Tonks and Miss Mortimer, the pixilated spinster ladies who lived in Bell Cottage and had, as long as anyone could remember, done the flowers in the church, began putting their heads together, pondering on the floral decorations that should be worthy of such an occasion. Mrs Bunford, the village dressmaker, bought three new pattern books so as to be completely up to date in the event of a summons from the house, and the vicar, scholarly Mr Morland who had christened Rupert, was touched and happy at the idea of marrying him.

As for the Mersham servants, it was only when the weight of anxiety was lifted that they realized how great it had been. Proom had secretly had no doubt that they were refurbishing Mersham only to put it up for sale and, while he himself only had to hint that his services were on the market for offers to come flooding in, his mother was hardly an exportable commodity. Mrs Park's anxiety had been for Win, her simple-minded kitchen maid. Louise, though she seldom spoke of it, was the sole support of an invalid brother in the village. So, as they drank to the health of Miss Muriel Hardwicke in the earl's champagne, emotion and goodwill ran extremely high.

'And if the wedding is to be at the end of July I shall still be here,' said Anna, whose engagement had now been extended to the end of that month, 'which I shall like very much because I have never been to an English wedding and Russian weddings are very different, with people standing under high crowns for two hours and everybody falling down and fainting.'

As for the dowager, she left her planchettes and her ouija board, drew back the curtains of her twilit boudoir and began to make lists. She made lists for Mrs Bassenthwaite about the catering and lists for Proom about the disposition of the house guests. She made lists of the relations she was going to invite to the wedding and the acquaintances she was going to inform of it, and as soon as she made the lists, she lost them. Yet out of the fluffy cloudiness of her mind and the chaos of her boudoir there emerged the design, masterly and graceful as Mersham itself, of a country wedding in high summer. A wedding in which everyone in the house and the village would most joyfully share.

*

The first person to call and congratulate Rupert was his friend and best man, Tom Byrne, driving over from Heslop Hall.

Heslop was less than ten miles from Mersham, a great Elizabethan pile, sumptuous and tatty, which had harboured broods of roistering Byrnes for centuries. The Byrne children had played with George and Rupert, had ridden in the same gymkhanas, been to the same parties. It was natural that Tom, who had miraculously survived four years in the infantry without a scratch, should be Rupert's best man, and he came now also to offer his family's help in welcoming Muriel. But both Rupert, coming forward to greet him, and the servants, peeping out of the ground floor windows, forgot the wedding and everything else for they saw that Tom had brought no less a person than the Honourable Olive.

Ollie Byrne was just on eight years old and anyone speaking ill of her within fifty miles of Heslop or of Mersham would have found themselves lying flat in a gutter with a bloodied nose. The Byrnes had already had three lusty, red-headed sons: Tom, the eldest, Geoffrey and Hugh, when Lady Byrne, though in failing health, found herself pregnant once again. She only lived long enough to give birth to a premature and hopelessly delicate daughter before she died. The baby, hastily christened Olive Jane, spent the first year of her life in the prison-like wards of a famous teaching hospital, more as an aid to medical research than because the pathetic, screwed-up bundle seemed to have any chance of life. As for Ollie's father, Viscount Byrne, presented with three sons to bring up and an infant daughter in distant London, he sought for a new wife with a frenzy he made no effort to conceal.

His choice fell, somewhat arbitrarily it was felt, on an American, Minna Cresswell, the daughter of a New York shipowner whom he happened to be standing next to at Goodwood. Confronted by a new step-mother, within a year of their mother's death, Tom, Geoffrey and Hugh glared, scowled and swore eternal enmity. Minna was small, quiet and mousy-looking and seemed to have nothing but her fortune to commend her to anyone's attention.

The new Lady Byrne made no attempt to ingratiate herself with the boys. She didn't ask them to call her 'Mother', they were in no way bidden to love her, nor did she hand out expensive gifts. Her practical actions were confined to quietly modernizing those parts of Heslop which were in danger of collapse; and even this she did so discreetly that new bathrooms and radiators appeared as if by magic, without upsetting either her lord's hunting or his meals. And every week she motored to London to breathe her will into the tiny, jaundiced bundle that was the Honourable Olive.

Within a year, the boys were rushing into the house calling 'Mother!' before they had even taken off their coats. When she was away, Byrne prowled his mansion like a labrador deprived of game – and Ollie, spewed up from her teaching hospital at last, decided to live. Not only to live but to conquer. At three, a pair of huge round spectacles perched on her freckled nose, she departed gallantly for weekend visits in the English manner (clutching, however, a rolled-up rubber sheet in case of accidents). At four, though still tiny, she learned to ride.

So when, at the age of five, she contracted tuberculosis of the hip, the blow was shattering. Once again, Ollie went away from home to be immured for two interminable years in a Scottish sanatorium, where she lay, her little pinched face peering above the blankets, on freezing verandas, immobilized in a series of diabolical contrivances. It was in that sanatorium that the nurses, seeing how the child bravely coped with the recurring, debilitating fever and the agony of secondary osteomyelitis, turned the meaningless prefix, 'the Honourable', into a badge of office – and the Honourable Olive she was destined to remain.

Once again, laying the ghosts of all the wicked stepmothers since time began, Minna travelled to and fro, read to the child, sang to her, went back to Heslop to entertain the American troops stationed nearby, saw Tom and the second son, Geoffrey, off to war.

When Geoffrey was killed at Paschendale, Minna lost her look of youth for ever. But the gods were appeased, Ollie was cured and returned to Heslop. The fact that one leg was shortened and in callipers was a small price to pay. She was *alive*.

Lifting her out of the Crossley and setting her down on the gravel, Rupert gathered that Muriel, in response to his call last night, had been in touch with her already. For Ollie, her big blue eyes glinting behind their round spectacles, was clearly in a state of ecstasy.

'Rupert, she rang my mother. Muriel did. She rang Mummy and she said you wanted me for a bridesmaid and she wanted me too. It's true, isn't it? I'm going to be a bridesmaid, aren't I? It's really true?'

'Yes, Moppet, it is,' said Rupert, taking her hand but making no other attempt to help her up the steps to the front door. Helping the Honourable Olive with the simpler tasks of life was not a thing one did twice.

'I've never been a bridesmaid before. Never,' said Ollie. 'There are going to be two others, Mother says, grown-up ones and me. And you know what I'm going to wear?'

'I don't, Ollie. But I should dearly like to know. Or is it a secret?'

Ollie sighed in ecstasy. 'Muriel told me. Rose-coloured satin. It's true. That's pink, you know,' she added obligingly. 'And a matching rose-coloured velvet muff stitched with pearls.' She stopped for a moment, quite overcome. 'And in my hair – honestly, Rupert – a wreath of roses and steph . . . something with "steph" in it that's white and smells lovely. And to go to the church, a white cloak lined with the same pink and trimmed with swansdown.'

Rupert looked down at the little upturned face with its mass of freckles and marigold curls and a wave of tenderness for Muriel engulfed him. She could so easily have wanted to choose someone of her own.

'I think you're going to be absolutely beautiful,' he said.

Ollie, who perfectly agreed with him, nodded her head. 'Can I go and tell Proom and Cookie and James while you talk to Tom? And Peggy and Louise?'

'Of course. You can tell Anna too,' said Rupert pensively. 'She's a new maid and she's Russian.'

Ollie was impressed. 'Like the ballet?' she said. 'Mummy likes the ballet very much. She's going to invite them down.'

'Very like the ballet,' said Rupert gravely.

It was fortunate that Peggy, polishing the brasswork in the hall, had overheard this interchange so that by the time the Honourable Olive reached the kitchen and had been installed on her favourite stool beside Mrs Park, everybody was suitably primed.

'Guess what I'm going to do!' said Ollie, when she had had her traditional spoonful of plum jam, felt James's brachial muscles and been introduced to Anna.

The servants looked at each other in simulated amazement.

'Go to a birthday party?' suggested Mrs Park.

'No,' said the Honourable Olive, her eyes gleaming with importance.

'Go away on holiday?' suggested Louise.

'No!' said Ollie, wriggling with excitement. 'Better than that!'

'Go to the pantomime?' hazarded Proom.

'No!' So intense was her delight that she seemed

likely to slide off the stool altogether. 'I'm going to be a *bridesmaid*!'

'Never!' exclaimed Mrs Park.

'Not for his lordship's wedding?' said James in awed tones.

'Yes.' Ollie's smile shone through the kitchen like Inca gold. 'And guess what my dress is going to be made of.'

Once again, the staff shook bewildered heads.

'White muslin?' suggested Mrs Park.

'No. Better than that.'

'Yellow organdie?'

'No.' She waited, holding back with an innate sense of drama while they floundered hopelessly among lesser materials and commonplace outfits. Then yielding at last, '*Rose pink* satin an' a pink muff with pearls and a head-dress of roses and a cloak with swansdown on it!' She paused, suddenly anxious. 'You will be there?' she said. 'Won't you? You'll all see me?'

'We'll be there,' said Mrs Park, giving her another spoonful of jam. 'There isn't one of us as you could keep away.'

While Ollie was holding court in the kitchen, Tom Byrne was offering his stepmother's help in introducing Muriel to the neighbourhood.

'She wants to give a ball at Heslop in Muriel's honour. She thought a few days before the wedding, so that house guests could stay for both. Would Muriel care for it, do you think?'

'I'm sure she would! I can't imagine a greater compliment.' Rupert was flattered and touched, for Minna, like many unassuming and self-effacing women, was a marvellous hostess.

'She'd have come over today to discuss it with your mother but she's gone up to Craigston to see Hugh.'

'How *is* Hugh these days? Happier?'

Tom's young brother had paid for his happy home life with excrutiating attacks of homesickness when he first went away to school. Rupert's last memory of him was of a small, carrot-headed boy in a brand new uniform being wretchedly sick on a clump of waste-ground behind Mersham Station.

'Oh, he's fine now, he's really settled at last. He's made a new friend this term who seems to be a paragon of all the virtues. He's bringing him down to stay after the end of term. If the wedding's on the twenty-eighth he should be here in time for it – and for the ball.'

'In that case, would he like to be an usher, do you think?'

'He'd love it, I'm sure. Thirteen's just the age for that to be a real honour. Now tell me exactly what you want me to do. Lavinia Nettleford's chief bridesmaid, I gather . . .'

The talk became practical. It was only as he rose to go that Tom, his cheerful, freckled face very serious, suddenly said, 'I haven't told you how very happy I am for you. Really. For all of us at Heslop there's nothing and nobody too good for you.'

Rupert flushed. 'Thanks, Tom. To tell you the truth,

I can't quite believe in my own luck. And knowing that it's not just for me. That because of Muriel all the people here will be looked after.'

'You'd have had to sell otherwise?'

'I think so. I promised George I'd hang on, but quite honestly I saw no hope.'

'And you'd have minded?'

'Not for myself,' said Rupert who had recently and regretfully refused an invitation from his erstwhile tutor to join him in an expedition to the cave monastery near Akhaltsikhe on the Black Sea. 'Not even for Mother; she's always said she'd be happy in a cottage. Only . . . when I was thinking I'd have to sell I kept remembering such silly things. Once I came back on leave and there was Proom in the pets' cemetery – you know, that place behind the orangery where all our dogs are buried. He'd dug a new grave and he was burying a pair of unspeakable khaki socks that Mother had knitted for the troops. They were past unravelling, he said, and our soldiers had enough to contend with!'

Tom laughed. 'Yes, Proom's a paragon all right.'

'And when I was still at Cambridge there was this maid – a spindly, pert little thing. Louise. She's head housemaid now but she was very young then. I once found her coming out of Uncle Sebastien's room with her cap all askew and it was obvious he'd been pestering her. I was really angry and I began questioning her. And she snubbed me – oh, so politely, so chivalrously. And she was right, of course, he means no harm. He just went on loving women when he should have stopped and somehow she understood this. It's people like that I didn't want to "sell".'

'Yes, I can see that. You'll be a good master for Mersham, Rupert. Better than George though you'll hate me for saying so.'

'Don't! If you knew the guilt I feel. Just to be alive . . .' He broke off, seeing Tom's face, remembering Geoffrey, Tom's shadow, blown up at Paschendale. 'God, what an idiot I am! Forgive me.'

Tom shook his head. 'We're both in the same boat, I guess. Guilt for the rest of our lives.'

'If it teaches us humility . . .'

Tom smiled. 'You don't need teaching it, Rupert. It was always your gift. Come, let's find Ollie.'

They found the Honourable Olive already sitting in the Crossley, in a state of evident bliss, holding a cardboard box on her knees.

'It's a baby hedgehog. Anna found it and she's given it to me. She's got it to drink milk from a saucer so it's old enough to go out into the world, she says. She's very nice, isn't she? I think she's beautiful.'

'Beautiful?' said Rupert, and there was something in his voice which made Ollie look at him, her brows furrowed.

'Yes, she is. And I like the way she talks and she told me a poem in Russian because I asked her. It's about a crocodile walking down the Nevsky something. She's going to teach it to me next time.'

'Who is this girl?' asked Tom, looking curiously at Rupert.

'A new maid.' Rupert was still brusque.

'I should like to meet her.'

'You will,' said Rupert. 'It's almost impossible *not* to meet Anna somewhere in this house.'

3

On the following day Rupert returned to London to fetch his bride and Anna and Peggy were sent upstairs to make ready Queen Caroline's bedroom, which had been assigned to Miss Hardwicke until the wedding.

It was in the midst of these preparations that Anna received a letter from her beloved Pinny:

My dear Anna, I am writing to give you some news which I know will delight you. Your cousin, Prince Sergei Chirkovsky, is safe! When the White Army was routed at Tsarytsin he managed to escape and reach Odessa and eventually made his way to London. He arrived last week, very exhausted, of course, but basically in good health. As you know, his parents are still with Miss King and their joy as he walked in may be imagined. Sergei wouldn't stay more than a few days since it is true that Miss King's flat is rather overcrowded and he has gone off to look for some kind of employment – out of London, if possible, since the grand duchess does not seem to have abandoned her scheme for marrying him off to that dumpy lady-in-waiting of hers. He called to see us and was particularly anxious for news of you. I told him where you were but not what you were doing. You know how protective he has always felt about you and I had visions of him posting off to Wiltshire and challenging your employer to a duel!

Petya's letter I enclose. As you see he is settling down very well and has made a friend who has invited him to stay after the end of term, so you need not be afraid about missing his return. As for your mother, she is reasonably well but a little vexed with me for refusing to buy six vats of buttermilk from the United Dairies. The Baroness de Wodzka has convinced her that she could market it as pregnant mares' milk from Outer Mongolia at a considerable profit. I was obliged to tell her that in my view the *koumiss* cure is not sufficiently well known in West Paddington to ensure the success of the scheme.

I hope that you are not finding your new duties too onerous and look forward very much to your return.

Yours affectionately,

Winifred Pinfold

'What's the matter with Anna now?' enquired James, coming into the servants' hall at lunchtime.

'She's happy,' said Louise gloomily.

'It's because her cousin's safe,' said Mrs Park. 'She thought the Bolshies had got him but they haven't.'

'Well, you can send someone else up there with her after dinner,' said Peggy. 'She's like a bloomin' tornado up there, getting ready Miss Hardwicke's room. She's had all the feather beds out in the courtyard an' poundin' the daylights out of them and now she's at the mirrors with some brew she's mixed from that dratted Selina Strickland and you can't get her to stop for a minute.'

The Honourable Mr Sebastien Frayne, padding past the door of Queen Caroline's bedchamber, was arrested by a young and ecstatic voice trilling Mozart's *Hallelujah*.

'You seem in very good spirits this morning,' he said.

Anna turned, jumped off the chair and curtsied all in a single movement.

'I am sorry, I shouldn't sing, I think, though I cannot remember if Selina Strickland has said one may or not. But I am so happy!' said Anna, added 'sir,' – and spoilt the effect completely by throwing her arms round the old gentleman's neck and kissing him on the cheek.

'Well, well,' said Uncle Sebastien, blushing and entranced at the first unsolicited kiss he'd had in twenty years. 'And what has happened to make you so happy?'

'My cousin, Sergei, is safe! He was fighting with Denikin in the Crimea and we had no news for so long that we thought he had been killed. He was *exactly* like a brother to me and to Petya and now, because I am so happy, I am going to make Miss Hardwicke's room so beautiful that she will be *amazed*!'

Anna was as good as her word. Queen Caroline's room was one of Mersham's loveliest, with its hand-blocked wallpaper of azure fleur-de-lis, its Venetian fourposter, white-curtained and white-valanced like a cloud bed on Olympus, and its exquisite view of the lake. Like all the rooms in the main block, however, it had been shut up during the war and now showed signs of neglect.

Anna blackleaded the grate and annointed the bed-springs with sulphate of ammonia, she took down curtains and scrubbed drawers and, to add the final touch, she purloined from the other rooms, bringing in a finely wrought candlestick here, a Dresden shep-herdess there, working for this unknown girl with skill and love. Nor was her task made easier by the fact that Baskerville, the earl being absent, was again persist-ently padding after her, only pausing with his customary howl of despair every time she disappeared down the service stairs and through the green baize doors.

'Why are you so *stupid*?' she berated him. 'Why don't you come through into the kitchen when I have finished so that I can scratch you properly, but now I must *work*.'

'You'll never get that dog to go through that door,' said Proom, encountering her at bay with a bucket of suds. 'He must have swallowed *Debrett's Peerage* when he was a pup.' Then, addressing her in a way in which so kingly a person seldom addressed a house-maid, he said: 'Mrs Proom was wondering whether you'd have a moment to look in after supper tonight. Only if you're not busy, of course.'

Anna, whom he had at last trained not to sink to the ground every time he encountered her, smiled and said: 'Yes, I shall like to come very much. Only . . .' She broke off and looked shyly at the august figure of the butler. 'I don't know if it is permitted, but this after-noon I must polish the toilet set in Miss Hardwicke's room and also the candlesticks and the inkwell . . . many things. And I have noticed that Mrs Proom has strong hands still and she told me she was once in ser-vice. So do you think I might perhaps take them over with the polish and a lot of newspaper so that there is no mess and we could do them together? She would truly help me, I think, and it would not take longer.'

Anna stopped, misinterpreting Proom's silence as one of disapproval. She had been foolish, the silver was valuable . . .

Proom was fighting down a number of emotions. Gratitude to this young girl for detecting, behind his mother's eccentricity and tantrums, her desperate desire still to be of use. Shame that he himself had so seldom made this possible.

Clearing his throat, which seemed to have become a trifle choked, Proom said magisterially, 'Very well. You have my permission. Just see that nothing is mislaid.'

*

71

Mrs Bassenthwaite, inspecting Queen Caroline's bed-room when Anna had finished, was moved to praise.

'You've done very well, my dear.'

'But who will do the flowers?' asked Anna, knowing that everything depended on this.

Mrs Bassenthwaite hesitated. She had always done them herself, but she was very tired these days and there was a niggling pain in her side which never quite seemed to go away.

'You will,' she said. 'Go to Mr Cameron. Tell him I sent you.'

So Anna, her face screwed into what the other servants had learnt to call her 'monkey look', pondered massed delphiniums in delft-blue and white or low bowls of peonies in alabaster jars; but in the end as anyone who thinks of a bride in the month of July must do, decided on roses. Cutting short her lunch hour, she went to find the deaf and misanthropic old Scotsman who had ruled Mersham's gardens for three decades.

Walking with delight between beds of celery, nascent cauliflowers, strawberries nestling like little crimson eggs on their beds of straw, she came to a green door in a high wall, pushed it open – and stood, spellbound.

The rest of the garden at Mersham, though incorrigibly beautiful, suffered from the neglect and understaffing caused by the war. But the rose garden was a miracle of husbandry and care. There were roses as dark as spilt blood and roses with the delicate pink of a baby's fingernails. There were beige and blowsy roses and mysterious golden roses, tightly furled. Roses climbed the stone walls, rambled across arbours or stood in dark green tubs, as demure as Elizabethan miniatures. And as Anna started to sniff her way ecstatically from bloom to bloom, Mr Cameron, who had seen her enter with foreboding, began to hunt for his ear-trumpet, finally tracking it down in the bottom of a watering can, and to jam it into his whiskery ear, a rare sign that he was willing to communicate.

'I thought they should be very pale and gentle, like flowers in a dream, you know?' said Anna when she had explained her errand. 'Not strong roses, not red – though of course his lordship will wish to give her red roses for passion and so on,' said Anna, waving a dismissive hand. 'But for now I want everything very soft and welcoming and a little loose, you know? Those roses that seem to be shaking themselves out a little?'

Mr Cameron nodded. 'You want the old-fashioned ones . . . The Bourbons and the Damasks. There's Belle de Crecy; she'd do you fine. And Madame Hardy over there. Or Königan van Denmark – there's no one to touch her for scent.'

They wandered about in total amity, selecting, discussing, rapturously smelling, while Anna's little Tartar nose turned yellow with pollen and her Byzantine eyes glowed with contentment.

Arriving at a single bush, growing quite by itself in a centre bed of fresh-mulched earth, Anna stopped dead.

'Oh!' she said. 'How *beautiful*! I have *never* seen such a rose as this.'

The old man's eyes shone with pride. 'She's new,' he said. 'I bred her myself.'

The new rose was white. At first sight it appeared pure and flawless white, and yet this was a contradiction, for somehow, most strangely and marvellously, the whiteness was irradiated as if from within by a hint, a blush of pink.

The old man became technical, explaining fertilization problems and grafting, while Anna, who had lifted the other roses towards her with questing fingertips, knelt before this one, reverent and untouching.

'I need a name for her,' he said. 'It's difficult, that.'

'She's like snow in Russia,' said Anna. 'Snow in the evening when the sun sets and it looks like *Alpenglühen*, you know? And if snow had a scent it would smell like that; so pure and yet so strong.'

Mr Cameron scratched his head. 'I could call her that,' he said. '"Russian Snow". It's a good name, that.'

Anna's face was sombre. 'People wouldn't like it. They are angry with us because we made peace too soon.' Suddenly she straightened and turned towards him, her face illumined. 'I have had such a good idea!' she cried. 'Why don't you call her after his lordship's fiancée? Call her Muriel Hardwicke? Or just Muriel? Consider the *honour* of such a thing!'

'Hm.' Mr Cameron was taking this in. 'If it would please his lordship . . .'

After Anna had left, with instructions to pick what she wanted dew-fresh at dawn, he jammed his ear-trumpet into a trellis to show that conversation was over for the day, and stood for a long time contemplating his much-loved new rose.

Somehow she didn't *look* like a Muriel? But why?

Later that evening, Anna received a summons to the dowager's room.

It was a critical time below stairs, for Mrs Park was planning a brand-new dessert for Miss Hardwicke's engagement party. This concoction, which had been stirring in her mind since the engagement was announced, was nothing less than a great swan made of meringue. But inside the swan – a challenge not to be denied – she wanted to put a filling of *crème Bavaroise*. And for this she knew (with her instinct and her fingertips, as she knew everything) she would need a cupful of Tokay. What's more, not just *any* Tokay, but the 1904 Aszu puttonyos, which alone combined the necessary delicacy with a touch of earthiness. Proom was being uncooperative about supplying this admittedly priceless wine, declaring that it was absurd to open a whole bottle of the stuff just for a few spoonfuls.

When she was compelled to do with lesser ingredients, Mrs Park never sulked, but she nevertheless *suffered* and her suffering was reflected in Win's uncomprehending and adenoidal melancholy and a general 'atmosphere', which prevented Sid from whistling and

James from giving his biceps their usual evening canter down his forearm.

But when Anna's summons came, the kind cook was able to put her own troubles aside for a moment.

'Now don't look like that, dear,' she said encouragingly. 'It's nothing to be afraid of, I'm sure.'

Mrs Park was right. The dowager had sent for Anna to inform her that she was to wait on Rupert's fiancée till a new lady's maid should be engaged.

Anna stared at her, her huge, tea-coloured eyes turning quite stewed with despair.

'But I do not know enough to do this, my lady!'

'Nonsense, my dear, I'm sure you'll do it splendidly. Mrs Bassenthwaite speaks very highly of your work.'

'But in Selina Strickland there are *terrible* things in the part concerning lady's maids. Like . . . for example, gophering irons. I do not know,' said Anna desperately, 'how to gopher!'

The countess was unimpressed. 'I think that must be rather an old-fashioned book, dear,' she said. 'And anyway, my maid, Alice, will be only too willing to advise you. It's just to help Miss Hardwicke dress and keep her room tidy and bring her breakfast tray. Proom will explain your duties, but I assure you there's nothing that's at all difficult.'

Anna, however, was hard to console and returned to the kitchen in a state of dejection which it took the combined efforts of Mrs Park, James and Louise to overcome.

'For heaven's sake, it's an *honour*,' said Louise. 'Why aren't you pleased?'

Anna launched into an explanation, from which the bewildered servants gathered that she was afraid of becoming like some character in a book who had been tossed up by the earth and rejected by the heavens.

'Shall I still be able to have my meals downstairs?' she asked tragically.

It was Proom himself who disposed of Anna's fears of a life spent in limbo, informing her that she was still a housemaid who would be expected to carry out her usual duties, as well as lending her services to Miss Hardwicke when required, adding that if she had nothing better to do she could go and see to the shutters as it was coming on to rain.

It was not only in the house and in the gardens that preparations were being made to welcome the new bride. Potter, the head groom, had been entrusted by his lordship with a commission that brought a spring to his step and sent him whistling round the stables. He was to purchase a mare for Miss Hardwicke's use. And not just any mare – but one of Major Kingston's white Arabs from the stud in Cheltenham that was the envy of the world.

'Pay anything you like, Potter,' the earl had said before he left for London. 'It's the bridegroom's present to the bride and to hell with being sensible. We may be broke, but we'll hold our heads high over this one.'

So Potter, leaving for Gloucestershire, was a happy

man. Only the earl's old hunter, Saturn, and the dowager's carriage horses now remained of the fine stables they had kept before the war. Potter himself had been wise, refusing to join in the traditional battle of groom against chauffeur. He had learned to drive and been as willing to convey the dowager to the station in the Rolls as to drive her to the village in the brougham she still preferred when paying calls. But now he saw good times ahead for the new earl who, for all his quiet ways, was a brilliant horseman and, as he called in at the kitchens to say goodbye, there was pride in Potter's bearing and a sparkle in his eye.

'It is like a fairy story,' said Anna, who had got over the shock of her promotion. 'Three presents for the bride: a white rose, a dappled mare, a snowy swan . . . and now she comes!'

'Let's hope she's a bloomin' princess, then,' said Louise, whose feet were hurting her, 'or there'll be ructions!'

4

Muriel Hardwicke had been, quite simply, a perfect baby. Born to parents already rendered wealthy by the gratifying sales of Hardwicke soups, Hardwicke sausages and a similar assortment of canned goods, her plump, pink limbs, golden curls and hyacinth-blue eyes were the wonder of all who beheld them. Her mother, an unremarkable and rather nervous woman, never ceased to be amazed at the physical perfection of her child; Muriel's father, as though to prove himself worthy of what he had produced, redoubled his efforts at work, made mergers, formed companies and quite quickly became a millionaire.

Only Muriel herself, gravitating naturally to the ornate mirrors in the plush Mayfair mansion where she grew up, was not surprised at the flawlessness of the image which greeted her. It was as though she knew from the start that she was not like other children. She hated to be dirty, could not bear mess or torn clothes and once, when a stray kitten brought in by the cook scratched her hands, she shut herself in the nursery and refused to come out until it was removed.

She had reached a full-breasted and acne-less adolescence when her mother, as though she knew she could do no more for her lovely daughter, contracted pneumonia and died. Five years later, her father collapsed at a board meeting with a perforated ulcer and, at twenty-two, Muriel Hardwicke found herself sole heiress of a group of businesses valued at some three million pounds.

She did not let it go to her head. She kept the Mayfair house, engaged a chaperone and – the year was 1916 – herself volunteered as a VAD. Her loathing of illness and her detestation of squalor were put aside in the interests of her grand design. For now was the chance to cross the great barrier between the *nouveau riche* and the aristocracy. In the war hospital, with a steady stream of wounded officers passing through her hands, she would – she was quite certain – find a worthy mate.

In the event, it had taken two years; but when the Earl of Westerholme was wheeled in she had known her quest was ended. The title was an excellent one, the young man was undeniably attractive and his wounds, though severe, were not disfiguring. Nor did the fact that Mersham was impoverished displease her: it would make her own position more secure, for his family would welcome a bride who was going to restore their home.

Muriel's own taste would have been for a fashionable wedding in a London church, but she had been quite happy to agree to Rupert's offer of Mersham and a village wedding. For, studded about in impossible Yorkshire hovels which they refused to quit, were some ancient and deeply unsuitable relations of her father's. Grandma Hardwicke with her rusty bonnet and clacking teeth might have dared to brave a big London church, but she would hardly turn up, uninvited, at Mersham. And after all, even a simple country wedding could be conducted with order, propriety and style.

This being so, Muriel was determined to make a clean start. Her house was to be sold, her servants dismissed. Only her chaperone, Mrs Finch-Heron, would travel with her to Mersham and then she too would be sent away.

But first she would go and say goodbye to the man who had clarified all her aspirations, the man whose ideas had come to her as though all her life had been leading towards such a goal. Dr Lightbody was giving a lecture tonight at the Conway Hall. She would go to it as a perfect preparation, a kind of blessing on her new life. And tomorrow, Mersham.

Slipping into her seat, Muriel noticed with irritation that the hall was half-empty. It was truly appalling what this gifted, handsome man had had to endure in the way of calumny and indifference. Dr Lightbody had a Swedish grandmother from whom he had inherited his fair hair and pale blue, visionary eyes. A devoted grandson, the doctor had most naturally decided to visit the old lady on her farm near Lund. The fact that his departure for Sweden happened to take place just two days before the outbreak of war was obviously a complete coincidence, yet there were people vile enough to accuse him of cowardice. The Swedes themselves had been so unreceptive to the implications of his 'New Eugenics' that the poor man had had to uproot himself immediately after the armistice and return to England.

And yet his doctrine was as uplifting as it was sensible and sane. Briefly, the doctor believed that it was possible, by diet, exercise and various kinds of purification about which he was perfectly willing to be specific when asked, to create an Ideal Human Body. But this was not all. When his disciples had made of their bodies a fitting Temple of the Spirit, it was also their obligation to mate with like bodies. In short, Dr Lightbody wished to apply to human beings those laws which farmers and horse breeders have used for generations. For as the great man was now most persuasively arguing, what was the use of producing swift racehorses, pigs with perfectly distributed body fat and chickens whose egg-boundedness was only a distant memory – while permitting the human race to perpetuate idleness, physical deformity and low intelligence by unrestricted breeding?

Muriel, her full lips parted, her pansy-blue eyes fixed admiringly on the doctor's blond head, sighed with satisfaction as he reiterated his well-remembered

82

points. Everything made sense to her. There were people who, by physique and training, were somewhat superior and she would have been foolish not to recognize herself as one of them. That these people had a duty to the human race seemed to her clear. Muriel was serious about her beliefs and if Rupert had shown any flaws, mental or physical, or any insanity in the family, she would have set aside her inclinations and refused to become engaged. Fortunately, Rupert had in every way passed the test and as Countess of Westerholme it would be her privilege and duty to see that the doctor's ideas were carried out.

Dr Lightbody was now drawing to a close.

'All of us, ladies and gentlemen,' declaimed the doctor, looking round to see if, among the sea of swelling bosoms, there *were*, in fact, any gentlemen, 'have it in our power to acquire – by Right Diet, Right Living and the avoidance of lechery and vice – a body that is a flawless and an unsullied chalice, a hallowed temple for the human spirit. Can we doubt that, having acquired it, it is our duty to pass it on to our unborn children and make of this island race a nation of gods? Valhalla is in our grasp, ladies and gentlemen. Let us march towards it with confidence, unity and joy! Thank you.'

'Get a taxi, Geraldine,' said Muriel to her chaperone. 'And buy some of those diet sheets on the way out, won't you? They didn't sell too well last time. I'm going backstage to congratulate the doctor and say goodbye.'

*

Dr Lightbody left the Conway Hall in an excellent frame of mind. The lecture had gone well; the audience had been appreciative and the diet sheets had sold better than usual. He had particularly enjoyed the visit of Miss Hardwicke afterwards. Now there was a disciple worth having! Other women had to strive to *become* a chalice, but not she! A few followers like that and he could make of this dispiriting country a Mecca and a place of joy. She had invited him down for the wedding. Might there be something for him there? A chance to work under a wealthy patroness? To set up an Institute of Eugenics at Mersham, free from the financial anxieties that plagued him? Yes, he'd have to keep that very much in mind.

His mood of elation lasted until he turned into the dingy street in Ealing where he rented lodgings. But as he let himself in it collapsed, pricked by a weary exhausted voice asking, in the appalling Midlands accent he had never been able to eradicate: 'Ronnie? Is that you?'

'Yes, Doreen, it is I,' said Dr Lightbody in the careful voice, as of a teacher speaking to a backward child, that he always used when addressing his wife.

Doreen sat in a shabby armchair, her glasses on the end of her nose, darning one of his socks. She looked pale and exhausted, there was a spot on her chin and her shoulders were hunched in their usual pose of resigned weariness. Angrily, he waited for her to cough and, sure enough, after a short struggle to hold her breath, she began the dry, infuriating coughing that always seemed to assail her these days.

'There's some coffee on the stove,' she said when she could speak again. 'And a piece of chocolate cake, if you want it. It's freshly baked.'

Dr Lightbody went through into the tiny kitchen. How had it happened that he, with his vision of what the human body could be, had been trapped into this appalling marriage? Why had he been so weak as to listen to his parents when they insisted he marry the girl and why, having done so, had he not left her two months later, when she miscarried? It wasn't just that she was socially completely his inferior – a lowly clerk's daughter in whose house he had lodged in his last year at college – it was that all along Doreen had been antagonistic to his ideas. First, she had not wanted to accompany him to Sweden and had produced some nonsense about sharing the fate of her countrymen. Then, when in the purity of the Swedish air and the freedom from conscription he had at last been able to formulate his ideas, Doreen had mutely and obstinately misunderstood everything he was trying to do. And when they returned to England and his teaching had at last begun to gain ground, had she been behind him, helping him, building up his image?

She had not. When he had suggested she come with him on a tour of the docks, to encourage the dock workers to marry only when there was healthy blood on both sides, Doreen had said she didn't think it was any of her business. No wonder that when she had

85

half-heartedly followed his diet sheets, it had done her so little good. One had to *believe*. Not only was Doreen's body not a temple, Doreen's body was a disaster. Lately he had not even asked her to come to his lectures. It was better for people not to know that he, to whom they turned for leadership and guidance, had to share his life with someone whose very appearance was a denial of all that he was working for.

And, deep in self-pity, Dr Lightbody bit into a large slice of Doreen's feather-light chocolate cake and sighed.

5

Unlike Rupert, Muriel was spared the reception by massed servants on the grand staircase. This did not mean, however, that the servants did not watch her arrival. Perched on various strategic stepladders and in convenient look-out posts, Mersham's staff gazed curiously at the Daimler and saw the earl hand out a tottery lady, whose motoring hat and swathed veils suggested high winds and the keeping of innumerable bees. But before despondency had taken root, the earl handed out a second lady, full-breasted and voluptuous, in a flesh-coloured duster coat tasselled with skunk tails.

And over Sid on a ladder in the west landing, over Louise and Mrs Park wobbling on stools in the store room, over everyone, there spread a look of pure satisfaction. Not only was the new countess beautiful, but there was also plenty of her and James, balancing Mr Sebastien's telescope on a Roman urn, summed up the general feeling when he said simply and lustingly: 'Cor!'

'This is your room, dear,' said the dowager, leading Muriel into Queen Caroline's bedchamber. 'We thought you'd like it, it has such a pretty view of the lake.'

Muriel looked with pleasure at the graceful, airy room, the low bowls of roses. 'But it is delightful! Charming! I have never seen a lovelier room.'

The dowager smiled affectionately at her beautiful new daughter-in-law. 'And this is Anna, who will wait on you till you have engaged a maid of your own.'

Anna curtsied. The depth and intensity of her curtsy, which had so disconcerted the earl and his butler, in no way troubled Muriel, who felt it to be only her due. She turned back to the dowager. 'The guests are invited for eight o'clock, I believe you said?'

'That's right. It's just a small party of our intimate friends to welcome you and drink your health. With the wedding so soon, we didn't want to delay in introducing you to the neighbourhood. You have the whole afternoon to rest.'

'Thank you, but I am seldom tired,' said Muriel composedly.

The dowager could believe it. She had never seen a more magnificent creature. She turned to go, but at the door she paused and said to Anna: 'The flowers are quite beautiful. You have a real feeling for this kind of work. Mrs Bassenthwaite told me how much trouble you took.'

A slight crease furrowed Muriel's forehead. She had never heard a servant addressed in such familiar and affectionate terms.

'You may unpack, Anna,' she said. 'You'll find a picture in a silver frame in the crocodile-skin case. I want that on my bedside table.'

'Yes, miss,' said Anna, and set to work.

Hanging up a dance dress of green accordion-pleated chiffon, a tea gown of coffee-coloured lace, a magenta boucle suit with a fringed hobble skirt, she presently came on a silver-framed photograph. This turned out to be, not as Anna had expected a portrait of the earl, but of a fair man with sticking-up hair and visionary eyes. The signature: 'From Dr Ronald Light-body with kindest regards', meant little to Anna but, obedient to her mistress's instructions, she placed it on the bedside table.

'I shall wear the orange *crêpe de Chine* tonight,' said Muriel from the chaise-longue, where she was lying with closed eyes, drawing deep and systematic breaths of air into her lungs. 'The one with the crystal beading. See that it is pressed. And with it the match-ing bandeau and ostrich feather fan . . .'

'Well?'

Slipping into her seat in the servants' hall for a quick meal before the party, Anna faced a battery of faces . . .

She did not fail them. Clasping her hands in her best annunciatory-angel manner, she said: 'She is beautiful *all over*. I can tell you this absolutely because I have seen her in the bath.'

James put down his knife.

'She wished, you see, that I should wash her back and also rub her with some cream of Dr Lightbody's and I assure you she is like a *goddess*,' said Anna, delighted to have such happy tidings for them all.

'Who's Dr Lightbody when he's at home?' enquired Louise.

'He is a very important man whom Miss Hardwicke admires very much and wears his hair *en brosse* and is the president of the New Eugenics Society.'

'The what?' asked Sid.

'Eugenics,' said Proom in his most professional manner, 'is the science of selective breeding. It is an extremely important field of study and Miss Hardwicke's interest in the subject is entirely to her credit.'

'Yes, I think so too,' said Anna, her eyes ablaze with enthusiasm, 'because in Russia, in the country, about twenty versts from us there lived a farmer who suffered very much with his chickens because when they were roasted they always had blisters on their breasts and . . .'

'Anna!' Louise had long since made her peace with the Russian girl, but there were words which, as head housemaid, she had no intention of permitting her underlings to use.

'I'm sorry,' Anna apologized. 'If I say *chest* blisters

is it all right? So he went to see a professor of eugenics in Kazan and—'

But Anna's account of the chicken farmer's triumph in eliminating breast blistering was destined to remain unfinished. For Mrs Park, who had been lingering in the kitchen, now arrived at the door, shy and blushing like a bride, and said with simple dignity: 'Will you come, everybody, and see . . . ?'

Among her other anxieties, Mrs Park suffered from the conviction that guests at Mersham were in danger of starving to death. For the fifteen or so intimate friends invited that night to a buffet supper to celebrate the earl's engagement, she had prepared three freshwater salmon grilled and garnished with parsley butter, a *mousseline* of trout adorned with stuffed crayfish heads and a pike poached in court *bouillon*. There was a *fricassée* of chicken with morels and cream, half a dozen ducklings, a York ham and a piece of *boeuf royale* which took up the whole of a side table . . .

But it was none of these that held the servants' gaze. For, in the centre of the huge table, drawing the eye as inevitably as the *Winged Victory* compels the eye of those ascending the main staircase of the Louvre, was the dessert that Mrs Park had created in homage to Muriel Hardwicke.

The gentle cook had seen in her mind's eye a great swan made of snow-white meringue – The Swan of Mersham, which was part of the Frayne coat of arms. She had visualized its wings made of the palest almonds, furled and slithered to feathered authenticity and its beak and eyes picked out in silver. She had imagined the inside of this mighty, heraldic bird as consisting of the most delicate and subtle *mousse Bavarois* which, at the touch of a knife on the creature's heart, would ooze out in a fragrant mouthwatering slither . . . She had conceived of a great lake of *crème Chantilly* with islets of whipped syllabub for the swan to float upon and, surrounding it, an emerald shore of fringed angelica . . .

And what she had seen she had created.

For a moment, the servants marvelled in silence.

'You'll be sent for after this, Mrs P,' said the butler, 'so make sure you're ready to go upstairs. Miss Hardwicke'll want to see you, no doubt about it.'

'Oh no, surely?' Mrs Park, flushing rosily, demurred.

But secretly, modest as she was, she *did* think she'd be sent for. The swan had kept her and her devoted amanuensis, Win, from their beds for the best part of a week; but for once it seemed to her that she had made something of which Signor Manotti himself need not have been ashamed.

At Heslop Hall, Lady Byrne, already dressed for the party, was saying goodnight to Ollie, sitting like a small sunflower in her white-canopied bed.

When she had first come to Heslop, Minna Byrne had left untouched the bleeding stags, dismembered antlers and dripping, severed heads of John the Baptist which adorned the halls and corridors of Lord Byrne's enormous Elizabethan mansion. But when she had discovered that her infant stepdaughter was supposed to sleep under a malodorous tapestry of St Sebastian being quite horribly stuck with arrows, Minna had acted with decision and despatch. Ollie's room was now simply furnished, but looked delightful with its American patchwork quilt, bentwood rocking chair and gaily painted chests and it was there that the Byrnes tended to congregate at the end of the day.

'You look *lovely*, Mummy,' said Ollie.

Minna smiled. She always dressed plainly and had retained the Quaker air she had brought from her New England childhood. But for Muriel Hardwicke, who had saved Mersham from ruin and chosen Ollie for her bridesmaid, she had added the Byrne pearls to her cream silk dress and put diamond drops in her ears.

'I wish I could come,' said Ollie wistfully. 'I haven't seen Muriel yet.'

'I know, lovey. But it's really a very *late* party.' While encouraging Ollie in every way to be independent, Minna secretly guarded her like a lioness against fatigue. 'You'll meet Muriel next week when you go to fit the dresses.'

'Yes.' Ollie gave a blissful sigh. Heslop had of late abounded in trapped housemaids pinned against walls, resigned under-gardeners and delayed tradesmen, all receiving, at Ollie's hands, the details of her outfit.

Tom Byrne now wandered in in his evening clothes,

93

to ruffle his sister's hair and receive her compliments on his appearance.

'You look very cheerful,' said Minna, smiling at her eldest stepson.

Tom grinned. 'I am. I can't wait to meet this paragon of Rupert's. Beautiful *and* devoted *and* saved his life *and* an orphan so we can have the fun of the wedding down here! It seems almost too good to be true. Not that anything's too good for Rupert.'

'No, he's a dear and just the person for Mersham,' said Minna, to whom Rupert's war record had come as no surprise. 'And Mary seems to have quite abandoned all those spirits of hers now he's home and there's a wedding to plan for.'

'Well, not quite,' said Tom. 'Last time I called I had to take a message for Mrs MacCracken at the school-house from a Passed-On Lady who was having trouble with her knitting on the other side.'

Minna sighed. She dearly loved the dowager, whose kindness when she first came to Heslop had been unceasing, nor was she disposed to mock anyone who sought comfort in the knowledge that the death of the body is not the end. If only the spirits, just once in a while, would come up with something *interesting*.

'You won't forget to give Anna the letter I wrote?' Ollie asked her brother. 'It's very important. It's all about the hedgehog.'

'I won't forget,' promised Tom, looking tenderly down at the little marigold head.

'What an interesting girl she sounds,' said Minna. 'Is she really Russian?'

'So I understand.'

'What a hard time they must have had, all those poor people. I was wondering whether I might ask Mary if she'd let me borrow her for the ball. I'm going to ask some of the Ballets Russes people down; leaven up the County a bit. A Russian maid would be invaluable. Remind me to mention it.'

'All right, Mother. Oh, by the way, are you and Father going in the Rolls tonight?'

'I imagine so. Why?'

'I thought I'd take the Crossley over to the Rabinovitchs and ask them if they'd let me pick up Susie.'

Tom spoke as naturally as if his courtship of Susie Rabinovitch had not set the whole neighbourhood by the ears. When Tom had first clearly shown his interest in the plump and outwardly unprepossessing daughter of a Polish Jew, Tom's father had not been pleased. Lord Byrne personally liked Leo and Hannah Rabinovitch, who, having amassed a fortune in the rag trade, had settled in a large and mottled mansion called The Towers a couple of miles from Heslop. All the same, it had been with some force that Lord Byrne had pointed out the presence in the neighbourhood of the Honourable Clarissa Dalrymple, of Felicity Shircross-Harbottle and a score of other girls left bereft by the loss of so many of their future husbands in the war. Tom, with his nice smile, had acknowledged their worth and continued to court Susie.

Gradually the Byrnes, led by Ollie, who thought The Towers, with its gilt bathrooms, thick, plush carpets and lamps shaped like swans, to be the most beautiful home she had ever seen, came to see Tom's point of view. Exactly what it was about Susie was hard to say, but not to like her was impossible. It was therefore with slight chagrin and considerable amusement that the Byrnes watched the dismay that Tom's courtship had evoked in Mr and Mrs Rabinovitch. Confronted with the despairing remnants of Jewish orthodoxy, the Byrnes could only smile and wait. Tom was twenty-five, Heslop was entailed and even if it hadn't been, Lord Byrne would not have dreamt of dispossessing a son whom he loved deeply and who was eminently suited to succeed. For the rest, time would tell.

This philosophical attitude was not one that came naturally to Hannah Rabinovitch, dressing for the engagement party in her bedroom at The Towers, which she had furnished, in all innocence, like a luxurious brothel of the *Belle Époque*. The thought that Tom Byrne, as Rupert's best man, would be very much in evidence that night brought a frown to the kind, middle-aged face which she was methodically rubbing with cold cream.

How had it happened? Why did good-looking Tom Byrne, the heir after all not only to a viscountancy but to a considerable fortune from his delightful American stepmother, have to fall in love with Susie? And, as if to find some clue to the secret, Mrs Rabinovitch pulled her wrapper closer and went into her daughter's room.

Susie's maid was busily laying out the red lace dress, the kid shoes and embroidered shawl that Susie was to wear that evening. Susie herself, quite oblivious of these preparations, was curled up in an armchair reading *The Brothers Karamazov*. As she looked at her only daughter, Hannah shook her head and sighed.

For Susie was plain. Not perhaps ugly, though she had been spared neither the big nose nor the frizzy hair which so often characterized her race, but undoubtedly plain. Plain and plump and bookish to a degree that surely should have put off an attractive young aristocrat who had practically been born on a horse. What right had Tom Byrne to discern, within a month of their meeting, that Susie had a heart of gold, a sterling sense of humour and the kind of creative common sense that can smooth out personal crises in a moment? So Susie was the light of their life, the joy of their declining years – but what business was that of Tom Byrne's? Why hadn't he and his family cut them dead when they moved into the district? A Jewish rag trade merchant like her Leo? Not only a Jew, but a Polish Jew, who, everyone knew, was the lowest of the low?

How nervous she had been when Leo decided they should move into the country from Golders Green. She'd been prepared for years of ostracism and suspicion, not to mention the twenty-mile drive to the synagogue, for Leo's mother had been alive then and she was very strict. But first the Village Institute had started pestering her for recipes for *kugelhupf* and *gefillte fish* and then the County had come. Of course, Lady Byrne was American and one had to expect a certain amount of liberalism from someone educated in New York, a city in which anti-Semitism would leave one somewhat isolated. But the Countess of Westerholme had called too, and soon the Rabinovitchs had found themselves accepted as part of the Mersham scene.

But acceptance was one thing – to come courting one's daughter was another.

In a way, of course, it was her own fault, Hannah could see that. She shouldn't have made such a pet of Ollie. It had been her own idea to employ the Honourable Olive as their *Shabbat Goy* and the sight of the little girl arriving each Friday evening on her tricycle with the single, built-up pedal, her face beaming with pride as she lit their candles, had given their festival new meaning. Each time she came, Leo had given her a single pearl to string on a necklace which, as everyone agreed, would make her the most beautiful girl in the world long before she came of age.

But really it was ridiculous to blame herself. How could one do anything except love that most gallant of human beings? Except that in Ollie's wake, bringing her down when the weather was bad, had come Tom Byrne, on leave from the Guards . . .

'Oi,' thought Hannah Rabinovitch, 'Oi, oi . . . An uncircumcized viscount, what sort of a grandson is that?' Sighing, she went to wake the paunchy, velvet-eyed leprechaun that was her husband Leo.

Hannah had been seventeen when her father came to her in the Polish village of her childhood and told her that she was to be a bride. She had only seen Leo once before they stood together under the *huppah* and exchanged their rings. Since then, it was only Hannah's constant battles with the germs which assailed him, the irregular food that was served him and the accidents which threatened him, that prevented a jealous God from destroying the happiness he had caused her by giving her in marriage to such a man.

Anna was enjoying the party very much. She had been on her feet since six that morning but now, dressed most becomingly in the black alpaca dress and snowy muslin that was her evening uniform, she surged among the guests, attracting more attention than she realized by her palpable longing to give, bestow and *share* the earl's best sherry.

How beautiful the house looked! How nice the guests were! Mr Morland the vicar, with his wise, scholarly face; Mrs Rabinovitch, who had taken her aside to beg her help in keeping a second glass of wine from the Vale of Tears that was her husband's stomach, Tom Byrne, who had slipped a note into her pocket and thanked her for her kindness to Ollie . . . How happy everyone looked, how pleased they were at the earl's good fortune!

And how magnificent was Muriel Hardwicke,

Anna's own handiwork, standing and holding court in the centre of the room.

Anna herself, sensitized by her upbringing, would not have chosen, for a simple supper party in a country house, an orange dress both embroidered with crystal beading *and* lined with bands of monkey fur; nor would she have found it necessary to have added diamond-studded vulture quills to the bandeau which supported her hair. But she had faithfully carried out Muriel's orders and the result was dazzling. The earl himself seemed unable to take his eyes from her.

This was true. Fetching Muriel downstairs, Rupert had indeed been dazzled. He had seldom seen Muriel out of uniform – to him she had been a calming presence dressed in white, ready with a merciful injection when the pain grew too great. Now it occurred to him how little he really knew of his bride's thoughts and hopes and fears.

Anna surged towards them, illumined and slender, like a votive bronze from the more ecstatic sort of tomb, and proferred her tray, which Muriel waved away. What a strange girl she was, thought Rupert, following her with his eyes. He had not spoken to her since the evening beside the lake, but her spoor was everywhere: in Uncle Sebastien frowning at the piano over a Stravinsky score, in James caught rescuing a trapped Peacock butterfly from the study window and producing an embarrassed and somewhat garbled version of Tolstoy's theory of Reverence for Life; in his

100

mother's new hairstyle based – and becomingly – on that of Diaghliev's beloved Karsavina.

'Is that the Russian girl?' Minna asked the dowager.

'Yes, that's Anna. She's a dear girl and such a hard worker.'

Lady Westerholme was looking delightful in a dress of dove grey chiffon which Mrs Bunford, the village dressmaker, had finished just two hours before. The dowager always had her clothes made by Mrs Bunford, not because that excellent lady was a good dressmaker – she had, in fact, a most unfortunate way with the set of a sleeve – but because Mrs Bunford was the sole support of an invalid husband and a delicate son. Fortunately, the dowager's fine bones and wide-set grey eyes enabled her to get away with anything and no one who patronized Mrs Bunford *expected* to be able to lift their arms above their head.

'Ollie can't stop talking about her,' said Minna, watching Anna approach Uncle Sebastien and receive a fatherly and affectionate smile from him. The earl's uncle, cleaned up by Sid and poured into his evening clothes, was on his best behaviour. Not only was he to give away the bride at the wedding ceremony, but tonight it was he who was to propose the health of the happy couple and only the briefest lunge at Pearl's entrancing bottom as he passed her in the corridor had marred his conduct during the whole evening.

'I was wondering,' Minna continued, 'do you think I might borrow her for the ball? I've got some Russians coming and it would be such a help.'

'But of course, my dear. Borrow anyone you like.'

'You're an angel, Mary. And now you really must introduce me to that *gorgeous* girl!'

'This is Lady Byrne, Muriel, our dearest friend.'

Minna smiled warmly at Rupert's lovely bride. 'I can't tell you how happy you've made Ollie by letting her be your bridesmaid. It's her first time and she's over the moon.'

'I'm so glad she's pleased,' said Muriel graciously. 'I look forward very much to meeting her. Rupert seems so very fond of her.'

'I'll bring her over as soon as I possibly can,' promised Minna. 'I suppose you'll have to be thinking about the fittings soon with the wedding only five weeks away?'

'Yes, indeed. I've made an appointment with Fortman and Bittlestone next week. The dresses should be ready to try on by then.'

'You're not getting them made locally, then?' asked Minna, repressing a pang for Mrs Bunford, who had been glimpsed in her front parlour night after night, pouring over copies of *Bride* magazine.

'Definitely not,' said Muriel, casting a glance at the dowager's chiffon. Nothing, Minna noted, escaped those peacock-blue eyes. 'I never see why a country wedding should be *shoddy*, do you?'

'No . . . no, of course not.' She changed the subject. 'Rupert will have told you about the ball I am giving at Heslop for you. I'm asking people for the twenty-fifth so as to give you a couple of days' rest before the wedding. It's rather short notice, but almost everyone seems to have accepted. Fortunately, the victory celebrations will be over by then.'

Muriel seemed to be hesitating. Then, 'I was wondering, is the ball to be in fancy dress?' she asked.

'I hadn't thought of it as such,' said Minna. 'You know what it's like getting men to dress up. Why do you ask?'

'Well, it just happens that I have a particularly beautiful costume – a perfect replica of the one the Pompadour wore to the Silver Ball at Versailles. I had it made for a charity gala which was cancelled. So, naturally, if there was a chance to wear it I would be very pleased.'

Minna's heart sank. The thought of getting her dear old Harry to dress up as a pirate or a cavalier was too painful to contemplate. To get Lord Byrne into his tails was bad enough, and Tom wasn't much better. And most of the invitations had been issued: she'd have to make innumerable telephone calls. Then she looked at the lovely creature who was going to save Mersham and make Rupert happy and said, 'Well, I don't see why not. I'm sure people will collaborate if they know it's your wish. You can't imagine how much goodwill you've collected in the neighbourhood.'

'Thank you.' Having gained her point, Muriel was ready to turn her attention to something that had been puzzling her and, as Tom Byrne came to join his stepmother and be introduced to Muriel, she said: 'Tell me, those people over there, by the window – who are they?'

Minna's face creased into a smile. 'Oh, those are the Rabinovitches. Have you not met them yet? They're great friends of the Westerholmes and of ours. When old Mrs Rabinovitch was alive they used to employ Ollie as their *Shabbat Goy*.'

'So they *are* Jewish. I thought they must be.'

'Oh, yes, very much so and proud of it. Leo came from Poland quite penniless and made a fortune in the rag trade. He's got some marvellous stories, you must get him to tell you.'

Rupert had crossed the room to talk to the vicar and so it was in a confidential tone that Muriel said, 'And they are really intimate friends? They visit here quite frequently?'

'Is there any reason why they shouldn't?' broke in Tom Byrne.

Minna looked anxiously at her stepson. On all other matters Tom was easy-going and courteous, but on this particular subject . . .

Muriel, however, realized she had gone too far. 'No, of course not. I just thought they might be embarrassed over dietary problems and so on.' She laughed charmingly. 'I wouldn't like to make a mistake and offer them pork!'

'They're not strictly orthodox any more,' said Minna, 'though they kept the festivals for Leo's mother while she lived. In any case,' she went on, striving for lightness, 'Proom knows everyone's foibles. It isn't

Mersham they'll envy you for after your marriage, Muriel – it isn't even Rupert – it's Proom!'

And as though on cue, Proom himself appeared in the double doorway and announced that supper was served.

The guests had eaten, the covers had been removed and now, in the majesty of polished satinwood and gleaming silver, the Westerholmes and their chosen friends awaited the climax of the evening, Mrs Park's *chef-d'oeuvre*, the dessert she had created in homage to Muriel Hardwicke.

Below stairs the atmosphere was tense, fraught with the anxieties that attend the launching of a great ship. But the swan, on its gigantic platter, held steady as James lifted it, his scrupulously tended biceps never more worthily employed. Win, her mouth agape, ran to open the door; Louise bundled Mrs Park into a clean apron, ready for the expected summons . . .

'The Mersham Swan, my lady,' announced Proom – and as James marched forward to set the bird down before Miss Hardwicke, the guests rose to their feet and clapped.

'My dear, what a *triumph*!' said Minna Byrne. 'Really, there is no one in the world like your Mrs Park!'

'Oi, but that is *genius*!' cried Hannah Rabinovitch, while Miss Tate and Miss Mortimer, the pixillated spinsters, hopped like little birds.

Proom, like a great conductor, waited *in* silence *for*

silence. Then he took up the knife and, with a flourish which nevertheless contained no hint of ostentation, pierced the noble creature's heart. Exactly as Mrs Park had foreseen, the filling, softly tinged with the pink of an alpine sunset, oozed mouthwateringly on to the plate. Deftly, Proom scooped out a piece of meringue breast, a section of almond-studded wing and with a small bow handed the plate to Muriel Hardwicke.

Everyone smiled and waited and Anna, standing in the doorway with her tray, gave the exact sigh she had given when, at the age of six, she saw the blue and silver curtains part for the first time at the Maryinsky.

Muriel picked up her spoon in her soft, plump hand. She raised it to her mouth. Then she made a little *moue* and put it down again.

'You must forgive me if I leave this,' she said, turning to the dowager.

The stunned silence which followed the remark was total.

'You see,' Muriel explained with a charming smile, 'it has alcohol in it.'

Muriel was correct. There *was* alcohol in it. The Imperial Tokay Aszu 1904 which Proom, yielding to Mrs Park's palpable need, had after all allowed her to have.

The dowager, after an agonized glance at her butler, seemed to be in a state of shock. By the doorway, Anna and Peggy made identical gestures, their hands across their mouths. Proom's face was as sphinx-like as ever, but a small muscle twitched in his cheek.

106

Something about the atmosphere now made itself felt, even by Muriel. She turned to her fiancé.

'You don't mind, I'm sure?'

Rupert tried to pull himself together. 'No . . . no, of course not. I knew you didn't drink wine or spirits but not that even in food . . .' He broke off as the full implications of Muriel's embargo sank sickeningly into his brain.

'Dr Lightbody showed me a piece of cirrhosed liver once. I have never forgotten it,' said Muriel simply.

But now the shock which had held the guests silent began to wear off. Each and every person present had a memory of some good deed done by Mersham's gentle, well-loved cook and, led by Minna Byrne, with her fine social sense, they threw themselves on to the dessert, begging and imploring Proom for helpings of the bird. The vicar, Mr Morland, remembering the feather-light delicacies the cook had sent down during his wife's last illness, disposed of the swan's neck and beak in an instant and asked for more. Tom Byrne, whose childhood visits to Mersham had always taken in a session of 'helping' in the kitchens, however busy Jean Park might be, consumed virtually an entire wing in fair imitation of Billy Bunter. Hannah Rabinovitch, though it cost her dear, abandoned her guard on the tenuous, pitted organ which served her husband for a stomach and allowed him to consume lethal doses of *crème Chantilly* . . .

Downstairs, Mrs Park sat in her clean apron and waited. Waited for ten minutes, for twenty, her eyes on

107

the bell board, while hope and confidence and antici-
pation slowly drained away.

Until Proom himself, believing concealment to be
impossible, came down and broke the news.

6

The night after the engagement party, Anna could not sleep. She had been on her feet from six in the morning until midnight, and even then Miss Hardwicke had expected her to wait up and help her into bed. By the time she reached her attic, Anna was in that state of exhaustion in which sleep, though desperately desired, is impossible to reach.

For a while she endured the heat and stuffiness of the little room, tossing and turning in the narrow bed. Then she gave up, slipped back the covers, and throwing a cotton shawl over her shoulders, began to creep quietly downstairs.

On the second floor landing she stopped abruptly. Here the back staircase crossed a panelled corridor on which were a series of small guest rooms used for visitors who came for shooting parties: simple, bachelor rooms that she had hardly seen.

And from behind the door of one of these had come the sound of someone moaning, as though in pain.

But who? Surely the rooms were empty? And then she remembered. The earl had moved into the end one temporarily while the grand master suite was being spring-cleaned for the wedding.

The sound came again: a low cry, followed by a spate of indistinguishable words. And, hesitating no longer, Anna pushed open the door.

By a shaft of moonlight coming from the uncurtained window she could make out a tousled head on the pillow. The Earl of Westerholme was groaning. He was also fast asleep. In familiar country now, Anna moved over to the bed and switched on the lamp. Then she leant over and shook her employer's shoulders.

'Wake up,' she said. 'Please wake up. *Completely*.'

Rupert opened his eyes, but the slim figure in white with the heavy braids of hair made no sense to him.

'It is very foolish to sleep on your back,' Anna said firmly. 'It is *always* foolish, but when you have been in a war it is foolish beyond belief.'

The earl looked at her with unfocused eyes. He put out a hand and as he found hers, small-boned, infinitely flexible and rough as sandpaper, recognition came.

'Yes,' he said. 'You. Of course.' Then, suddenly ashamed, 'I'm sorry. A nightmare . . .'

'What was it about?'

The earl shook his head.

'Yes,' said Anna firmly. 'You must tell me. I always made Petya tell me his dreams and then he was better.'

'Who is Petya?'

110

'My brother. He used to see anarchists on the ceiling. There was an icon lamp in his nursery which threw shadows. Tell me about your dream.'

'It's always the same. It's after the crash . . . I was a pilot in the war, you see.'

She nodded. 'I know.'

'I'm in the tree . . . hanging,' Rupert went on, speaking with difficulty, 'and he's down there on the grass, dry grass like Africa, and the flames are crackling. He's on fire, burning like a rick. I try to get to him. I have to.'

'Who is he?'

'Johnny Peters. My navigator. I'm responsible for him.'

'And then?'

'I struggle and struggle, but the cords of the parachute are tangled round my neck and I know if I cry out . . . If I warn him, the flames will go out and I try to call but nothing comes.'

Anna's work-roughened hand still rested in his. 'Was it really like that?'

'Yes . . . No . . . A little. He was burned earlier, in the plane. The flames weren't like that. It was muddy . . . a turnip field. The flames are a pyre.'

'Yes, I see. All men dream like that, I suppose, after a war. Women, too,' she added ruefully. 'It will be better when you are married.' Suddenly she freed her hand and said eagerly: 'Of course! How stupid I am! I will fetch Miss Hardwicke – she will want to be with you.'

111

'No!' Rupert was wide awake now, sitting up. 'Good heavens, no! It would be most improper.'

'Improper?' said Anna, shocked. 'She will not think of that when you are troubled.'

'Anna, I forbid it,' said the earl. 'I'm all right now. I'm fine.' But as she made as if to go he said pleadingly, like a child, 'Stay a little longer. Tell me about your father.'

She smiled, her face tender in the lamplight. 'I wish you had known him. He could make just being alive seem like an act of triumph. People used to smile when they saw him coming . . . he made everything all right.' She swallowed. 'He was in the Chevalier Guards,' she went on, letting pride overcome caution. 'It was one of the tsar's crack regiments. When the revolution came the men mutinied and killed their own officers, so we tried to be glad that . . . he died when he did.'

'What was his name?'

'Peter Grazinsky. He was a good man and he hated war.' She jumped up. 'And now I'll make you a hot drink and then—'

'No, please. I don't want a drink. Just stay a little longer.' One of her thick braids had come unplaited at the ends and he was reminded, foolishly, of the fronded bracken he had uncurled with his fingers as a boy. 'Tell me about yourself. Where were you born?'

Relieved by the impersonality of the question, she said, 'In St Petersburg. I can never think of it as Petrograd.'

'Ah, yes. The city built on the bones of a thousand serfs.'

'Yes, it was built by Peter's dream and many people suffered for it. But it is not a sad city. The streets are so wide and the houses are such lovely colours: apricot and moss green and that colour that is like coffee with cream in it, you know? And everywhere there is water. The Neva, of course, and the canals, the Moika, the Fontanka . . . so that it's as if there were mirrors everywhere and one can see two cities with golden domes, one floating over the other.'

'Go on. Tell me about the snow.'

She smiled. 'Ah, yes, the snow . . . We were always happy when the snow came, isn't that ridiculous? But it made everything so smooth and quiet and . . . joined together. The whole city became one thing and the sledges were so swift and silent after the rattling of the *droshkies*. And in the country it was even better. We used to wait for the cranes to fly south and then we knew that in a very few days the snow would come. It has to fall three times before it lies, did you know that? The first fall melts and the second – but the third, that stays.'

She fell silent, her eyes full of memories, and Rupert, setting a trap for her, said quietly: '*Qu'est-ce qui vous manque le plus?*'

She frowned, thinking. Then, in a French more fluent and better accented than his own, she answered: '*La sensation d'immensité, probablement. La Russie est si enorme que cela change tout.*'

'Yes.' He could see that she might miss just those things: the sheer size of a land, its limitless skies, and the breadth of vision that such size might bring. And she had not even noticed the change of language!

Prompted by some demon to destroy the confidence he had carefully built up, he took hold of her wrist and said: 'Do you realize if this were two hundred years ago I could keep you here? Exercise my *droit de seigneur*. What would you do then?'

'I should scream,' said Anna, disengaging her wrist. She got up and went lightly to the door, then she turned and said, grinning, 'I 'ope!' – and was gone.

The following day was a Sunday and the family had the pleasure of hearing Mr Morland read the banns and of introducing Muriel to those members of the congregation who had not managed to get a glimpse of her as she drove from the station. The future countess, in a Nile green satin suit and pearls, seemed relaxed and serene and bowed most graciously to her parishioners as she walked down the aisle. The earl, on the other hand, looked tired – but then he hadn't been long out of hospital and men were always nervous about weddings.

It was also noted that very few Mersham servants were present. The dowager, unlike many employers, was not in the habit of marshalling her staff on a compulsory church parade. Today, most of the regulars had decided they could serve God best by staying at home and succouring Mrs Park.

The gentle cook had had a sleepless night and now sat like a broken-stemmed flower, reproaching herself, while Win, devoted and uncomprehending, tried to ply her with cups of tea.

'It's my fault; I should have found out,' said Mrs Park. 'Signor Manotti wouldn't have done a thing like that.'

'Give over, Jean, do,' said James, abandoning protocol to use, for once, her Christian name. 'Why, you know Signor Manotti had the brandy uncorked and half a pint in the bowl before 'e even thought what he was going to cook.'

'I just don't know what to do,' said Mrs Park in a low voice. 'It's everything, you see. No syllabub 'cos of the sherry, no jugged hare 'cos of the wine. No trifle, no *crepes Suzettes* . . . No beef stews, no *coq au vin* . . . Why, even Welsh Rarebit's got ale in it.'

And as she sat there, seeing the whole rich vocabulary of dishes she had striven so hard to learn brought suddenly to nought, a large tear gathered in Mrs Park's round, blue eyes and rolled slowly, unheeded, down her cheek.

It was too much for the others. 'But she will not *want* you not to cook most beautifully for everyone else!' cried Anna. 'It is *impossible* that she does not want others to eat as they wish. It will only be necessary to prepare something extra that has no alcohol in it for her, and as she is very rich and there are many more people to help you, this will not matter.'

'Anna's right,' said James. 'Don't you remember old

Lady Byrne? She was a Quaker, never touched a drop herself but kept one of the best tables in the country.'

But Mrs Park was not to be consoled. Though trained by a great international chef, she belonged to the old-fashioned country tradition which bound a good cook, by a thread of skill and understanding, to the mistress of the house. Muriel's rejection had left her desolate.

'I'll have to give in my notice, Mr Proom,' she said. But even as she spoke, she looked at Win standing hunched and bewildered by the range. At the orphanage they had said Win was unemployable. 'Defective' was the word they used – a word that made no sense to Mrs Park, whose patient, loving kindness had turned the girl into a second pair of hands. But would a newcomer be able to take her on? If she herself left Mersham, what would become of Win?

And worn out by strain and sleeplessness and disappointment, Mrs Park let her head fall on her arms, and sobbed.

'So these are your ancestors?' said Muriel, looking with pleasure and interest at the serried ranks of Westerholmes in the long gallery.

Returning from church, she had found laid out for her a simple dress of blue linen which matched the colour of her eyes. She had taken the hint and also allowed Anna to arrange her golden hair in a low chignon. Steering her through the armoury, the library and the music room, Rupert thought he had never seen her look fresher or more beautiful and his misgivings of the previous night vanished in the sunlight. Of course Muriel would fit in at Mersham, of course she would love his people and his home.

'Yes, those are the Westerholmes and the women fool enough to marry them,' he said, smiling. 'That's Timothy Frayne, who founded the family fortune in all sorts of disreputable ways. And that's his son, James – he was the first earl. James was one of the fair, roistering Fraynes, always in trouble! Then this one's William – he's one of the other kind, dark and dreamy. William landscaped the park and furnished the music room – music was his passion. And George here is a throwback to James – a devil with the women and always getting into scrapes. My brother was like him, they said.'

'And you're like William,' said Muriel, looking at the scholarly face above the lace collar. 'Goodness, who's this one? He looks *very* strange!'

Rupert grinned. 'That's our black sheep, Sir Montague Frayne. He was a cousin of the fourth earl's. He's the only one of my ancestor's who's had the distinction of becoming a fully fledged ghost.'

'Really?' Muriel's tone was not encouraging. 'What did he do?'

'He murdered his wife's lover,' said Rupert, looking at the wild-eyed young courtier nonchalantly posed with one hand on his hip. 'Or the man he believed to be his wife's lover: a young architect who built the Temple of Flora and the gothic folly in the woods.'

'And where does he do his haunting?' said Muriel,

humouring her fiancé, for she did not, naturally, believe in ghosts.

'Oh, not in the house. Out in the folly where the dark deed was done. It's quite a big place, a sort of tower with three rooms one on top of the other with a dome on the top. No one uses it now and it's kept padlocked. The servants swear he howls and wails in repentance, and of course no one will go near it in the dark.'

'One must allow for foolishness and superstition in the uneducated classes,' said Muriel.

'Yes, I suppose one must,' said Rupert, a little bleakly.

He looked at his watch. In an hour, Potter would be back with the mare. The excitement in the groom's voice on the telephone had told Rupert all he wanted to know and, at the thought of the gift he was giving Muriel, his spirits soared. He had taken so much from her already, was so greatly in her debt, but the bridegroom's present to the bride would at least be a worthy one!

'Shall we go outside?' he suggested. 'You must have seen enough of my ancestors to last you a lifetime.'

'Not at all, dear,' said Muriel, who was peering intently at the portraits, 'I find them very handsome.' She turned to smile coquettishly at him. 'Just like you. And there don't seem to be any taints or blemishes, which is unusual in so old a family.'

'Taints?' said Rupert, puzzled. 'What exactly do you mean?'

'Well, you know . . . deformities, inherited diseases,' said Muriel, drawing her skirt away from Baskerville. 'Hare lips and so on,' she continued. 'Or mental illness. Though that would hardly show up in a painting, I suppose.'

Rupert was looking at her in rather an odd manner. 'I don't know of any; they were a very ordinary lot as far as I know. But if there were, Muriel, would it really matter to you?'

Muriel smiled and patted his arm with her plump, soft hand. 'You must remember my great interest in eugenics. And once you have met Dr Lightbody, which I hope will be very soon, I know you will become as interested as I am.'

As they walked towards the garden door they met Pearl, carrying coals to Uncle Sebastien's room.

'That reminds me,' said Rupert, as she bobbed a curtsy and scuttled respectfully away. 'How is Anna making out? It's early, I know, but are you satisfied with her?'

Muriel frowned, a neat and parallel gesture. 'Yes,' she said doubtfully. 'She is deft and painstaking but I confess, dear, that I don't really care for her. There is something not quite right about the girl.'

'You don't find her disrespectful or anything of the sort? Because I don't think she means—'

'No, I can't say she's disrespectful,' said Muriel, who prided herself on her fairness, 'but for a servant she is too *interested*. A good maid should be like a piece of furniture: there, but unnoticed.'

'Yes,' said Rupert, who saw exactly what Muriel meant. You could say a lot about Anna, but not that she was like a piece of furniture. 'She's only temporary, you know; part of the intake to prepare for the wedding. I'm looking to you to engage what servants you will afterwards.'

'I'm glad to hear you say that,' answered Muriel as they prepared to cross the stableyard, 'because I do think quite a lot of changes will be needed. For example, I really think we should have matched footmen. In a house of this quality, to have footmen of different sizes gives a very untidy appearance. I should like them about six foot two, but I daresay we had better content ourselves with six foot, so many people having been killed in the war.'

Rupert looked up quickly to see if Muriel was joking, but her lovely face was placid and serene.

'Isn't that a little grand for us?' he said. 'They have them at Longleat and Blenheim, I know, but Mersham is hardly a palace. And James, who's been with us for years, can't be nearly six foot and yet he's an excellent servant; quick and willing and conscientious. It would be very wrong to turn him off.'

'Of course it would, dear. Don't worry, just leave everything to me. You see, I so much want things to be *perfect* at Mersham and – Good gracious, what's that?'

'That' was an enormous tea-cosy which had just flown out of the first floor window of a cottage built into the stable block, narrowly missing a bed of petunias. It was followed by a strange whooping noise and

120

a shower of spoons, clattering on to the cobbles at their feet.

Muriel, looking with horror at Rupert, was surprised to see him smile like a child experiencing a familiar but long-forgotten treat.

'It's Mrs Proom! My goodness, that takes me back! We ought to go and see her, Muriel, she'll be so pleased.'

'Mrs Proom? You mean your butler's wife?'

Rupert shook his head. 'His mother. She must be well over ninety. She was a very active woman once and now she's bedridden. It makes her a little fractious sometimes and then she throws things.'

Muriel frowned. Mad old women who threw things were no part of her plans for Mersham. But Rupert was already leading the way into the trim little cottage and she had perforce to follow him.

Mrs Proom was sitting up in bed, her lace cap askew, her little shrunken chest heaving angrily.

'I'm bored,' she said. 'Where's the Russian girl? Cyril said she was coming.' The words were hardly decipherable because Mrs Proom, in deference to the weather, which was warm and sunny, had removed her teeth.

Rupert had walked over to the bed and taken her little brown-spotted hand in his. 'Mrs Proom! How good to see you. Do you remember me?'

The change in the shrunken face was touching. 'Master Rupert,' she mumbled. 'His lordship, I should say, and me without my teeth.'

'I've brought my fiancée to see you,' said Rupert, smiling warmly down at her. 'This is Miss Hardwicke.'

Muriel came forward, ready to be gracious.

'My, what a beauty!' said the old lady. 'Cyril said as how you was good-looking, but you're lovelier than a queen.'

'Thank you,' said Muriel, smiling charmingly at the old lady.

But as they were leaving, Mrs Proom turned querulous again. 'I want the tweeny,' she said. 'Anna, she was called. She's telling me about the Bolshies. I like fine to hear about the Bolshies.'

'I'll pass on the message,' promised Rupert. 'I'm sure she'll be here soon.'

'I don't want her soon,' said Mrs Proom. 'I want her *now*.'

It was as they were strolling along the lake that Rupert was reminded of a practical matter he'd meant to mention to his betrothed.

'Muriel, after we're married, I wonder if you'd look into the business of bathrooms for the top floor. The servants' attics. There don't seem to be any at all.'

'Don't they have ewers and basins?' asked Muriel, surprised.

'Well, yes. But some of them seem to feel they'd like something more. Housework is a pretty dirty business after all.'

'Rupert, none of your servants are *socialists*, I hope?'

'Good heavens no, I shouldn't think so. I mean, I haven't asked. Surely you don't have to be a socialist to want to have a bath?'

'It often goes together,' said Muriel sagely.

Rupert did not pursue the matter. Three o'clock had just struck and it was time to go and meet his groom.

'Muriel,' he said, his face alight, 'we have to turn back now. I've got something to show you . . . a surprise.'

An hour later, Anna, passing the stables on her way to visit Mrs Proom, came upon the Earl of Westerholme standing alone by Saturn's loose box, stroking his old hunter's neck. She would have gone past, but something about his expression, a look of weariness, made her hesitate.

'Don't,' he said as she halted. 'I forbid it.'

'Don't what,' said Anna, startled.

'Don't curtsy. I've had a hard afternoon and I can't stand it.'

Anna was indignant. 'But I am a *maid*, my lord! And in Selina Strickland—'

'And don't speak to me about Selina Strickland either. I have developed a profound dislike of Selina Strickland. Come here, I want to show you something.'

Anna came. The earl walked down the long line of loose boxes, most of them empty now, and drew back the bolt of a door at the end.

'*Oh!*' said Anna. 'She has come!'

'Potter told you I was buying a mare for Miss Hardwicke?'

'Yes.' Anna could not take her eyes off the mare as she pranced and cavorted, shy yet trusting, white as snow, with the narrow head and marvellously held neck of the true Arab. 'She's like Mr Cameron's new rose.'

'And, like Mr Cameron's new rose, she needs a name.'

Anna was stroking the velvet muzzle now, apologizing tenderly for her sugarless state . . . modulating, as the mare grew more affectionate, into her own language. That damnable language, thought Rupert, that turns everything into poetry – and catching one word, he said: '*Dousha?* That means "soul", doesn't it?'

'Yes. But it is also what you call people you love. We say "my soul" like you say "my darling" or "my dearest".' She looked up to give him one of her sudden, life-enhancing grins. 'We are very interested in souls in Russia.'

'So I understand.' Rupert let his long fingers run through the mare's silken mane. 'Shall I call you Dousha?' he asked her. Then. 'But after all, I shall not call her anything. I'm going to sell her again,' he added, trying to keep his voice light.

'Oh no!' Anna's face was puckered in despair. 'Why?'

'Miss Hardwicke doesn't ride. I knew that. But I thought she would want to learn. That's why I chose the mare, for her gentleness. The bridegroom's present for the bride. Silly of me. Muriel wants sapphires.'

The bleakness in his eyes, contrasting with the light voice, was too much for Anna, who buried her face in the horse's neck.

'Do you ride?' Rupert asked suddenly, and watched – his depression lifting – the expressions chase across her face as she decided whether or not to lie.

'Everyone rides in Russia,' she compromised at last.

'Of course,' he agreed gravely. 'Particularly the housemaids. Oh, God, I wish I could . . . but really I can't. It wouldn't do.'

Anna was wise enough to ignore this. Instead, seemingly at random, she said: 'Have you heard of the Heavenly Horses of Ferghana?'

Rupert caught his breath.

'Yes,' he said, 'I have heard of them. And of the Emperor Wu-Ti who sought them all his life because he believed they would carry his soul to heaven.'

It had grown very quiet in the stable. Only the mare's gentle whickering broke the silence.

'She is one of them, I think,' said the girl softly. 'One of the brave ones who gallop till they sweat blood.'

'Perhaps I could send her home,' mused Rupert, 'to browse on fields of alfalfa in an emerald valley watered by crystal streams from the Pamirs . . .'

'Until the servants of the emperor come to harness her to the Chariot of Immortality—'

'And she gallops off into the sky bound for the Land of Perpetual Peace.'

For a while neither of them spoke. Then he said: 'It was my dream once, to go out there. To Afghanistan or further and bring back some of those horses. There's a strain there still . . .'

'It was a good dream,' said Anna quietly.

'No. Not now, not any more.'

'But *yes*! One must hold on to dreams. My Cousin Sergei was like you – all through the fighting, while he could still get letters, he wrote of the splendid horses he would breed when there was peace again.'

Rupert turned to her, his own troubles set aside. 'Ah, yes, Uncle Sebastien told me how happy you were that he was safe. Do you have any news of him?'

Anna nodded. 'I had a letter yesterday from my mother. He has become chauffeur to a very rich and important duchess!'

'That sounds promising.'

Anna gave a theatrical sigh. 'I'm afraid it will end badly,' she said. 'You see, the duchess has five daughters and Sergei is *very* beautiful!'

'Lucky Sergei!' said Rupert, smiling down at her.

And, relieved to have paddled back into the shallows, he led his housemaid from the stables.

7

Fortman and Bittlestone's reputation as 'England's Premier Department Store' rests on a number of specialities. On the food halls, where bowler-hatted gentlemen's gentlemen may be seen of a morning prodding their way through a selection of exotic cheeses; on the jewellery department, where maharajahs have not scorned to pick up a trinket to take back to their palaces in Rawalpindi or Lahore; on the restaurant, where, in a décor resembling the bathrooms of the Topkapi Palace, ancient duchesses consume English mutton at prices so astronomical that it stills all possible criticism of the food.

But above all, on its bridal department. For over a hundred years, Fortman and Bittlestone have been making wedding dresses for the élite of Britain. Conveniently situated for bridesmaids' lunches at the Ritz, there was hardly a morning when a bevy of brides and their attendants did not take possession of the opulent fitting rooms with their oyster-silk booths and draped curtains, their ankle-deep carpets and obsequious sewing girls. For here was the end of the road for those girls who, having safely weathered the storm-tossed agitations of 'The Season', came matrimonially to rest.

And here, at twelve noon just four weeks before the wedding, Muriel Hardwicke had arranged to meet her bridesmaids: Miss Cynthia Smythe, The Lady Lavinia Nettleford – and Ollie Byrne.

For Ollie, the proposed expedition to London was a source of desperate excitement. Not only was she to meet Muriel at last and try on The Dress, but she was also to join the two grown-up bridesmaids afterwards at the luncheon that Tom Byrne, as best man, was giving them at the Ritz. And to complete the glory of this day, Tom himself was going to drive her up to town.

Rupert, proposing to escort Muriel by train, was less enthusiastic. He had hoped to spend the day catching up on the business of the estate but, in her quiet way, Muriel had been insistent about the purchase of her sapphires, and sapphires were not to be found in Maidens Over, the local market town.

'You know the little rhyme, dear,' she said playfully. '"Something old, something new, something borrowed, something blue." To walk down the aisle wearing *your* sapphires would make me very happy.'

She was prepared to be generous over land and settlements; indeed she had taken some trouble to have Rupert financially dependent on her even before the marriage. Just in case anything *should* go wrong, no man of honour could possibly break an engagement to a woman to whom he was beholden in that way. But she wanted people to see that she was admired and courted and the discovery that the dowager had, over the years, quietly sold off the Westerholme jewels, in order to pay Lord George's gambling debts, had not pleased her in the least. She was sorry, of course, that Rupert had bought a horse which was apparently very valuable, but horse riding was something she had no intention of indulging in. It was a sport which, unless begun in childhood, would inevitably set one off at a disadvantage and there was something displeasing about these prancing, perspiring animals.

One other person was travelling to London that morning. Anna had served a full month at Mersham and was having her whole day off – a day which she proposed to spend with her mother and Pinny at West Paddington.

She was walking down the village street bound for the station and the milk train to town when a loud hoot from behind made her turn round. Done up to the eyes for motoring, the Honourable Olive, in a long muffler, leant out and said: 'Anna! I'm going to London! I'm going to try on my bridesmaid's dress and I'm going to lunch in a restaurant and I'm going to see Muriel and—'

Tom, grinning, interrupted this spate. 'Can I offer you a lift? Are you going to the station?'

Anna nodded. 'Thank you, you are very kind.'

She climbed into the back, deciding on this

wonderful summer morning to give Selina Strickland and protocol a rest. 'It's my day off,' she said, 'so I'm going to London to see my mother and—' She broke off, peered at Ollie and said gravely, 'I find you *extremely* elegant, Miss Byrne.'

Ollie beamed. 'It's my best coat. And my best gloves. And,' she slewed round to whisper to Anna, 'there's *real lace* on my petticoat. Honestly.'

They passed the turning to the station and Tom, unconcerned, drove on.

'Oh, please, you must put me down here!' cried Anna.

'Nonsense, we'll take you up to town.'

'Yes, you must come, Anna, because I have to tell you about the hedgehog and you promised to tell me about when Sergei was naughty and fell through the ice and the poem about the crocodile walking down that street and . . . Tom, can I go and sit in the back with Anna?'

Anna gave up. As for Tom, he smiled, well pleased with this development. He was the friendliest of men and would have taken Anna up to town in any case. But today Susie was working at the London Library, a place so respectable that her parents allowed her to attend it unchaperoned. If Anna should happen to be willing to take Ollie to Fortman and Bittlestone and leave her there, it would give him half an hour which he might snatch with Susie. A half hour which, in view of the bridesmaids' lunch he would later have to endure, he felt he deserved.

*

130

In the chattery of Fortman and Bittlestone, the two adult bridesmaids were eating ices and waiting for the bride.

Muriel had chosen her bridesmaids with the care and concentration which characterized everything she did. Cynthia Smythe, the only friend Muriel had made at school, had earned the honour of following Muriel down the aisle by a kind of servility and obsequiousness which made Uriah Heap look like the all-in wrestler, Hackenschmidt. She was a pale girl, long-necked and goitrous, with crimped, light hair over a low forehead and an insipid mouth. Untroubled by either intelligence or will, Cynthia had thought it 'spiffing' to be asked to be a bridesmaid, 'super' to be invited to lunch with Tom Byrne, and could generally be relied upon not to trouble Muriel with a single original remark or independent action.

The Lady Lavinia Nettleford was a different matter. The eldest of five daughters, whose mother's attempts to marry them off had passed into folklore, she was an equine looking girl with blue eyes set close together, an expression of incorrigible hauteur and that misfortune known as the Nettleford nose. Lady Lavinia scarcely knew Muriel, with whom she'd nursed during the war, and what she did know she thoroughly disliked. Along with the other debutantes at the hospital, she'd felt nothing but chagrin and contempt for Muriel's campaign to entice the Earl of Westerholme, severely wounded and in a state of shock, into an engagement. She herself was made of sterner stuff than Larissa Ponsonby and Zoe van Meck, who had cried their eyes out when the engagement was announced, but her annoyance was no less. Nor did she have any illusions about why Muriel had asked her to be a bridesmaid. Muriel, whose father was, to all intents and purposes, a grocer, wanted (and Lavinia thought this perfectly natural) to be followed down the aisle by the daughter of a duke.

But though she disliked Muriel and saw through her, it had not occurred to Lavinia to refuse. For attached to every wedding is that font of hope, that potential piece of manna, the best man. She did not personally know Tom Byrne, for the Nettleford seat, Farne Castle, was on a distant, wave-lashed Northumbrian shore but, though heir to a mere viscountancy, he was reputed to be both personable and rich. Lavinia, pursued by the hot breath of her four sisters Hermione, Priscilla, Gwendolyn and Beatrice, had been seventeen times a bridesmaid. This time, the charms of the new chauffeur notwithstanding, she intended to become a bride.

'Ah, there you are!' Muriel had left Rupert at the Flying Club and now strode confidently into the chattery. 'You've introduced yourselves, I see.' Her appraising deep blue eyes raked the bridesmaids and she nodded, well satisfied. The girls were of roughly equal height and similar colouring and would make a well-matched pair to follow her up the aisle. If Ollie was half as sweet and pretty as Rupert made out, the procession ought to be a great success. 'Come along,' she continued, 'we won't wait for the little girl, she's coming up by car.'

Followed by her bridesmaids, Muriel charged, unseeing, past the world's most impressive cheese counter, through 'handbags' and 'haberdashery' and was wafted in the lift to the sanctity of the bridal department, where Madame Duparc, whose varicose veins were stabbing like gimlets, schooled her face into a welcoming smile and, flanked by Millie and Violet, the underpaid and undernourished sewing girls, gushed her way towards Muriel.

'Everything is ready, Mees Hardwicke and I think you will be very, very pleased. With one fitting, we should complete. Of course mademoiselle's measurements are so satisfying . . . the perfect figure . . .'

Soothing, flattering, joined now by the chief *vendeuse*, Miss Taylor, Madame Duparc led the entourage towards the three luxurious fitting booths at the far side of the room with their ornate mirrors and plush-lined stools.

Into the centre booth there now vanished Muriel Hardwicke, to be followed by Madame Duparc herself. Into the right-hand booth passed the Lady Lavinia Nettleford, humbly accompanied by Millie. Into the left-hand booth, its curtains held aside by the obsequious Violet, stepped Cynthia Smythe. From a mysterious upper region there now appeared three more girls in the Fortman uniform of pale green carrying, in swathes of tissue, the bridesmaids' dresses and the wedding gown itself. Directed by the chief *vendeuse*, they vanished into the appropriate booths, from which came twittering noises of admiration as the little seamstresses pinned and flattered, measured and soothed.

Meanwhile Anna and the Honourable Olive had arrived downstairs and were wending their eager and interested way through the food hall. Tom's plan had succeeded. In exchange for a promised taxi afterwards to take her to West Paddington, Anna had expressed herself delighted to deliver Ollie at Fortman's. Now the two girls were sniffing their way appreciatively between jars of Chinese ginger, beribboned chocolate boxes, marzipan fruit . . .

'Isn't it a *lovely* shop, Anna!'

'Beautiful!' said Anna, her eyes alight. 'How many things can you smell, Ollie?'

The little girl wrinkled her nose. 'Cheese and coffee and a sort of sausage-ish smell and soap . . .'

'And freesias and cigars and duchesses . . .'

Ollie giggled. 'Duchesses don't smell.'

'Oh yes, they do,' said Anna. 'It's a very *rich* smell with fur coats in it and lap dogs and blue, blue blood.'

They were still laughing as they went up in the lift, but as they approached the opulent silence of the bridal department and passed an amazingly disdainful look-ing dummy swathed in white tulle, Ollie suddenly became quiet, overcome by the importance of the occa-sion.

'Could you . . . stay till Tom comes back?' she asked, letting her hand creep into Anna's.

Anna nodded, glad that she had not given Pinny a definite arrival time.

'But of course.'

Madame Duparc, momentarily relegating Muriel to two minions, now came forward to welcome them. 'Ah, this is the little flower girl for whom we have been waiting,' she said, smiling down at the child with her flame coloured curls and brave limp.

'Come, *ma petite*, your dress is ready. The others are next door so we will go into this room and give them a surprise.' She turned to Anna, in no way deceived by the plainness of her clothes and said: 'You will wish to accompany your little friend, mademoiselle?'

'Thank you.'

Ollie stepped into the booth. Anna helped her out of her coat, her dress. Very small, utterly expectant, wearing her petticoat with *real* lace, the Honourable Olive stood and waited.

Then they came, two girls, ceremoniously carrying the ensemble that for weeks now had been the stuff of Ollie's dreams. They carefully unwrapped the rose pink dress, the velvet cloak, the pearl-encrusted muff.

'Oh, Anna, *look*!' said the Honourable Olive, holding her arms up. 'Oh, *gosh* . . .'

Next door things were proceeding less smoothly. Cynthia Smythe, it was true, oozed meekness and gratitude as she turned and twisted at the fitting girl's behest and the Lady Lavinia, in her booth, staring over the heads of the assistants with the bored hauteur of a thoroughbred being decked out for a minor agricultural show, gave relatively little trouble.

The same could not be said of Muriel Hardwicke. Muriel had the clearest possible ideas about the way her dress and train and veil should look and these ideas, though she expressed them forcibly, the staff of Fortman and Bittlestone were failing to realize.

'No, no . . . that dart is in *quite* the wrong place. And the sleeves are much too full at the wrist.'

'But when mademoiselle has her bouquet—'

'I'm not carrying a bouquet,' snapped Muriel, 'flowers are far too unreliable. I'm carrying a gold-bound prayer-book, so please don't use that as an excuse.'

The girls grew hot and flustered, Madame Duparc's varicose veins throbbed and pounded across her swollen legs . . . But at last, though grudgingly, Muriel declared herself reasonably satisfied.

'If the others are ready, tell them to come out, please. I want to see the effect of the whole ensemble.'

The door of the left-hand booth now opened and there emerged, like one of the puppets in *Petroushka*, the apologetic and slightly goose-pimpled figure of Miss Cynthia Smythe.

The door of the right-hand booth followed – and the Lady Lavinia Nettleford, lofty and indifferent in her eighteenth bridesmaid's dress, stepped out.

After which Madame Duparc, the little sewing girls and the chief *vendeuse* gave the same experienced and slightly weary sigh.

For her bridesmaids Muriel had chosen identical dresses of rose pink satin with a bloused bodice, a pink velvet sash and the three-tiered skirts which the great Poiret had just introduced in Paris. A wide frill of pink accordion-pleated chiffon lined the hems, encircled the cuffs of the short sleeves and edged the square neck – and dipping low on their foreheads like inverted tea cups, the girls wore close-fitting, pink satin-petalled caps.

Pink is a lovely and becoming colour and the image of a rose is never far from the minds of those who contemplate an ensemble of this shade. Unfortunately, there are other images which may intrude. Cynthia Smythe, emerging soft-fleshed, goitrous and apathetic from her ruffles, suggested a prematurely dished-up and rather nervous ham. The Lady Lavinia had other troubles. Though the bodice was generously bloused, the Lady Lavinia was not. With her stick-like arms, jerky movements and the tendency to whiskers which has been the Nettleford scourge for generations, she relentlessly reminded the onlookers that pink is not only the colour of budding roses, but of boiling prawns.

But now the door of the centre booth was thrown open and there emerged – to the sound of imagined trumpets – the bride herself.

Muriel had chosen not white, but a rich brocade of ivory which better took up the colour of her creamy skin. Cleaving to her magnificent bosom, clinging till the last possible moment to her generously undulating hips, the dress fanned out dramatically into a six-foot train, embroidered with opalescent beads and glistening *pailettes*. Richly elaborate threadwork also spangled the bodice and, eschewing the simple white tulle so beloved of ordinary brides, Muriel had set her diamond tiara over a veil of glittering silver lace.

And seeing her, Madame Duparc and her staff broke into the expected applause, but half-heartedly, for *weddings* were their business and Muriel, in her metallic splendour, looked more like some goddess descending from Valhalla than a bride.

A very small noise, like a cricket clearing its throat, caused them to turn their heads.

In the doorway leading from the other fitting room stood a tiny figure in rose pink satin – and pushed gently forward by Anna, who then stood aside – the Honourable Olive, *en grand tenue*, began to walk across the deep pile of the dove grey carpet towards Muriel and her retinue.

And as they watched her the tired sewing women began to smile, remembering suddenly what it was all about. The sheer joy of a wedding: the sense of wonder and humility and awe . . . the newness of it and the hope . . . all were there in this child, limping with a shining morning face towards the bride.

Holding in one reverent hand the flounces of her dress, clutching in the other the pearl-encrusted muff she had not been able to relinquish, Ollie advanced. Apart from a head-dress of fresh flowers for which Minna had begged, Ollie's outfit was the same as the other bridesmaids', but her radiance and delight had transfigured it. The pink ruffles nestled beguilingly against her throat; she listened with parted lips to the rustle of her skirt as if it were the sound of angel's wings. One of the fitting girls, forgetting her place, had sent downstairs for rosebuds, which by some alchemy blended, instead of clashing, with her flaming hair.

Now Ollie was close enough really to see Muriel and the blue eyes widened behind the round glasses. Ever since she had heard Muriel spoken of, Ollie had seen her as a fairy tale princess. Here in reality, she surpassed all Ollie's dreams. Untroubled by considerations of suitability or good taste, Ollie gazed at the glittering, shimmering figure with its diamond crown. And forgetting about herself completely, she came to rest in front of Muriel, looked up adoringly, and said:

'Oh! You do look *beautiful*!'

Muriel seemed not to have heard. Ever since Ollie had appeared in the doorway she had been staring in silent fascination at the child. Now she drew in her breath and as Anna, guided by some instinct, stepped forward and Tom Byrne entered to fetch the bridesmaids, she hissed, in a whisper which carried right across the room:

'Why did no one tell me that the child was crippled!'

8

Ollie had heard. As though the words had been a physical blow, the colour drained from her face, she bent her bright head and the small hand which had been proudly holding up the flounces of her skirt dropped to her side. In shocked silence, Madame Duparc and the shopgirls stared at the woman who had done this deed.

Tom Byrne had checked his first steps towards his sister to control a rage so murderous that it terrified him. He wanted to shake Muriel till her teeth rattled, to press his fingers into her throat. Horrified to find these feelings in himself, he stood stock-still in the middle of the floor like a bewildered bull.

It was the Lady Lavinia, with her well-bred indifference, who saved the moment by suggesting an alteration to Muriel's train and the fitting continued.

But when it was over and it came to carrying out the next part of the programme, Ollie quietly refused to cooperate. To the suggestion that she should now

140

join the other bridesmaids for luncheon at the Ritz, the Honourable Olive gave a low-voiced but unalterable 'No'. She wasn't, she said, hungry and, clinging to Anna's hand, she added that she thought she would like to go home.

'I can't take you home yet, love,' said Tom, desperately distressed – turning, with appeal in his nice brown eyes, to the Lady Lavinia Nettleford and Cynthia Smythe. Surely they would release him, let him attend to his sister? But in the eyes of Muriel's adult bridesmaids there was only a desire, implacable as the urge of a wildebeest towards a water hole, for luncheon at the Ritz.

'Well, really,' said Muriel, 'all that fuss just because I said—'

But even she did not repeat what she had said.

Anna now took charge. Her rage had been as instant and murderous as Tom's, but it had been extinguished by an emotion even more intense: a deep pity for the man who had linked his life with a woman such as this. Now she rejected this too, bent only on helping Ollie.

'Perhaps it would be nice if you came home with me and we made cinnamon toast and I showed you a little dog that has in his stomach the diamond that the Empress Elizabeth gave to Rastrelli and also a stuffed grandmother?'

Ollie, though she did not speak, indicated her approval by nodding into Anna's skirts and Tom looked at her with gratitude.

But, in the event, they shared Lord Westerholme's taxi. Arriving as planned to escort Muriel to lunch, Rupert was told that she preferred to stay behind and shop.

'Oh?'

Muriel glanced up at him sharply. It had been her intention to punish her fiancé by depriving him of her company, for it seemed to her that in concealing Ollie's handicap he had been deceitful and underhand. Now, too late, she saw her mistake. The flash of anger in Rupert's eyes had only lasted a moment, but it had been unmistakable.

'In that case I'll get myself off to Aspell's,' he said, turning away. 'I've got a taxi waiting. Does anyone want a lift?'

So it was arranged that Rupert would drop off Anna and Ollie, before proceeding to the queen's jewellers to purchase Muriel's bridal gift.

'Who was that girl?' asked the Lady Lavinia, looking after Anna as she led Ollie away. 'The foreign one?'

Muriel shrugged. 'Just one of the Mersham domestics. She seems to have forgotten her place and cadged a lift to town. A Russian refugee. Why do you ask?'

'She reminds me of someone.'

'Who?'

'Actually, our new chauffeur. He's a foreigner, too.'

And the Lady Lavinia sighed. For Sergei was rather more than a foreigner . . . To have the fur rug tucked round one's knees by him, to have him hold open the car door and see him smile that devastating yet protective smile, to catch the warmth in those dark, long-lashed, gold-flecked eyes was to feel so cherished, so curiously excited, that it was best not to think of it. Not that she made an idiot of herself like her four sisters did, likening him to Rudolf Valentino, carrying on like kitchen maids. Sergei was, in fact, a great deal better-looking than Valentino – taller, stronger, in every way more manly – but that was neither here nor there. Whatever he had been in his native land, a chauffeur was a chauffeur. It was a good job she had given him the afternoon off. With Mama and the younger girls still in Northumberland, Hermione and Priscilla were quite capable of ordering him to take them on joyrides round the park.

But Tom Byrne was waiting – and with Cynthia docilely in attendance, Lavinia swept off to the powder room to prepare for the luncheon which she hoped would seal her fate.

Ollie sat between Rupert and Anna in the taxi as it crawled down Piccadilly, festooned with bunting for the victory parade. She was still very white and quiet and Rupert, sensing her distress, was too wise to ask what had happened. Instead he watched as Anna, summoning up all her forces, turned to attack the little girl.

'So. You wish to sit there like a small, wet blancmange because someone has said a word to you.'

'It's not a very nice word,' said Ollie, in a thread of a voice.

'Nice, nasty . . . It's a word,' said Anna shrugging. 'It means someone who is lame. Well, you are lame. You are also pretty and good and have about one hundred and twenty people who love you very much and a hedgehog called Alexander. To be frightened by a word is an idiocy and you know this very well. In fact, I think I am a little bit ashamed of you.'

'Are you?' said Ollie. A trace of colour was returning to her cheeks.

'Yes, I am. Of course, if you wish to be sad on *purpose* that is all right. We can all be sad. Lord Westerholme can be sad because under his shoulder is a piece of shrapnel and this gives him pain when he lifts his arm,' said Anna, ignoring Rupert's quick look of surprise. 'And I could cry almost immediately because my father is dead and they have taken away all our houses—'

'Did you have a lot of houses?' asked Ollie, momentarily diverted.

Anna bit her lip and Rupert, at his most silky, said, 'In Russia all the housemaids have a lot of houses, Ollie.'

Not quite understanding, Ollie nevertheless responded to the feeling of warmth and affection which had grown up, almost tangibly, in the back of the taxi. And able, now, to put the dread question into words, she asked:

'Will Muriel still want me to be a bridesmaid?'

Rupert, not knowing the reason for the question, answered it in a voice that she had never heard him use.

'Ollie,' said Lord Westerholme, taking both her hands in his, 'if you are not a bridesmaid at my wedding then there will *be* no wedding, and that I swear!'

Ollie sighed and let her head fall back on to the seat. 'I'm sorry,' she said. 'I was silly.'

Anna nodded, conceding this. Then, allowing the tenderness to come back into her voice she said, 'Do you know what is best of all? When one has been hurt or saddened, then suddenly to turn everything upside down and be very happy. So I think we should have an absolutely beautiful afternoon – an afternoon that you can lie in bed and remember for years and years.'

'Can we do that?' asked Ollie.

'Most certainly,' said Anna.

Anna was as good as her word. It was into an enchanted world that she now led Ollie Byrne.

Pinny, opening the door of her little mews house, did not need Anna's hurried aside to see that the child had had a shock. To the information, tendered by Ollie, that she was not tired or hungry and almost never went to the lavatory, Pinny listened attentively and with respect. Half an hour later, Ollie, having drunk two glasses of milk and eaten a large helping of macaroni cheese, was lying on the sofa feeding the budgerigar the strips of cinnamon toast that were his passion.

But Pinny's house was only the beginning. Anna had run upstairs to change into her only 'good' dress – a green velveteen which Kira had sent from Paris. The Countess Grazinsky gathered up shawls, leaking packets of tea and lorgnettes, and when Pinny was satisfied that the little girl was properly rested they set off for the Russian Club.

For the rest of her childhood, if anyone asked Ollie what she wanted to be when she grew up, she always replied: 'A Russian.' The club was on the first floor of a large, dilapidated house behind Paddington Station, but the trains which shook its foundations every few minutes might have been travelling, not to Plymouth but to Minsk, not to Torquay but to Vladimir the Great, so exotic and foreign were its delights.

For there really was a stuffed grandmother. She lived – so everyone swore – in a most beautiful and gaily painted chest which stood under one window. The chest was heavily padlocked and covered with a crimson gypsy shawl and no one would have dreamt of putting down a tray of glasses or a plate on it without saying, 'Sorry, Baboushka', or 'Forgive me, Ancient One'. Nor was there anything *sad* about her, as Anna was quick to explain. For the old lady had belonged to the two pale young men, Boris and Andrey, who now owned the house the club was in and spent their time at a corner table playing Halma and planning to assassinate Lenin. Boris and Andrey had adored the old lady and when she died had, with the help of a famous Egyptologist, found this way of keeping her with them when they fled their native land. Or so they said.

Above the Baboushka there hung an icon of St Cunouphrius, the saint who grew a beard to cover his

146

nakedness and whose stick-like arms and little, white legs were all that protruded, wistfully, from behind the curlicues of coal-black hair. Beside him, there was another picture showing forty martyred bishops busily freezing to death in their shifts on an ice floe, and beneath them was a small shrine containing a crimson icon lamp, a bunch of withered marigolds, a lump of bread and a packet of Cerebos salt. There was an enormous, stuttering, smouldering samovar of fluted brass . . .

And there was Pupsik himself, the mythical dachshund, his sagging extremeties hanging exhaustedly over the edges of a low footstool which had become a kind of altar. Pupsik, to whom his owner the Baroness de Wodzka had fed, in a moment of panic on the Finnish border, the Rastrelli diamond embedded in a chunk of liver sausage. A priceless diamond, the baroness's only remaining jewel, which somehow, mysteriously, the ancient, wheezing animal had managed to retain in some diverticular abnormality along the clogged and malodorous drainpipe of its body . . . Every day during the six months of his quarantine, the baroness had rung the kennels, terrifying the kennelmaids with her imperious, '*Vell*? 'ass 'e voided?'

But Pupsik, though functioning normally in other respects, had not voided the jewel.

Bets had been laid, horrendous physiological disputes had split the club – but Pupsik, returning from quarantine to find himself famous and feted, continued to deprive the baroness of the jewel which would have

147

reunited her with her children in America, secured her a livelihood, a home.

Anna's entry, with her mother, her governess and Ollie, was the signal for an explosion of hugs, kisses and endearments. The Princess Chirkovsky, Sergei's mother, enveloped her in an enormous motheaten chinchilla stole; a grey-bearded poet who had been writing verses to her since she was six years old rushed forward with his latest ode. Colonel Terek, who had parked his taxi in the mews, went for more vodka . . .

For a few moments, Anna gave herself up to the joy of being welcomed. Then she held up her hand and, switching to English, said: 'I have brought you a very special friend of mine, Miss Olive Byrne. She has been a little bit sad and I have told her that here it is possible to be instantly and completely happy. Was I correct?'

And the party began.

An hour later, Ollie had reached unimaginable heights of glory. Her health had been drunk and the glasses thrown away so that no lesser toast could ever be drunk than the one dedicated to her. Gentlemen behaved in this way in the presence of beautiful women, Anna explained, and she must accustom herself to it. Now she was not only sitting *on* the stuffed grandmother, but holding in her arms the greater part of the dachshund, Pupsik, bestowed on her by the Baroness de Wodzka herself. On either side of her, as unobtrusively watchful as the Praetorian guard, stood Pinny and Sergei's erstwhile governess, Miss King. Boris and Andrey, the pale young counter-revolutionaries, were playing the balalaika; Princess Chirkovsky, waving her arms, was expounding to Anna's mother her latest, absolutely sure-fire method of retrieving the family fortunes: the setting up of a *piroshki* stall on Paddington Station.

As for Anna, she was everywhere – dancing with a huge blond Cossack, flirting with the eighty-year-old admiral who had lost an eye in the Tsushima Straits, picking up her mother's shawls – but always returning to Ollie to give the little girl a hug, a smile.

'Everyone wants to be with Anna, don't they?' she said to Pinny, to whom she could have said nothing that would endear her more.

But suddenly something happened. Anna had stopped dancing and was standing stock-still in the centre of the room, her face turned to the door. The colour drained from her cheeks; her clasped hands flew to her mouth . . .

Then everyone saw what Anna had seen; a tall, tanned, staggeringly handsome man in a dove grey uniform with a high collar, standing in the doorway. The next second, pandemonium broke loose. The Princess Chirkovsky rose, let out a scream and rushed forward, overturning her glass of tea. Miss King, the Countess Grazinsky and a crowd of others followed. Pupsik woke, barked, and slithered out of Ollie's arms on to the floor.

Only Anna stood still in the centre of the room, hugging her joy.

Then Sergei saw her and parted the people that were between them and she was in his arms. They had shared a childhood and a country. They had not seen each other for three years and, for two of them, Anna had believed him lost. Now, even their excited ebullient compatriots were silent, awed by the measure of their joy.

'Annushka! *Milenkaya . . . dorogaya . . .*' He put up a finger, brushed away her tears. 'Is it you . . . is it really you?'

Anna could not speak. She just stood looking up at him, letting the tears run down her face, while Sergei pulled her close to hug her, then away so that he could see her, and closer once again.

But even in this moment of homecoming and happiness, Anna did not long forget the little girl whose wound she had set herself to heal, and presently she dried her eyes and led her cousin over to where Ollie sat.

'Sergei,' she said, 'I want you to meet a very special friend of mine. Miss Olive Byrne.'

Sergei, from his great height, looked down on Ollie. He clicked his heels and bowed. Then he reached for Ollie's hand, turned it over and kissed the palm.

'*Enchanté*, mademoiselle,' he said gravely. 'Permit me to say that all my life I have wanted to meet a girl with hair the colour of a sunset over the steppes.'

Ollie tilted her head at him. Sergei's gold-flecked eyes were warm and tender, the smile that lit his lean, tanned face and showed his dazzling teeth was unforced, caressing and perfectly sincere.

She stared down at her kissed palm and up again. And unhesitatingly, uncomplainingly, joined the long, long line of women that were in love with Anna's Cousin Sergei.

While Ollie was being feted at the Russian Club, Rupert was being led into an upstairs room at Aspell's, the discreet and world-famous jeweller in Bond Street. Mr Aspell had intended to deal with a client such as Lord Westerholme himself, but Rupert was early; Mr Aspell was still at lunch and it was to old Mr Stewart, whose dry and scholarly exterior hid a deep and romantic passion for rare stones and their history, that Rupert explained his errand.

'Sapphires . . . Ah, yes.' The dry fingertips met, the gold pince-nez fixed themselves on the good-looking young nobleman. 'What kind of sapphires had you in mind, my lord?'

Rupert smiled. 'I'm afraid I thought sapphires were just sapphires.'

'Oh, dear me, no! No, no, not at all.' Mr Stewart, shaking his bald head, looked quite upset. 'There are sapphires so dark as to seem almost black in certain lights. Siamese sapphires are like that. So much so that they have been used as mourning jewels during certain periods of history. Then again the Australian stones are almost turquoise with a light, translucent quality that is very characteristic. They're not quite so valuable, but very pleasing. Whereas certain star sapphires are quite grey in tone . . .'

'I see. Well then I'm afraid the limitation may be one of price. I'm not very well off.'

Mr Stewart nodded sympathetically. 'Yes, quite. Well, this is an exceptional time to pick up a bargain. We are getting some quite outstanding pieces at a very reasonable price from the Russian emigrés. For example, we would be in a position to offer you the Galychev necklace of one hundred and seven cabochon sapphires, each stone weighing not less than thirty carats. Or we are acting as agents for Madame Bogdanin – she is selling off a chain of Burmese stones with an exceptionally fine gold-beaded mounting by Fabergé. No one, in my view, can set jewels like the Russians.' He sighed. 'Of course, if I could have offered you the Grazinsky sapphires . . .'

Rupert leant forward, wondering why his heart had begun to race. 'The Grazinsky sapphires?' he prompted.

Mr Stewart nodded. 'I have never seen such sapphires. Never. It was as if God had at that moment invented the colour blue and wanted it preserved for ever in those stones. It was almost a religious experience to look at them.'

He glanced up, suddenly anxious, for he was aware that of late he had begun to reminisce and ramble in a way that betrayed his age. But the earl's silence was one of total attention.

'All the Grazinsky jewels were like that. Beyond

price, beyond belief . . . There was a triple row of pearls with which I suppose one could now purchase Blenheim Palace. I've never seen such pearls anywhere. Even in Russia they were a legend and what country understands pearls like the Russians do? Every nurse-maid pushing a perambulator has a *kokoshnik* studded with them. But these . . . They had the Potempkin pendant, too, and of course the emeralds. They were one of the great showpieces of the world, the Grazinsky emeralds.'

'You sound as though you have seen them yourself?' said Rupert.

The old man nodded. 'Yes, I went out to Russia . . . oh, twelve years ago it would be now. The autumn of 1908. I was collecting material for a monograph on eighteenth century court jewellery. The period of the Empress Elizabeth.' He smiled apologetically. 'It's my speciality. It may seem dry to you, but I assure you—'

'No, no, not at all,' said Rupert. 'I'm extremely interested. Did you actually meet the Grazinskys?'

'I didn't just meet them, I stayed with them. They invited me for as long as I wished. People tell me,' said Mr Stewart, removing his spectacles and polishing them, 'that Russia was corrupt, that the revolution was necessary – and I have no doubt that they are correct. But all I can say is that never in my life have I experienced such hospitality . . . such *democracy* as I experienced in that house. But I must say their attitude to their jewels amazed me.'

'In what way?'

'It's not easy to put it into words. To a certain extent, all Russians are like that. They treat their jewels – not carelessly, exactly – on the contrary, they glory in them. After all they're halfway to the Orient. But it's almost as if they thought of them as . . . family friends or household pets. For example the Grazinskys didn't keep anything in the bank – it was all just lying about the house. Once – I really couldn't believe my eyes – I was invited into one of the upstairs salons and found the baby lying on a bearskin rug – and playing with the Crown of Kazan!'

He looked up to gauge the effect of this on his client.

'I'm afraid you'll have to enlighten me,' said Rupert. 'I'm very ignorant about jewellery. What is the Crown of Kazan?'

'You may well ask, my lord. It's a fifteenth century piece; it ought to be in a museum, let alone a bank. Enamelled, gold-studded with uncut rubies and dia-monds . . . The countess used to wear it to costume balls – and there was the little boy dribbling on it! His sister had given it to him because it was so pretty, she said, and would help him to cut beautiful teeth.'

Rupert waited, willing him to go on. 'She sounds a very enterprising child,' he said.

'Oh, she was, she was,' the old man continued. 'A most unusual child. Not pretty exactly but . . . it was difficult to leave a room that she was in. Her parents thought the world of her, of course. I remember her mother going out to a charity gala one evening. She was wearing the diamond tiara that Alexander the Second bought for the Princess Dolgoruky – and a necklace of *sunflower seeds*! Anna had made it for her, so she wore it to the tsar's box at the Maryinsky!' He paused, shaking his bald head. 'I've often wondered what happened to them. There were rumours that they'd lost everything – robbed by their old wet nurse, I've heard. She was an incredible woman – used to wear the finger of some Georgian saint round her neck; nasty looking thing. Her people came from a cave village near the Turkish border; there must have been dreadful poverty there. I suppose the temptation was just too much for her.'

'None of the Grazinsky jewels have reached the European market, then?' asked Rupert.

'None, my lord, you can be sure of that.'

'And if they did?'

'If they did, I fancy you could buy an English county with what they'd fetch. And now to business. In my view you'd do best to consider the Bogdanin *parure*. The stones are a little pale, perhaps, but magnificently cut and the price is not at all unreasonable. If you would care to come with me to the strongroom . . .'

Muriel had stayed behind at Fortman's. As an engaged woman within four weeks of marriage, she considered it perfectly seemly to dispense with a chaperone and the thought of making good the deficiencies of her trousseau without the clucking of Mrs Finch-Heron was most agreeable.

Even Fortman's, however, was not immune to change. Walking into what had once been 'lingerie', Muriel found that the great store had embarked on a new venture: a pet department. An area had been separated off with a trellis and where once there had been calming displays of *crêpe de Chine* cami-knickers and *négligés* of guipure lace, there was now a circle of cages with silver bars. Inside, there tumbled litters of soft puppies, clusters of kittens, a bush baby with stricken eyes. There were fish tanks with darting, thumb-sized fish; crocodile-skin dog leads hung from a rack, woven poodle baskets lined with velvet were stacked on the floor . . .

Muriel frowned. Fortman's was her favourite store and the intrusion of livestock into what had once been a sanctuary of bust bodices and suspender belts displeased her.

She was about to turn away when she saw, standing by a sanded aviary full of brightly coloured parrots, a man whose back seemed familiar. Tall, broad-shouldered, with springing, straw-coloured hair . . .

She approached.

'Dr Lightbody?'

Ronald Lightbody turned.

'Miss Hardwicke!' His pale eyes gleamed – and indeed Muriel, in peach satin, flushed from the heat of the store, was a sight to make any eugenecist rejoice. 'I had supposed you to be down in the country, preparing for your wedding.'

Muriel smiled with unaccustomed warmth. 'I am, really. I just came up for the day to try on my wedding dress.' She looked at him enquiringly. 'You are not considering purchasing a parrot?'

'Not a parrot, no.' And, following his gaze, Muriel saw that what the doctor had been rapturously contemplating was not a parrot but a bird, pinioned and heavily chained to an iron bar – a fierce and yellow-eyed predator with a death-dealing beak.

'It's a golden eagle,' explained the doctor, and realized suddenly that he could confide in this beautiful woman as he could never confide in his wife. 'There is a Persian who lectures on the need for inner harmony. He has the hall on Thursdays and Saturdays and he always comes on to the platform with a falcon perched on his shoulder. The effect,' said the doctor bitterly, 'is considerable.'

'I see. So you thought an eagle . . . ?'

'Not for my own sake,' said Dr Lightbody. 'Ostentation is anathema to me as you know. But for the sake of the Cause . . .'

As he had expected, Muriel understood. Side by side, Master and Disciple stood and gazed at the eagle and each saw the same vision – the doctor striding on to the stage with the King of Birds sitting lightly on his shoulder. It was a fine vision. To Muriel's practical mind, however, certain considerations presented themselves. Delicately, she voiced them.

'Yes,' he said, sighing. 'You're right, of course. And Doreen is so uncooperative.'

'How *is* your wife?'

'Don't ask, Miss Hardwicke. She seems to be incapable of making any effort at all. Some mornings she simply doesn't get out of bed. It is wrong to complain, I know, but sometimes I feel so terribly *alone*.'

Muriel was deeply moved. She knew of the vision which had sustained the doctor ever since he had realized that his name was no coincidence – that in his body there really *was* a light, a shining image of perfection which could save the world. And to help him, to succour him, he had only a low-born slut.

She laid a plump, kid-gloved hand on his arm. 'Dr Lightbody, I'm just going up to the restaurant for luncheon. I have an account here. If you would care to join me . . . ? I am unchaperoned,' she dropped her eyes demurely, 'but with you I know I will be perfectly safe. And to tell you the truth, I too have troubles.'

Dr Lightbody's eyes lit up. A free lunch! With a last regretful look at the eagle, he gave his arm to Muriel.

They ascended in the lift and settled themselves in the restaurant, which abounded in nodding, feathered toques and swelling, net-encrusted bosoms. A pianist played soft ragtime; daylight had been excluded by silken drapes and replaced by pink-shaded lamps. It was an atmosphere for intimacy and confidences.

'And how do you find your future home, Miss Hardwicke?' enquired the doctor when they had ordered.

Muriel took a sip of Vichy water and dabbed at her mouth. 'It's very beautiful. Quite, quite lovely. Only I had expected – perhaps it was foolish of me – far higher standards . . . a much greater formality and propriety. Perhaps it was unreasonable of me?'

'No! No! How could it be unreasonable to want the highest and the best? In what way does Mersham fall short?'

Muriel sprinkled salt over her haddock mousse. 'It is not easy to be specific, but both morally and hygienically there is . . . a kind of *laxness* which I had not expected.'

Dr Lightbody leant forward. The discussion of hygienic and moral laxness with a beautiful woman in a softly shaded restaurant was exactly to his taste.

'Can you give me examples?'

'Well, take the servant problem. A house, after all, is judged by its staff. And at Mersham there is a most appalling and totally senile old woman who has been given a cottage in the stable block, not two hundred yards from the house. She *throws* things, Dr Lightbody! And my fiancé seems to find this perfectly natural. Indeed, he seems to enjoy it.'

Dr Lightbody made noises of sympathy.

'I can give you so many examples . . . I've discovered that they *knowingly* employ a mental defective in the kitchen; the girl can't even speak, I understand. And even in the family itself . . .' She flushed. 'Rupert's old uncle . . . I have seen it with my own eyes. He actually . . . *handles* the maids!'

Hungry for details, Dr Lightbody laid down his fork but Muriel was off on another track. 'I could give you a hundred instances . . . Rupert has this great dog who is allowed everywhere, even into the *bedrooms.*' She shuddered. 'And even socially . . . They entertain Israelites of a kind that would not have been permitted over my father's doorsteps.' She lifted her blue eyes to his face. 'You see why I am distressed?'

Dr Lightbody reached across to take her hand, thought better of it and took, instead, the Sauce Tartare.

'Indeed I do.'

But he saw, in fact, a great deal more. Ever since Miss Hardwicke had invited him down for the wedding, the conviction had been growing in him that this was his chance. To found an institute in one of England's most famous houses, to spread the doctrine of the new eugenics free from the endless financial anxieties that had hitherto pursued him – here, clearly lay his destiny. He had seen pictures of Mersham – the library, for example, would make a perfect lecture theatre.

That was if Miss Hardwicke really had, as she seemed to, the upper hand . . .

'Don't you see, my dear young lady,' he said now, 'you have a task. A mission. You have been singled out!'

'Yes, I know. And of course I shall act. After the wedding I mean to—'

'*After* the wedding?' said the doctor. 'My dear, I beg

of you, don't wait, don't procrastinate! Remember you are acting in the best interests of these unfortunate people. Take the lady with senile dementia. There is a paper by Schuster and Filemann which shows *conclusively* that the old are better off with others like themselves, protected from stresses and strains which they can no longer endure.'

Muriel nodded. 'It is certainly what one always feels when confronted with such people,' she said, remembering the broken flowerpot, the appendix in its glass.

'And the defective kitchen girl . . . What if she should get herself into trouble, as girls of that kind are so apt to do? Another deformed human being brought into the world. Would you ever forgive yourself?'

'No, indeed. You are right; you are perfectly right. You have helped me so much.' She smiled up at him and this time the doctor did permit himself a quick squeeze of the soft, plump hand.

'It is hard, I know,' he said. 'All reformers must endure opposition and calumny. I myself . . .' He sighed.

'I know, I know . . . You must forgive me,' said Muriel. 'I'm afraid I'm not quite myself this morning. You see there is this little girl who is to be a bridesmaid . . .'

She launched into a description of the morning's events.

Dr Lightbody was shocked. 'You have been

abominably treated. You mean you had no idea that the child was so severely handicapped?'

'None at all. Rupert just kept saying how pretty she was, how sweet.'

The doctor's blond eyebrows met together in a frown. 'To have a conspiracy of silence on such a topic is gross dishonesty indeed. Still, if as you say, your fiancé is so fond of the child, tact and diplomacy will be needed. Let me see . . .'

Two hours later, the doctor let himself into his flat. He was in the best of spirits. Though he regretted the eagle, Miss Hardwicke had been right. Dagos and for-eigners could risk an accident, but not he. And Miss Hardwicke had extended her invitation not only to the wedding but to the house party for the ball which pre-ceded it. If only Doreen wasn't so unpresentable. He supposed he'd have to take her along, but the embar-rassment would be almost unendurable.

'Doreen?' he called now.

There was no answer. Instead, his landlady came puffing upstairs, her fat, powdered face full of self-importance.

'She 'ain't 'ere. They bin and took her away in an ambulance.'

'An *ambulance*?'

'Aye. She bin coughin' somethink 'orrible – well, you know how poorly she was. But she would go out and go and get you a pork chop for your tea and in the butcher she 'ad this turn. Blood comin' out of her mouth an' all. So they sent for an ambulance and they

162

took her away. In the Samaritan she is, on Edgware Road.'

Dr Lightbody stared at her. He caught himself wondering what had happened to the chop.

'How terrible!' he said. 'How absolutely terrible!'

9

Rupert returned from London nursing a single and obstinately held idea. Anna must go. She must go now, immediately, before the wedding. She must be given the four weeks' wages she would still have earned and be sent back to London. He was simply not prepared to have coal carried to his study by a girl whose brother had cut his teeth on the Crown of Kazan. The thing was intolerable and in any case Anna herself, as he now saw, had been a disruptive force ever since she came to Mersham. Once Anna went, reasoned Rupert with impeccable logic, everything would be all right. He would stop having nightmares, Uncle Sebastien would stop playing Stravinsky, Potter would sell the mare. Above all, Muriel, his chosen bride, would be loved and appreciated as she deserved to be.

He began, therefore, by tackling his mother.

The dowager was in her boudoir, dealing with some last-minute wedding invitations. There were dark circles under her fine, grey eyes and rather more chiffon scarves than usual seemed to have slipped from her shoulders to the floor.

'Dismiss Anna!' she said horrified. 'But why, Rupert? She's leaving anyway after the wedding.'

'After the wedding,' said Rupert, firmly if obscurely, 'is too late.'

Lady Westerholme looked in bewilderment at her son. 'Too late for what, dear?'

Rupert changed his tactics. 'I found out quite a lot about her background when I was in town, Mother. Apparently she comes of a very distinguished family indeed.'

The dowager received this information without surprise. 'Well, so I supposed. She has such lovely manners and speaks such pretty French. But really I cannot see that as a reason for sending her away before she wants to go. Look at the poor tsar. He couldn't have been more distinguished and now he's dead. And your Uncle Sebastien is so fond of her.'

'Yes, well, that's another thing—'

'No, you're wrong, Rupert. Uncle Sebastien doesn't lay a finger on her, I'm sure. She's like a daughter to him. And Baskerville adores her.'

A sudden memory of Anna held at bay by the lake, her hair tumbling in disarray over the desperately held towel, made Rupert momentarily shut his eyes.

'Are you suggesting that we employ our servants for the sake of my dog?' he asked savagely.

The dowager stared at him. 'Why are you so angry with her, Rupert?'

'I'm *not*, Mother.' He tried again. 'But you know Muriel doesn't care for her.'

'Oh?' The dowager's tone was distinctly cool. 'I should have thought Anna was working very well for Muriel. I've been past Muriel's room three nights running and found Anna sitting outside on a hard chair waiting up for her until well after midnight. And considering she's up again at dawn to exercise—' She broke off, put her hand to her mouth. 'Oh, dear.'

Rupert's face was like thunder. 'I see. So Anna's been exercising the new mare. I might have known it.'

'Now, Rupert, you mustn't blame Anna. It was Potter's idea – he'd been watching her with the mare and he guessed she could ride. You must remember he only has the one boy now and there's a great deal to do at present.'

'I told Potter to sell the mare again. He has my strict instructions.'

'Yes, of course; he's going to, dear. But you can't sell a horse like that to anyone.' Her eyes softened. 'She's a beauty, Rupert. I tried her. Potter sent Alice to ask if Anna could borrow my habit. Anna wanted to ride bareback – he was very shocked! So I went down to see and they persuaded me to take her out just for an hour.'

Rupert forgot his anger. 'I'm so glad, Mother. You've not been out since . . . George died, have you?' His face lit up. 'I'm an idiot! Of course, I'll keep her here for you. Then you can come up whenever you like and—'

'No, no, Rupert. That's out of the question. It's

166

sweet of you, dearest, but it would be quite wrong. If Muriel doesn't care to ride she certainly won't want to keep horses for her mother-in-law. I'll be very snug down in the Mill House, you'll see.' And the dowager frowned, for Colonel Forster was fussing about putting in a damp-course for her before she moved, not realizing that she *had* to be in there the day after the wedding. 'As for Anna, dearest,' she went on resolutely, 'you and Muriel must do what you think best, of course. It would be very wrong of me to interfere. Only remember, Mrs Bassenthwaite is not at all well.'

It was Proom, accordingly, that Rupert summoned to his study.

To the suggestion that his newest housemaid be sent away with a month's wages in lieu of notice, the earl's butler listened with a sinking heart. Since Anna's arrival, Mrs Proom had only thrown two flowerpots and they had been small ones.

'Might I ask why you wish her to be dismissed, my lord?'

Rupert frowned. 'Miss Hardwicke doesn't care for her.' And as Proom continued to stand impassively before him, he went on: 'But that isn't it. I found out certain things about her background which makes it most unsuitable that she should be employed as a domestic.'

Proom nodded. 'Mrs Bassenthwaite and I were, of course, aware that she was of gentle birth. For this reason we were extremely reluctant to employ her.'

'Well, then . . .'

'However, it must be stated, my lord, that Anna has done everything she could to overcome her handicap. This is not to say that her adherence to the views of Mrs Selina Strickland has always been beneficial. In fact, only this morning James was threatening to throw all three volumes of the *Domestic Compendium* into the lake, Anna having asked him for calcined magnesia to polish Miss Hardwicke's bedside grapes. But—'

'Asked him for *what*?' interrupted Rupert.

'Calcined magnesia, my lord. It is a substance which is used in certain circles,' said Proom dismissively, 'to bring a heightened bloom to the fruit. A process analogous to the annointing of plums with Reckit's Blue. Needless to say, I have never permitted such practices at Mersham. The fruit here is *never* tampered with.'

Rupert put down the paper knife with which he had been demolishing a number of hapless envelopes.

'I can't help wondering why they accept her, Proom? They must know she comes from a totally different world.'

'Yes, my lord. They do.' He paused, considering how much to put into words. 'Perhaps it's not generally realized that what a servant dreads is not hard work, it's boredom. Housework can be extremely monotonous. And Anna . . . well, you can say a lot about Anna, but not that she is boring.'

'No,' said Rupert, allowing himself a wintery smile. He got up, went to the window, started playing with the tassel of the blind . . .

'Things are not very easy at the moment,' continued Proom, who had left Mrs Park searching wild-eyed through her cookery books for an alcohol-free wedding cake. 'Periods of transition are always unsettling and Lady Westerholme will be greatly missed. To dismiss Anna now would not be at all good for morale. It would be regarded as a very grave injustice.'

'But if she were paid—'

'My lord, there is no way you could get Anna to accept money to which she would feel she was not entitled. She is extremely proud. She is also looking forward very much to the wedding. Russian weddings, as you are probably aware, are very different. Anna is planning to cut her hair.'

'No!' The earl had swung round, his voice, his whole manner so peremptory, that Proom looked at him in amazement.

'There is nothing in the regulations to prevent it, my lord and—'

'I forbid it,' said the Earl of Westerholme. 'I forbid it utterly and you may tell her so.'

To his own surprise, on going to talk to Muriel, who was writing letters in Queen Caroline's bedchamber, Rupert received no thanks for his efforts to get rid of Anna.

'Rupert, I beg you not to concern yourself with the indoor staff. I've told you that I mean to see to all that. After all, I don't interfere with the running of the farms

169

or the forests, do I, even though—' She paused delicately.

'Even though it is your money that makes it possible for me to go on running them,' said Rupert levelly.

'Yes, that's true. And I certainly have better things to do than interfere with the servants. But I knew you were not pleased with Anna and . . .'

Muriel put up a restraining hand. 'I admit that Anna is not what I call natural servant material, but I am not displeased with her work. Last night when we came back from London they sent a most unsuitable girl to wait on me – a long-nosed, frizzy-haired creature with a most impertinent manner.'

'That'll be Louise. She's head housemaid, you see and—'

'Please, dearest, there's no need to explain. Let it suffice that I am perfectly prepared to put up with Anna until the maid I have ordered from Switzerland arrives. What I did want to speak to you about was your dog.'

Baskerville, hearing himself referred to, turned his massive head. Among his many excellent qualities, the earl's dog did not number a quick intelligence. Even he, however, had gathered that, incredible as it seemed, his natural behaviour was not wholly pleasing to Muriel Hardwicke. Now, in a heroic effort to conform, he sat on his haunches by the door, repressing an almost overwhelming desire to examine the livestock under the fourposter, and ruining the patient, Landseer pose he had adopted with frequent and enormous yawns.

'What about my dog?' said Rupert lightly, momentarily letting his hand rest on Muriel's hair. Perfectly groomed, perfectly golden, with its metallic lustre, it looked more as if it had been mined than grown.

'You have often said,' Muriel continued, 'that my good nursing, my attention to hygiene, saved your life.'

'Yes, I have said it,' said Rupert, smiling. 'And I still do.'

'Well then, I know you will understand when I ask you not to bring Baskerville into my bedroom. Or into *our* bedroom when we are married.' The pansy-blue eyes looked up appraisingly and it occurred to Rupert, suddenly, how rarely Muriel blinked. 'I don't know if you're aware of the work by Bestheimer and his associates on the transference of canine worms to the back of the human eyeball, but I assure you if you were—'

'Baskerville goes to the vet every six weeks to be checked,' said Rupert, his voice deceptively quiet.

'I'm afraid it's not as simple as that.' She launched into a description of the lifecycle of *Toxacara canis* which would have given nightmares to Edgar Allen Poe. 'So you see, dearest, I really must insist.'

'Very well, Muriel; it shall be as you wish,' said the earl. 'Come, Baskerville.'

'I didn't mean—' Muriel called after him, disconcerted by the look in his eyes.

But Rupert had gone.

It was not unexpected that the earl's attempts to dismiss Anna should reach her ears. The following day, returning at dusk from an inspection of the haunted folly, the re-roofing of which his bailiff regarded as urgent, Rupert noticed that the door of the rose garden was ajar. Mr Cameron must be working late. He would just go in and have a word with him. Muriel had meant well, earlier in the day, when she offered to replace his ear-trumpet with one of the new-fangled hearing aids, but the old Scotsman was a crusty fellow and the moment had perhaps been unfortunate, for Mr Cameron had been showing them his new and lovely snow-white rose.

Putting his hand through Baskerville's collar, Rupert pushed open the door. Judders of ecstasy and a violent vibrato of the single, coal-black wart on Baskerville's blond cheek, prepared Rupert for what he would find – Anna, carrying a trug and a pair of seca-teurs, moving in a kind of dream among the flowers.

Tightening his grip on his dog, the earl advanced.

'Good evening,' he said pleasantly.

Ambushed, Anna stood her ground. Her head went up. 'Good evening, your lordship.'

Rupert recoiled. Not since she had deplored Mer-sham's lack of bathrooms had her 'r's rolled quite so terribly. It was her curtsy, however, that showed Rupert the full extent of her displeasure. Gone was the balletic homage, the dedicated servility. Anna had *bobbed*.

'Is anything the matter?'

Anna had decided on frostiness, on silence, on *le style anglais*.

'Nothing is the matter. As you perceive, I am pick-

172

ing flowers for Miss Hardwicke's room. Mr Cameron has permitted it. I am not stealing.'

Rupert looked at her, completely bewildered. 'No, of course you're not stealing. What's happened, Anna? Have I done anything?'

'No,' said Anna, still struggling with the concept of the stiff upper lip as purveyed in her infancy by Pinny and Miss King.

It was Baskerville, never an exponent of silent suffering, who put an end to this by twisting himself out of the earl's grasp. He would, so long after his suppertime, have marginally preferred a rabbit, but Anna was undoubtedly the next best thing. By the time he had made this clear to her, Anna, trying to save her basket, had lost both her cap and her *sang-froid*.

'Oh, *chort*!' she said, looking up at her employer through pollen-dusted eyelashes. 'You have made me so *sad*.'

'I? *I*? For God's sake, Anna.'

'I was in the dressing room when you boasted to Miss Hardwicke how you have tried to send me away. And I do not know why because I have really tried to work hard and it is true I did not know how to gopher but this turned out not to be at *all* necessary and though I did play a very little the piano in the music room last week when I was dusting it was only for perhaps three minutes because it was the B flat *étude* which is *very* short as you know and in Russia *always* when we sent away a servant we allowed them first to explain so—'

'Stop it! Stop it, Anna!' Rupert reached out, took her by the shoulders. A mistake . . . More of a mistake than he would have believed possible. He dropped his arms, stepped back. 'Please, for heaven's sake, Anna. It wasn't because I wasn't satisfied with your work. Your work is excellent. It was because I met someone who'd stayed with you in Petersburg.'

He recounted his conversation with Mr Stewart, to which Anna listened with growing amazement.

'You wished to dismiss me because Petya had cut his teeth on the Crown of Kazan?'

'All right, I know it sounds absurd but—'

'Absurd? It is crazy! Sergei has always said that the English aristocracy have brains like very small aspirins and now I believe it. In any case, the Crown of Kazan was very *heavy*. Niannka was always angry with Mama when she wore it because it gave her a headache.'

'Niannka? Is that the lady with the mummified finger?'

Anna dimpled, but her eyes were sad, for Niannka's desertion had hurt more than anything in the dark days of the revolution. 'Yes. It was the finger of St Nino, who lived in the monastery at Varzia, where she was born. He has *many* fingers, that one, perhaps three thousand – the monks are such rogues!'

'You've been there?'

She nodded. 'We stayed with Niannka when Mama took the waters at Borzhomi. It was very beautiful. We ate with our fingers and slept on the ground and washed in the Kuru, which is very cold and green and runs down from the Caucasus, and the men had great moustaches and got drunk and fell out of their caves,' said Anna, her face lighting up at the memory. 'Only the chickens I did not like,' she added, turning her thumb to reveal a white scar across its base.

'And it's certain that she robbed you?'

Anna shrugged. 'Kira's aunt saw her on the Anchikov Bridge, laughing with some soldiers of the Red Guard after we had fled. It is natural, perhaps. She was a woman of the people.'

'She undoubtedly seems to have been that,' said Rupert reflectively. Then returning to the attack: 'Anna, you must see how unsuitable it is, your being here.'

'No, I do not see it.' Her eyes kindled. 'I know. It is because I am a woman! It is all right for Sergei to be chauffeur to an amazingly stupid duchess, though he has *seize quartiers* and his grandfather was a grand duke, and it is all right for Colonel Terek to drive a taxi though his family has owned three-quarters of the Kara Kum, but I . . . I may not work. Naturally. In a country where women must be trampled to death by 'orses before they are permitted to vote one would expect this.'

'No, Anna, you're wrong. I worked with women in the war – I know very well what they're capable of.'

'Then why? Just because we are rich in Petersburg?'

'Not only rich – Oh, Anna try to understand. In Russia they probably wouldn't have allowed me over your doorstep.'

'*Pas du tout.*' She dimpled up at him. 'Mama was extremely democratic. Earls with large estates and many Christian names were frequently admitted. By the front door, even.'

'Oh, God.'

They had begun to walk between the fragrant bushes, drawn by the remembered perfection of Mr Cameron's new rose.

'You really like it here, don't you?' said Rupert wonderingly. 'Though we work you half to death, though your hands are raw and chapped, though you're cruelly short of sleep . . .'

They had reached the rose. 'Yes,' said Anna so quietly that Rupert had to bend his head to hear. 'Yes, I like it here. I like Mrs Park, who is so gentle and so good, and James, who has struggled and struggled to make himself strong. I like the courage of your mother, who is so patient with the spirits who plague her, and I like your uncle, who hears music as if each time it had been just composed. I like the warriors on your roof and your foolish dog and the catalpa tree that leans into the lake . . . And this rose, I like,' she said, bending in reverence to Mr Cameron's masterpiece. 'Yes, very much I like this rose.'

She fell silent. (And if I were to take the secateurs, thought Rupert, and cut each and every blossom from this incomparable bush and pour them in her lap, what then?)

Anna looked up at him. Her face crunched into its

176

monkey smile. 'And the appendix of Mrs Proom,' she continued, 'ah, that I *truly* love!'

Rupert lifted his hands in a mocking gesture of surrender. 'Then stay,' he said, 'heaven forbid that I should come between you and Mrs Proom's appendix,' – and left her.

The dowager was tired. She had spent the morning in the village, comforting Mrs Bunford, who was still very much upset at having been asked to make neither the wedding gown nor any of the dresses for the bridesmaids and, to console the widow, had ordered her own outfit of powder blue wild silk. To give Mrs Bunford wild silk to ruin was the act of a lunatic and the dowager was already regretting it. Then as she walked to her brougham she was accosted by tiny, tottery Miss Frensham who had played the organ in Mersham Church for forty years. Miss Frensham, rheumy-eyed and quavery, wanted to know if it was true that Miss Hardwicke wanted neither 'The Voice That Breathed O'er Eden' *nor* the 'Lohengrin March' like they always had, but something modern that Miss Frensham was almost sure she wouldn't be able to play since she couldn't see too well nowadays to read new music. Because if so, perhaps they'd like to get someone else to play, though it wouldn't be easy not to see Master Rupert married, not after she'd read him every single page of *The Prince and the Pauper* when he had the measles, because he always noticed when you missed a bit out, not like other children . . .

By the time the dowager had soothed Miss Frensham she was late for her appointment with Colonel Forster at the Mill House and must, she realized, have made a mess of explaining why she had to move into the Mill House *immediately* without waiting for the improvements that the Forsters were so kindly putting in for her, because Colonel Forster had looked at her very strangely and Mrs Forster had patted her hand in quite the wrong way when she left. And when at last she had gone home and sat down for a moment to rest, there had been the usual psychic vibrations and the voice of Hatty Dalrymple had come through as clearly as if she were still beside her in the dormitory all those years ago at school. Hatty, who had passed over as the result of a boating accident at Cowes, had always been a gusher and the information that she could see rays of aetheric ecstacy emanating from Rupert and his lovely, lovely bride did little for the dowager, remembering the look in Rupert's eyes these days.

And now she really *had* to make up her mind whether or not to send a wedding invitation to the Herrings.

Mr and Mrs Melvyn Herring and their twin sons, Donald and Dennis, were not so much herrings as sheep, and extremely black ones at that. The dowager came from an old Irish family whose pedigree was excellent, but whose upbringing, on a wild and lovely estate in County Down, had been unconventional and lacking in discipline. As a result, when the dowager's youngest sister, Vanessa, fell passionately in love with

the extremely handsome hairdresser who came to prepare her glorious, golden ringlets for her coming-out
ball, she had put lunacy into action and eloped with
him. For this attack of passion, poor Vanessa Templeton paid dearly, coming round, so to speak, a few
months later – to find herself pregnant, penniless and
desperate. Whether she died of a broken heart or puer-
peral fever following the birth of her son, Melvyn, it
would be hard to say. Whatever the reason, there now
began the long process of dumping Melvyn on anyone
who would have him which was to take up so much of
his father's life. For Vanessa Templeton's love child was
one of nature's genuine abominations: a deeply
unpleasant child who grew in deceit, temper and general sliminess into the kind of adult who can empty a
room within minutes of entering it. Melvyn's sojourn
at the Templetons' estate in County Down was burned
into the marrow of every one of its inhabitants, from
Lady Templeton herself down to the obscurest scullery
maid. The dowager, inviting him to Mersham in his
early adolescence, had been harrowed by this resemblance and by the fact that he looked like a smeared
and blotched version of her own Rupert. During this
visit, Melvyn had (at the age of fourteen) got the stillroom maid pregnant, lamed George's favourite hunter
with an air gun and stolen a hundred gold sovereigns
from her husband's desk. During a second visit, at the
age of sixteen, he had started a fire in the morning
room with an illicit cigarette and left with his aunt's
favourite Meissen figurine, which he sold to a dealer

before it could be traced. Fortunately, Nemesis over-took him in the form of a waitress called Myrtle who, finding herself pregnant by him, got him to the altar. The birth of Dennis and Donald squared the account for the twins, growing from pimpled, puking and over-weight blobs of dough into pallid, whining mounds of flesh, finally put the Herrings beyond the social pale. No one felt able to invite *four* horrible Herrings to their house and, after an abortive attempt by the Templetons to ship them off to America, Australia – anywhere – the Herrings dropped into obscurity in a Birmingham suburb.

But Rupert's wedding . . . The dowager, remember-ing her lovely, youngest sister, dangerously allowing sentiment to overcome reason, made up her mind.

'I'll ask them,' she decided. 'After all, Melvyn is my nephew.'

And so the gold-embossed invitation bidding Mr and Mrs Melvyn Herring and Donald and Dennis Her-ring to the wedding of Muriel Hardwicke with Rupert St John Oliver Frayne, Seventh Earl of Westerholme, in the church of St Peter and St Paul on the 28 July at 12.30 and afterwards at Mersham, dropped on to the threadbare linoleum of the Herrings' hall in 398 Hook-ley Road, Birmingham – with consequences which no one, at this stage, could possibly have foreseen.

The wedding preparations now accelerated towards their climax. Carriers drew up, continuously, deliver-ing antique wine coolers, *famille vert* bowls, ormolu clocks and a set of matching beermats showing views of the Hookley Road, which the Herrings, enchanted to be taken up again by their grand relations, had pilfered from their local pub. The Rabinovitches, exceeding even their usual generosity, sent a six-hundred piece armorial dinner service decorated in sepia and gold. Muriel moved among her wedding gifts with great efficiency, acknowledging everything meticulously as soon as it arrived and personally instructing Proom as to its display in the ante-room to the gold saloon. Old Lord and Lady Templeton wrote that they would come from Ireland. Minna Byrne most nobly offered to accommodate the Duke and Duchess of Nettleford and their four younger daughters, leaving only the Lady Lavinia to sleep at Mersham. The dowager wrote a friendly note to Dr Lightbody and his wife and was relieved, though surprised, that Muriel apparently had not one living relation who would wish to see her married.

But of course the bulk of the work fell on the staff. The influx of house guests for the wedding meant the opening up of rooms in the north wing and, once again, the maids were up at dawn, blackleading and dusting, washing the wainscot, taking curtains down and carpets up. Over the wedding breakfast itself, the dowager had made a stand. This was to be her last occasion as hostess at Mersham and there were to be no taboos. Only the best champagne and the choicest dishes would be served and, though there might be a few special alcohol-free dishes for Muriel and Dr

Lightbody, everything else would be as fine as Mrs Park could make it. So there was singing again in the kitchen as the gentle cook broke thirty-three eggs into her big bowl for the wedding cake and Win's round face beamed with relief, seeing her adored Mrs Park restored to happiness.

As for Rupert, he now did what troubled human beings have always done – he buried himself in work. Fortunately, there was enough of it. The estate had been neglected for years. Freed, now, from financial restraints, Rupert spent hours with his foresters, his farm manager, his bailiff. The new earl's capacity for listening, his high intelligence and quick concern, were a boon to the men who worked for him. They brought him their plans and hopes, their troubles and their prejudices. As he walked through his forests, pored over drainage plans, discussed cropping programmes and roofing materials, Rupert was content. Only at night, in the little room in the bachelor wing which he still preferred to his now spring-cleaned master suite, did the facade crack and into the landscape of his earlier nightmares there entered a new figure: a still, dark-eyed girl who stood with bent head, waiting – and when he reached for her, was gone.

Then, with less than four weeks to the wedding, he suddenly announced his intention of going to Cambridge 'on business'. While Muriel was still formulating her displeasure he had taken the Daimler and gone.

That afternoon, going into the housekeeper's room

to take tea as was his custom, Proom found Mrs Bassenthwaite sitting in her chair, doubled up and groaning with pain. The following day, in Maidens Over Hospital, she was operated on for the removal of her gall bladder.

At this crucial time, Mersham was without a housekeeper. Muriel saw this as her chance and, with characteristic efficiency, she took it.

10

Three days later, Mrs Park woke up aware that something was wrong. She looked at the round, brass clock on the chest of drawers. Half past six. Win should have been in half an hour ago with the cup of tea she always brought.

Mrs Park rose, put on her pink flannel dressing gown and carpet slippers and padded through her own snug sitting room behind the kitchens down the stone corridor to where Win slept, in a little slit of a room between the laundry and the stillroom.

There was no sign of Win. The bed was empty, the pillow uncreased, the grey blankets pulled tight over the iron bed.

Mrs Park's heart began to pound. Instinctively knowing that it was useless, she went through the kitchens into the servants' hall. The range had not been lit, the servants' breakfast had not been laid. Still searching and calling she went through the sculleries, the pantries, the larder . . . In the sewing room she

184

found Anna, changing out of her riding habit into her uniform.

'Anna, Win's gone! Her bed's not been slept in!'

Anna turned, her cap in her hand. 'It was her half-day off yesterday, I think? So she will have gone into the grounds, perhaps, and fallen asleep? The night was so beautiful. I have done this myself – *often* have I done it,' said Anna, but her eyes were grave.

Within half an hour every single member of staff was searching for the little dimwit who was as much a part of Mersham as the moss on the paving stones. Mr Cameron and his underlings searched the walled garden, the greenhouses and the orangery – for Win had loved flowers. Potter rode off to scour the woods; James and Sid circled the lake.

By lunchtime it was clear that the matter was one for the police and Proom, his face more than usually grave, went upstairs to inform the family.

The dowager and Muriel were in the morning room. Rupert had not yet returned from Cambridge.

'My lady, I have come to tell you that Win is missing. We have searched everywhere, but her bed has not been slept in and I'm afraid the matter is serious.'

He addressed the dowager as lady of the house, but it was Muriel who answered.

'Is that the simple one? The kitchen maid?'

'Yes, miss. Win is employed in the kitchens.'

'Oh, dear!' The dowager had risen. 'We must get hold of the police at once. And Colonel Forster, too. I'll go and—'

'No, wait!' Muriel spoke with authority. 'There seems to have been some mistake. Surely Mrs Bassenthwaite told you that Win was going away?'

Proom turned to her, his face impassive. 'No, miss. Nothing was said about it, I'm sure.'

'Going away?' echoed the dowager in surprise. 'But where to? Win has no family of any kind. She came from an orphanage in Maidens Over. As far as I know, she's been in the parish all her life.'

Muriel nodded. 'Mrs Bassenthwaite must have forgotten to mention it. It's often like that before a gall bladder operation – there can be almost complete amnesia. But I discussed it all with her very carefully.' She turned to the dowager. 'Rupert asked me to concern myself with the indoor staff without delay, as you know, and I felt that something should be done for the poor girl.'

'What sort of thing?' asked the dowager, puzzled.

'Well, you must have noticed how she lives? Almost like an animal. No speech, no rational thought.'

'Win has been very useful to Mrs Park, miss,' said Proom. 'Mrs Park is very fond of her. She doesn't say much, but she's got a way of knowing what Mrs Park wants almost before Mrs Park knows it herself. Mrs Park'll be very upset at losing Win.'

'I know. But of course I mean to replace Win immediately. There is to be a considerable increase in kitchen staff. And if Mrs Park is fond of Win – and I'm sure she is – she will want what is best for her.'

'I still don't quite understand,' said the dowager.

'Where has she gone? And how did she go so quickly without anyone knowing?'

Muriel smiled reassuringly. 'Fortunately, with my connections as a nurse and with the help of Dr Lightbody, I found an excellent institution where they give first-class guidance to girls of her sort. Speech therapy, training in handicrafts, everything. You'll see, Win'll be fit for something much better than kitchen work when she's been there a while . . .'

'But why was it so sudden, Muriel? Surely Mrs Park should have had some warning?'

Muriel's placid face turned towards her mother-in-law. 'People don't always understand what's best for them. A distressing scene would have been so bad for Win. It's like a child going to boarding school; the mother's tears make it impossible. So I arranged with Mrs Bassenthwaite that she should be fetched away quietly by someone sympathetic and experienced.'

'Mrs Park will want to know where she's gone, my lady. She'll want to be able to visit her.' To Muriel's irritation, Proom continued to address the dowager.

'And so she shall,' said Muriel. 'But the poor girl must be given a few weeks to settle down. I'll be in touch with Mrs Park myself. Just tell her she must be brave for Win's sake.'

'Though why,' Muriel continued, when Proom had bowed and left, 'one has to make so much fuss about the feelings of a cook, I don't understand. I hope Rupert will be pleased at least.'

But the dowager was silent.

Mrs Park accepted it. She accepted it for Win, trusting soul that she was. Nevertheless she suffered, silent and uncomplaining, berating herself for her selfishness in wanting Win around when the girl was learning to speak properly and take her place in the world.

'You'll see, she'll be back,' said James, unable to bear the stricken look in the cook's round, blue eyes, 'driving a big yellow motor as like as not and talking like a duchess.'

'There was a girl over my auntie's way,' Louise put in, 'she went to one of them training places and they taught her weaving and basket work an' all. She's got her own shop now.'

Mrs Park nodded. 'It's just I would have liked to say goodbye to her,' she said in her slow, soft voice. 'I'd just have liked to say goodbye.'

Muriel was as good as her word over Win's replacement. A new girl, sent down by Mrs Finch-Heron, arrived the following day. Mildred was bright and pretty and full of excellent suggestions for improving the routine. At night, kneeling by her bed, Mrs Park followed her prayers for Win's safety and happiness by asking God to forgive her her wickedness in wanting Mildred to shut up – or even better – go away.

Uncle Sebastien was playing the *Liebestod*. He thought that this was probably the last time he would play it, for he had been shamed and caught out and was to be punished. Muriel had seen him giving Pearl a squeeze as she sidled past him in the corridor. Pearl had squealed and jumped – she liked to act up a little – and he had turned to find Muriel standing in the doorway staring at him with contempt and disgust.

And she was quite right, of course. Right to despise him and to engage for him, as she had done, it seemed, a kind of jailor, a hospital nurse who would keep him from the maids.

How had it happened, Uncle Sebastien asked himself, sitting pink-faced and wretched by his gramophone? All his life he had loved women, but he was nervous and shy with those of his own class. It was the uncomplicated, half-glimpsed servant girls that had beguiled and enchanted him for three-quarters of a century. And just as a devoted gardener lingers at nightfall over his herbaceous border, so Uncle Sebastien, overcome by misery and Wagner, let his mind wander through the well-remembered treasury of serving maids.

There had been so many in his youth. The dairy-maids in blue caps like coifs to keep their curls out of the milk, their breath as sweet as that of the cows they tended. The dimity sewing girls in checked pink ging-ham with quick, pricked fingers . . . Scullery maids, patient as oxen with their hessian aprons and humped behinds, forever scrubbing pale circles in the darker stone . . . Laundry maids singing like blackbirds as they hung up the sheets . . .

He forgot so many things these days, but he could still remember almost all their names. Daisy, the little freckled nursemaid with streamers in her cap . . . Even

189

in his pram he'd loved Daisy. Netta, the poor little drudge at his public school who'd still managed to force a dimple into her pinched cheek when he'd passed her in the interminable, dank corridors with her buckets . . . And Elly, the Irish chambermaid, who'd given him so lightly and gaily what most youths had to buy with trepidation and risk from some professional. Ah, the panache of that girl who'd seduced him, not in some haystack or barn but on the needlepoint rug in the tapestry room, in the still hour between lunch and tea.

But of course it was wrong. Oh, one could find reasons, perhaps. Easy to say that if his parents had been able to show that they loved him, if the girl he'd asked to marry him hadn't laughed in his face, he'd have been different. Those were just excuses, thought the humiliated old man, while Isolde died and the gay and beguiling ghosts continued to walk inside his head.

The parlourmaids at his club, the tips of their delectable, shell-pink ears peeping from beneath their caps as they bent down to serve . . . The hoity-toity ladies' maids in rustling black silk . . . And down in the kitchen another world, hard to penetrate but glorious, with the flushed, busty and bustling girls and the delicious smells of the food caught in their white-bibbed aprons and later (if Fate was kind and they were willing) in their loosened hair . . .

Isolde was dead. Uncle Sebastien rose and took the needle from the record.

It was over.

There was a knock at the door. Not Mary, he hoped. The dowager, when she learned what had befallen him, had offered to take him with her to the Mill House. He'd refused, of course. There were only three bedrooms; he'd be impossibly in her way with his music and his insomnia. It wasn't even as though Mary was really his niece. He'd already been living at Mersham, a beached-up middle-aged bachelor, when she came there as a bride. She owed nothing to her dead husband's uncle. No, he wasn't as selfish as that but, all the same, he hoped it wasn't Mary. If she came now he might just weaken . . .

'Come in.'

A dark, enquiring head, a questioning: 'You are not busy, sir?' A curtsy.

Anna. He smiled. The dowager was right, he had not laid a finger on Anna. Too much of a snob, he told himself, for he had known her at once for what she was. Yet with this girl he felt none of the constraints he sometimes felt with women of his own class. And, as she stood before him, he understood what Rupert could not do: why the other maids, so quick to peck out an outsider, accepted her. For all her intelligence and breeding, Anna had something of their essence: a lack of self-regard, of priggery, a deep and selfless capacity for service.

'Miss Hardwicke is out and I have finished my work downstairs so Lady Westerholme has sent me to see if you require anything,' said Anna, paraphrasing the dowager's anguished: 'Go to Mr Frayne, Anna,' as she met her in the passage. She came closer. 'You are sad?'

'No . . . no,' said Uncle Sebastien, wondering what it would be like to have a daughter such as this. 'It's just . . . well, you may have heard, I'm to have a nurse. Miss Hardwicke feels I need looking after . . . that it's too much for the maids to keep carrying trays. It's very thoughtful of her.'

Anna nodded and tried to give him the concept back in an endurable form. 'Nurses are so *beautiful*,' she said. 'And they have such lovely uniforms, caps and cloaks and everything so starched and crisp.'

'This one is middle-aged and sensible. I'm going on a diet, too.'

Even Anna was daunted by this prospect. Then she came and slipped to her knees by his side and said, 'Please will you play for me? Not the gramophone. You, yourself. *The Waldstein Sonata*, perhaps, because I love it so much and particularly the last movement where the hands cross?'

The old man shook his head. 'I can't, Anna. I can't play properly any more.'

'*Please*,' said Anna, knowing that he must be led into his place of refuge – and waited.

Forgetting his own troubles, Uncle Sebastien looked at her, noting the weary droop of the shoulders, the dark smudges under her eyes, and something else, something that had not been there, he thought, when first she came to Mersham – a look, almost, of bewilderment, of puzzlement, as though she was troubled by something she did not yet understand.

'If you'll play with me?' he said cunningly. 'I have the Schubert duets. What about the *Fantasia in F*?'

'Ah, *yes*!' Her face was suddenly transfigured. 'But I cannot play with you, it is impossible.'

'Not Selina Strickland, I hope. Because—'

'No.' She sighed. 'I shall be gone so soon that it doesn't matter, I think. But you are a *professional*.'

In silence, Uncle Sebastien held out his hands, bent and swollen with rheumatism and age.

'Yes, you are right,' said Anna quietly. 'God understands these things. Come.'

And so they played some of the world's loveliest piano music – the exiled homesick girl, the humiliated, tired old man. Not properly. Better than that.

The next day, after taking up Mr Frayne's tea tray, Peggy came back to the kitchens heaving with an almost operatic rage.

'When I got up the stairs there was this blinkin' great cow all done up in white overalls met me at the door an' wouldn't let me past. "All trays are to be put down on the table outside from now on," she said.' Peggy's mimicry of the nurse's genteel tones was accurate and savage.

Anna turned. 'Was she beautiful?' she asked, clutching at straws.

'Beautiful! You must be joking. A nose like a hatchet and a huge black wart with whiskers on it.'

Anna sighed. Baskerville's wart, contrasting so poignantly with the blond undulations of his cheeks, was one of his greatest assets, but she could see that it might not be the same for a lady.

'None of us are allowed in the room from now on,' raged Peggy, 'not when Mr Frayne is in it.'

'Well, you used to grumble enough about the way he carried on,' said Louise. 'I'd have thought you'd be pleased.'

Peggy bit her lip. She seemed to be terribly upset. ''e didn't mean any harm,' she said.

'He'd never push it too far,' echoed Pearl. 'A proper gentleman he was, really.'

'Crikey, you talk as if he was dead,' said Louise.

''e might as well be,' said Peggy, and spoke truer than she knew.

While Mersham was preparing for the wedding, Heslop was no less busy preparing for the ball.

Heslop's butler, Mr Hawkins, had been trained by Proom himself and he brought to his work an iron rigour and indomitable sense of style. At Heslop, *The Times* was still ironed before it reached the breakfast table; the footmen, their hair powdered, wore their claret-coloured knee breeches and swallow tail coats even when the family dined alone; Monsieur Bourget, the chef, throwing off *quenelles fricassées* and temperaments with equal abandon, defended his kitchens, with their scurrying retinue of minions, as if they were Fort Knox. If Minna yearned sometimes for the simplicity of her American childhood or the easier ways of Mersham, she knew better than to interfere, and Heslop ran like clockwork.

Now, as she planned the ball in honour of Muriel Hardwicke with her housekeeper, her steward, her butler and her cook, no one could have guessed that the task afforded her anything but pleasure and delight.

And yet the truth was very different.

Welcoming Ollie back from her day in town, Minna had naturally been eager to know how her stepdaughter had enjoyed her day.

'Oh, it was *lovely*, Mummy. It was simply lovely!' Ollie's flushed face had been full of delight yet Minna, with her sixth sense for the child's well-being, had been uneasy.

'Was your dress very beautiful?'

'Yes, it was.' Minna, bracing herself for details, watched with surprise as Ollie's bright eyes slid away from her own. 'And then I saw Pupsik who is a sausage dog and he's got a huge diamond right inside his *stomach* and the lady let me hold him and he fell asleep on my lap and snored and snored and—'

'Pupsik? Is that the Lady Lavinia's dog? Did she bring him to the Ritz?'

'No, I didn't go to lunch with them.' Ollie's face had gone blank again, a look of defeat flickering in her eyes.

Still trying to make sense of all this, Minna asked,

'But why, honey?' Her voice sharpened. 'Surely they didn't forget about you?'

'No, they wanted me to come but . . . I wasn't hungry. Well, *later* I was hungry and I ate four *piroshki* that Anna's mother made and some little eggs that fishes lay, all black and slithery, but Pinny wouldn't let me have any vodka,' said Ollie, frowning at the only cloud on an otherwise flawless afternoon.

'But where was this, Ollie?'

'At the Russian Club. Anna took me there. It's where she goes, and her friends. It's lovely and Cousin Sergei was there and he has white, white teeth and he spoke to me in *French* and afterwards he gave me a piggyback to the taxi and he said—'

She was off again. Minna let her run on and said no more about the fitting or the bridesmaid's dress. But that night she tackled Tom.

'Tom. I can't understand what happened in London. Why did Ollie spend the afternoon with Anna? I thought she was supposed to be having lunch with you and the bridesmaids?'

'Yes. well . . .' Tom's shifty expression was so ridiculously like Ollie's that Minna, worried as she was, managed a smile. 'She got very tired, you know how it is in those hot shops. So Anna took her off to her place – it was her day off, you see, and I'd given her a lift to town. And I must say I was most grateful to her because it was absolutely grim at the Ritz. You can't imagine what those girls are like.'

And Tom flushed. Whether or not the hot, sharp

imprint that he had felt while eating his *vichyssoise*, wedged between a screen and a potted palm, had or had not been the Lady Lavinia's knee, the whole thing had been a nightmare. Only for Rupert would he have endured the company of two women who might have been hand-picked for all that was most objectionable in the female sex. And in the hope of diverting his stepmother he began, most entertainingly, to tell her about his lunch.

But though Minna listened with amusement, it was impossible to deflect her from any anxiety that touched her stepdaughter and when she had finished laughing and commiserating with Tom, she said, 'But all the same, something must have gone wrong at that fitting. You know how Ollie went on and on about her dress and how wonderful Muriel was and now suddenly she won't talk about it at all. She just shuts up like a clam. And though she obviously had a lovely time with Anna, I feel that underneath she's had some kind of shock.'

Tom was silent. Muriel was Rupert's chosen bride. Living at Mersham, she would be their closest neighbour and Minna would find it impossible not to be involved and friendly. There was no point in making mischief. So he shook his head and said: 'Nothing happened, Mother. As far as I am aware it all went perfectly well.'

Minna stared at her stepson. The Byrnes were bruising riders, passionate lovers and gallant soldiers. As liars, however, they had always been bottom of the class.

'Tom, I try not to fuss about Ollie, not to pamper her. But what she has to deal with is not easy. If anything goes wrong she can become bitter and twisted for life. And to help her, I have to *know*, I have to have the facts. What did happen at Fortman's?'

So Tom told her.

Minna said nothing then or later. No breath of criticism escaped her lips and she continued to prepare for the ball as if Muriel were a beloved daughter or dear friend. Only once, as she stepped into her huge, cavernous kitchens and Monsieur Bourget rushing forward, said excitedly: 'I 'ave just 'eard that Miss 'ardwicke eats nothing that 'as in it alcohol so I cannot cook, I cannot function, I cannot *exist*!' Minna, forgetting herself for the first and only time, said, 'Miss Hardwicke will eat anything that is served to her in this house. *Anything*.'

The news that the ball was to be in fancy dress had profoundly depressed Lord Byrne, who had at first been convinced that his wife was joking.

'You're not serious, Min? You mean I'm to dress up as some ridiculous cowboy or something? I won't do it!'

'Muriel asked me, Harry. She has a dress she particularly wants to wear.'

'Well, let her wear it then. But you can't expect me to go gallivanting round my own place making a complete idiot of myself.'

'I thought maybe you could wear one of the military uniforms out of the costume gallery. They're really not so different from your dress uniform for the Coldstreams. And it would please her so much.'

'Not sure that I want to please her all that much,' snorted Lord Byrne. 'Met poor little Miss Tonks coming out of the church today when I went to see the sexton about old Hunston's grave. Seems Muriel doesn't like her flower arrangements – says they're too countrified. Won't have "The Voice That Breathed O'er Eden" either, Morland tells me. Got Miss Frensham trying to read some newfangled hymn and she's as blind as a bat, poor soul.'

Minna sighed. She had not told her husband what Muriel had said to Ollie, but the fear that Muriel had done some real and permanent damage to the child was always present in her mind.

Lord Byrne looked at his wife. He'd married her blind, knowing nothing about her except that she had a quiet voice, a sensible manner and some spare cash. Now, eight years later, he would have died for her without a second's hesitation. To dress up as a hussar in Wellington's army would be harder, but he would do it.

'What about Tom?' he asked. 'Does he know about all this dressing up?'

Minna nodded. 'I'm relying on Ollie to bring him round. Hugh's the one who's made most fuss. He actually got the headmaster to let him ring from Craigston to complain. The friend he's bringing down doesn't

199

have anything to dress up in. So I said their cadet uniform would be all right.'

Lord Byrne nodded. 'Rabinovitch won't like it,' he said darkly, allowing himself a moment of glee.

Lord Byrne was right. Rabinovitch *didn't* like it. Informed by Hannah that he was to attend the ball at Heslop in fancy dress, Rabinovitch turned his liquid frog eyes on his wife and said: 'Hannerle, make not the stupid jokes.'

'I don't joke, Leo. Minna has asked that we dress up. It is for Miss Hardwicke who wishes to be the Pompadour.'

'And because some stupid *shiksa* wishes to be—'

'Leo! Miss Hardwicke is a most charming girl.'

The conversation now descended into rapid and agitated Yiddish, ending, as was to be expected, in defeat for Leo, who agreed to add a red cummerbund to his evening clothes provided it was understood that this, and this alone, would turn him into a bullfighter.

'But no *sombrero*! Absolutely no *sombrero*,' said Leo, going down fighting.

Surprisingly it was Susie, usually so easy-going and uncomplicated, who proved difficult, stating that she had no intention of making a fool of herself to please that opinionated blancmange who had ensnared Rupert.

'*Susie*!' said her mother, deeply shocked.

But Susie, to whom Tom had fled after his day in London, was unrepentant. In the end, however, she too yielded, seeing how much it meant to her mother; for

Hannah Rabinovitch, like Minna Byrne, was a woman who reaped as she had sown.

It was while Susie was bending her usual, quiet attention to the problem of whether she would look less ridiculous as a gypsy or a shepherdess, that a maid entered with a letter on a salver.

Hannah opened it. 'It's from Mersham. From Muriel,' she said, pleased and eager, and began to read. 'She thanks us most kindly for the wedding present.'

Leo, who had just paid the staggering bill for the six-hundred-piece Potsdam dinner service, was heard to murmur that he was glad to hear it.

'What is it, Mother?'

Something in his daughter's voice made Leo lift his head.

Hannah was standing by the window, the letter in her hand. She looked, suddenly, immensely, unutterably weary and as old as one of the mourning, black-clad women in the Cossack-haunted village of her youth. And indeed the hideous thing that had crept out from beneath Muriel's honeyed, conventional phrases was as old, as inescapable, as time itself.

It is always a mistake to go back – and to go back to a place where one has been wholly happy is foolishness indeed.

Knowing this, Rupert was nevertheless badly shaken by the intensity of the memories which gripped him. He had survived well enough at Eton, but it was at Cambridge that he entered his heritage. It was here that he had discovered his passion for scholarship, here that he learned to excel at the solitary sports he so greatly preferred to the endless team games of his adolescence: here, above all, that he had learned the meaning of friendship.

Now, crossing Trinity Great Court, passing the shabby rooms on Q staircase with the carved motto on the mantelpiece (*'Truth thee shalt deliver: it is no drede'*) which had been his own, he walked through a gallery of ghosts. On the rim of this fountain, Con Grainger, deeply drunk and wearing striped pyjamas had declaimed, verbatim, Demosthenes' *Second Philippic*, before falling senseless into the water. Over that ridge of roof, now bathed in sunshine, Naismith, besotted with love for an Amazonian physicist from Girton, had climbed at night to hold hopeless court beneath her red-brick tower. Naismith had been killed outright within a month of reaching France – luckier than Con, perhaps, who still lay, shell-shocked and three-quarters blind in a Sussex hospital. And Potts, the brilliant biochemist who had kept a lonely beetroot respiring in a tank . . . Potts, who was a 'conchie', and had been handed a white feather by an old lady in Piccadilly the week before he'd taken his stretcher across the lines to fetch back one of the wounded and been blown to pieces by a mine . . .

Rupert walked on through the arch on the far side and made his way down to the river, only to be led by its lazy, muddy, unforgettable smell into another bygone world: of punts moored behind willows, of picnics at Byron's pool – and girls.

But this, too, was forbidden country now and turning, Rupert made his way back to the master's lodge, where he had been bidden to take sherry before luncheon at high table.

Later in hall, among the napery and fine glass, the ghosts crept quietly away. Here time really had stood still. Kerry and Warburger were still splenetically dismembering a colleague's ill-considered views on Kant; Battersley was still laughing uproariously at his own appalling puns; the fish pie was still the best in England.

'Coming back to us, then?' enquired Sir Henry Forster, regarded by most people, himself included, as England's foremost classicist. 'Quite a good chance of a fellowship, I should think. I remember your paper for the Aristotelian Society. An interesting point you made there, about the morale factor in Horatius's victory over the Curiatii.'

'Keeping up your fencing, I hope?' said the bursar, who had won ten pounds from his opposite number at Christchurch when Rupert and his team had taken the cup from Oxford.

Rupert answered politely, but his mind was already on his interview with the man he'd come to see. Professor Marcus Fitzroy was not in hall, because he despised food as he despised sleep and undergraduates and anything else which prevented him from getting on with the real business of life, namely the total understanding and expert disinterment of those distant and long-dead peoples whose burial customs so powerfully possessed his soul.

As soon as politeness permitted, Rupert made his way to the professor's rooms in Neville Court. He found them marvellously unchanged. A shrunken head on the mantelpiece supported an invitation to a musical evening; jade leg ornaments, axes and awls, and Rupert's own favourite, the skeleton of a prisoner immolated in the Yangtse Gorge, lay in their former jumble. Among the debris, a more recent strata of half-packed boxes, rolls of canvas and coils of rope indicated signs of imminent departure. The crumbling, highly archaeological-looking substance on a saucer seemed, however, to be the professor's lunch.

'You're off tomorrow, then, sir?' asked Rupert when greetings had been exchanged.

Professor Fitzroy nodded. He was a tall man, sepulchrally thin, with a tuft of grey hair which accentuated his resemblance to a demented heron. 'Pity you couldn't come,' he said. 'I've got to take that ass, Johnson.' The professor's contempt for students had not extended to Rupert, who, on a couple of undergraduate expeditions, had shown himself to possess not only physical endurance and the investigative acumen one might expect of Trinity's top history scholar, but also something rarer – a kind of silent empathy with the tribesmen and mountain people they had encountered. That a man like this should be wasted on an earldom and a rich marriage seemed to the professor to be an appalling shame.

'You're making straight for the Turkish border?' enquired Rupert, holding down the lid of a crate for the professor to hammer in.

'Yes, it's only a quick trip,' said Fitzroy disgustedly, for his real passion was for the wastes of Northern Asia – and the Black Sea, professionally speaking, did not rank much above Ealing Broadway. 'I've been landed with a field course back here in September; these damned ex-servicemen are so keen.'

'You said in your letter you hoped to go up to the cave monastery above Akhalsitske?'

'That's right. It's an extraordinary place – everyone seems to have been there. Alexander, of course, and then Farnavazi when he set up court at Mtskhet . . . And then there's the Byzantine stuff plonked down on top of it all,' said the professor, waving a dismissive hand at the modern upstart that was early Christendom. 'I'm going to look at the rock frieze in one of the inner caves. I've been corresponding with Himmelmann in Munich and he's convinced there's a link there with the Phrygian tomb monuments at Karahisor.'

'But surely, sir, that'll take you across the Russian border? Isn't there some fighting still going on there?'

The professor shrugged. 'I don't suppose it'll bother me.'

Rupert thought this possible. Professor Fitzroy, who had carried a mummified goat across the Kurrum valley in Afghanistan while being shot at by both sides during the Ghilzai's rebellion, would probably not be greatly troubled by the remnants of a Russian civil war. In addition to a total indifference to hardship and danger, the professor possessed a brother who was something very high up in the Foreign Office and of whom he unashamedly took advantage to get his archaeological finds back through customs including – so rumour had it – a beautiful Circassian wrapped in a camel blanket whom he was said to have installed in his house at Trumpington.

For a while they talked of what interested them both. Then Rupert, aware that he was holding the professor up, came to the point. 'I was wondering, sir, if you'd do me a favour? A very considerable one, I'm afraid.'

Professor Fitzroy straightened from the bedroll he had been tying and looked at the Earl of Westerholme. Most of his archaeological colleagues had been German and he had hated and despised the war. Yet when they'd heard that Rupert Frayne, with exactly ten hours' solo flying to his credit, had won the MC for coming to the rescue of a wounded fellow pilot, Fitzroy had surprised himself by treating his whole staircase to champagne. Now he answered Rupert's query with a single word: 'Yes.'

An hour later, while making his way down King's Parade, Rupert heard his name called and turned. Beckoning him from beneath a muslin parasol was an enchantingly pretty girl with blonde curls and huge, blue eyes, dazzlingly arrayed in pleated white linen.

'Zoe!'

Delightedly, Rupert went over and took the hand she offered in both his own. Zoe van Meck had been the nicest, the most sensitive, of the VADs who'd nursed him, and he remembered with admiration the efforts she had made to overcome her tender heart and achieve the degree of efficiency the job required. 'My goodness, you look devastating! Going on the river?'

Zoe nodded. 'I'm just on my way to Cat's.'

'Unchaperoned?' said Rupert, pretending to be shocked.

'Well, not quite; I'm going with a party,' she said, smiling up at him, 'my aunt and uncle live here; it comes in very handy for May Balls and things.'

Her voice was a little breathless, for suddenly seeing Rupert like that had stirred up something she'd believed safely buried. The *tendresse* which so many of his young nurses had felt for the Earl of Westerholme had gone rather deeper with Zoe van Meck – so much so that she had been almost relieved when she was transferred from the officers' quarters down to the men's wards on the floor below. But after her move she had seen almost as much of Rupert as before, for as soon as he was even partially ambulant, Rupert had insisted on going down to talk to the men. The only time she'd seen Rupert lose his temper was when the bossy ward sister, obsessed by rank and protocol, had attempted to turn him back. She could see him now, sitting still as stone by Corporal Railton's bed until he died – and Railton hadn't even been one of his own men, just a lad he'd met on the hospital ship coming home.

'You're not married yet?' asked Zoe.

'At the end of this month,' said Rupert, his voice expressionless.

Zoe sighed. She'd had three offers of marriage at the Peterhouse Ball alone and a young merchant banker sent her roses every day – yet at this moment she would gladly have changed places with Muriel Hardwicke.

And partly from mischief, partly to give her thoughts a more cheerful turn, she said, 'And how do you like your new relatives?'

'What do you mean?' asked Rupert, puzzled.

'Muriel's family, I mean, up in Yorkshire.'

Rupert frowned. 'Muriel doesn't have any family, Zoe.'

Zoe dimpled up at him. 'Oh yes she does! I was up there for Verena's ball and she took me into the village. Old Mrs Hardwicke was truly splendid, especially after she'd had her morning stout, but I think my *favourite* was Uncle Nat . . .'

Rupert took her arm. 'I'll escort you to St Catherine's,' he said. 'And now, please *tell*.'

And Zoe, accepting his escort with alacrity, told.

Mrs Bassenthwaite's illness hit Proom hard. True, it was a while since the housekeeper had taken a very active part in the running of Mersham, but in her quiet way she had held the strings together. Deprived of a working companion of nearly thirty years' standing, Proom found that a great many extra tasks fell on his shoulders. Normally, in the spate of work building up for the wedding, he would have relied on his right-hand man, James. But James had been acting strangely of late. Nothing could make James incompetent, but these days Proom would often see him in his pantry, the polishing cloth hanging from his hand, staring list-lessly at the silver. He scarcely ever seemed to whistle, and when Peggy had enquired in her friendly way after his trapezius muscle he had turned from her without a word.

Then one morning he didn't come down to work at all. The new hallboy, engaged as a result of the affluence Muriel had brought to Mersham, was despatched to the men's attics and came down to say that he had knocked on the first footman's door and been told to scram, and scram fast.

Proom himself went to investigate.

James was sitting on his bed, wearing only his pyjama trousers. Over the years he had turned his attic into a replica of the gymnasium where his heroes built up, with patience and dedication, their splendid, monu-mental bodies. There was a long mirror, and a set of iron dumbells racked in pairs from the smallest five pounder to the hundred-pounder that James now worked with ease. There was a chest expander with coiled springs like the hawsers of an ocean liner, a sta-tionary bicycle it had taken him thirty weeks to save up for and a pair of scales discarded by the old weigh house at Maidens Over. And on the walls, everywhere, pictures . . . Pictures of Mhatsi Adenuga, the fabled 'Abyssinian Lion', his oiled and ebony muscles held in a classic 'double biceps' pose . . . of the great Sandow, supporting on his shoulders a platform containing nineteen people and a Pekinese . . .

And on the bed, James, staring blankly into space. James who, through years of unremitting labour, had turned his scrawny, undersized body into something that could be set with honour beside these giants. No one, not even Proom, knew what it had cost James. The freezing hours before dawn doing the endless leg curls, the agonizing bench presses, never giving up even when, week after week, the scales held steady and the next weight proved immovable. But he'd done it . . . and now . . .

Proom's footsteps, silent as always, made no impression.

'What's up then, James? Why aren't you down-stairs?'

No answer.

'Come on, lad, what is it? Are you ill?'

James shook his head.

'Well, if you aren't, there's work to be done. Sid's brought the Venetian glass down from the store room, but I'm not trusting anyone but you to set it out.'

Again that wretched shake of the head. 'What's the use?' said James tonelessly. 'What's the blinkin' use? All this stuff—' he waved his hands. 'I might just as well throw it in the sea. I'm fifty inches round the chest, Mr Proom, and that's not bad going seeing I was thirty-six when I began. But there's not a darn thing I can do about my height. I can flog my guts out and I'll still be five foot eight, and will be till the day I die.'

'Well? I myself am only five foot nine. I cannot see the relevance of your remark.'

James turned. 'Didn't she tell you? She's going to bring in matched footmen.'

'Miss Hardwicke did mention it. She's going to bring back powdering too. It's old-fashioned but you never minded it, if I recall.'

'No, I don't mind. I'm all for a bit of class. But I'm not going to *be* a footman. They've got to be over six feet. Six foot two she wants them, if possible.'

Mr Proom shrugged. 'It never seemed to me wise to employ servants for their size or the shape of their calves, but that is neither here nor there. Whatever happens, you'll still be first footman in this house.'

'No, I won't,' said James tonelessly. 'She's not going to *sack* me, you understand. "His Lordship speaks so highly of my work."' James's parody of Muriel's genteel tones was devastating in its accuracy. 'There'll always be some odd jobs I can do about the place. "Mr Proom will find you something useful to do, I'm sure."'

The butler was silent. No one more than he, who had trained James from the age of twelve, knew the blow Muriel had aimed at James. James's skill with the silver, the unobtrusive bravura of his work at the sideboard, his knowledge of wines, all had been

211

instilled by him. The little Cockney lad had turned himself from a scruffy lamp boy into one of the most highly trained servants in the land – and now this!

'You're ready for promotion, anyway,' said Proom at last. 'I'd hoped you'd stay and take over from me. I know her ladyship intended it. But . . . well, we'll have to do it different. It's no use speaking to Lady Byrne because Hawkins's got his own team, but there'll be a vacancy somewhere. When they hear you're on the market, offers'll come flooding in, you'll see.'

'I'd like not to go too far away. I reckon I've got used to it here,' said James, coming as close as he could to expressing his sense of desolation at leaving the companions of a lifetime and the man who'd made him what he was. 'Do you think her ladyship might take me on at the Mill House?'

Proom frowned. The dowager's departure from Mersham, the restricted circumstances in which she would find herself, were a hard cross for him to bear. 'I doubt if she'll be taking more than a gardener-handyman. But something'll turn up. Let's just get this wedding behind us, shall we? You'll stay for that?'

'Aye, I'll stay for that.'

Mr Proom returned to his cottage at dinner time with a heavy heart. Mrs Bassenthwaite was gone, James was going; he doubted if Mrs Park would last much longer with Win away. Miss Hardwicke had promised him an increased staff to train, but it was already clear that her ideas would not accord with those of Mersham.

He opened the door of his mother's room. The bed was perfectly tidy, the flowerpots intact, even the appendix floated quietly in its bottle, but Proom was at once aware that something was wrong. He went over to the bed. Mrs Proom was cowering back against the pillows, shrunken and tiny as a child, and she was crying.

'What is it? What's the matter, Mother?'

The suffused blue eyes stared wretchedly up at him, the tears continued to flow silently down the raddled cheeks.

Mr Proom was appalled. His mother furious, unreasonable, mad, he could cope with. His mother unhappy and pitiful was more than he could bear.

'I know . . . I'm . . . a nuisance to you, Cyril.' The tears continued to well up, spill over. 'But I'll try to be better, Cyril . . . You'll see, Cyril, I'll be better.' She stretched out a hand, clawed desperately at his arm.

'Mother, what is all this *about*?'

Another spate of those heartrending and silent tears . . .

'I won't do nothing bad no more, Cyril, I won't throw nothing. Only don't send me away. Don't send me to the workhouse.'

'The *workhouse*? Are you *mad*, Mother?'

'She said . . . as 'ow I must be lonely. But I'm not, Cyril.' The little speckled claw dug deeper into his arm. 'I'm not lonely, I'm used to it here.'

'Who said this?' asked Mr Proom but already, sickeningly, he knew.

''er that's going to marry 'is lordship. 'er with the eyes that don't blink. She said . . . 'as 'ow I'd be happier with people like myself. But I wouldn't, Cyril. I wouldn't . . .'

'I'm quite sure you wouldn't, Mother,' said Mr Proom, trying for a little joke.

But the terrified old woman was beyond his reach. The sobbing was building up now, she was beginning to gasp and choke – she'd make herself ill.

He began to pat her hand, to soothe her, but as she gradually became calmer Proom's own fears increased. Had anyone asked Proom what he thought about his mother, he would have said that the old lady was a nuisance the like of which had probably never been equalled. If Mrs Proom's Maker had seen fit to take her to his bosom one night as she slept, Proom, after giving her a fitting funeral, would have regarded himself as the most fortunate of men.

An honourable release through death was one thing. Putting the old lady into a home for deranged old people was another. Proom knew he could have gone straight to the earl and been listened to, but making trouble between a man and his intended wife was not something he cared to do. No, it looked as though he too would have to leave Mersham. Only where, with a burden such as this, could he possibly go?

The problem of what to wear at the fancy dress ball at Heslop did not concern the Herrings, for they had not been invited. Indeed, the Herrings had expressly been bidden not to arrive until the day before the wedding, and had been informed precisely from which train it would be possible to collect them. Even so, nothing could damp the pleasure of that family of layabouts and spongers at the thought of being taken up again by their posh relations.

For the Herrings' star, which had never been conspicuously high, had of late plummeted catastrophically. The Herrings owed rent to their landlord, their grocer had forbidden them his shop and they had been turned out of their local pub. The supply of suckers on which Melvyn relied to keep body and soul together seemed, in the weeks before his noble cousin's wedding, to have mysteriously dried up and, in the proposed visit to Mersham, Melvyn saw a clear sign that Fate was about to smile on the Herrings once again.

'Don't worry, Myrtle,' he said now. 'Aunt Mary's a soft touch, really. She'll see us all right.'

'Maybe, maybe not,' said Myrtle, who was standing by the stove in a mauve satin *peignoir* liberally sprinkled with grease, mixing the lethal concoction of peroxide and vinegar with which she dyed her hair. 'But 'ow the dickens are we goin' to get there? There isn't a hope in hell of raising the rail fare for the four of us.'

'I'll think of something,' said Melvyn.

'Well, not that locking us in the lavatory one while the guard comes round, because that's got whiskers on it,' said Myrtle. 'And what about clothes? I ain't got a stitch to wear and the twins'll have to have new trousers.'

Melvyn sighed and looked at his obese and pallid offspring sitting on either side of the sticky kitchen table reading comics. Donald was methodically sucking a long black stick of liquorice into his mouth. Dennis was licking at a dribbling bar of toffee. Like certain caterpillars whose short lives are dedicated to achieving simply the maximum possible increase in size, the twins seemed to have done nothing but eat and burst out of their clothes since they were born. Watching them, Melvyn had to abandon another of his half-formed schemes – that of smuggling them to Mersham in a cello case in the guard's van. Even a doublebass case would not take more than half of either of his sons . . .

'Don't worry, Myrtle,' he said again, giving her shoulder a squeeze. 'I'll think of something. You'll see.'

Dr Lightbody, on the other hand, was one of the favoured ones who, at Muriel's request, had been invited for all the festivities and therefore faced the problem not only of morning clothes for the wedding, but of acquiring a suitable costume for the ball. A hot afternoon just a week before his departure for Mersham accordingly found him standing in front of the long, fly-stained mirror in the dim, dusty shop of Nathaniel and Gumsbody, the theatrical costumiers in Drury Lane. An enormous tricorne hat with a cockade lurched over his left eye, he wore a blue military coat heavily braided in gold and his arm was folded in a characteristic gesture across his chest. Unmistakably, he was the Emperor Napoleon as immortalized in the famous portrait by David.

'What do you think?' he asked the pale young man in charge of rentals.

'It suits you, sir. It suits you very well.'

'I don't like it,' pronounced Dr Lightbody. 'It's the hat, I think.' He removed it to reveal his high and intellectual forehead.

'What about Admiral Nelson, sir? We do a very nice line in him. He comes in three sizes and the eye-patch is free.'

The doctor shook his head. To go as a person in any way injured or defiled, even in battle, was against his principles.

He allowed the young man to divest him of his uniform and, clad only in trousers and braces, began to walk along the rows of ermine-lined mantles and sumptuous velvet cloaks.

'You don't fancy a nice cavalier, sir? Those hats with the big feathers always go down very well with the ladies.'

Dr Lightbody shook his head. Though the ringleted Jacobean wigs were very flattering one never knew what went on *underneath*.

It was all so annoying, he reflected, pausing now by the leather jerkin and feathered head-dress of an Indian brave, Doreen still being in hospital. Doreen was a good needlewoman, he had to give her that – she'd

217

always made his shirts. It would have been no trouble to her to have run something up for him. Instead of which she just lay there in that awful ward full of disgusting, wheezing old women and yellow people with tubes in them, staring at him with those big, grey eyes of hers as though he could help her. The sister had given him an odd look when he'd asked if it would hurt Doreen to do a bit of sewing while she was in there, so he supposed it was no good pursuing the subject. As a matter of fact, the hospital visits were an embarrassment altogether – the staff who talked to him about Doreen's condition seemed to think that his title of 'Doctor' would make him understand their jargon. Whereas in fact his title was a courtesy one, the courtesy being one that he had, so to speak, bestowed on himself when, in the drudgery of his last year at the catering college, he had first glimpsed his vision of the perfectibility of man.

'These are nice, we always think,' said the assistant, holding up a Viking helmet and breastplate. 'With a red beard, perhaps – and thongs?'

Again Dr Lightbody shook his head. He wanted something which would suggest what he saw as his threefold role: of teacher, of healer, of leader of men. Something in white and gold, possibly? A High Priest? A Zoroastrian?

Suddenly he had an idea. 'What about the Egyptians? Akhnaton, the Sun King – do you have him?'

'I don't know if we have him specifically, sir, but our

Egyptian section is very well stocked. If you'd just come through here . . .'

Ten minutes later, in the many-layered, pleated linen skirts, the curved sandals and golden, cap-shaped crown, Dr Lightbody stood before the mirror again.

It was closer, much closer – but there was something a little bit *effeminate* about the whole ensemble. Not surprising, really – when all was said and done there was a touch of the tarbrush about the Egyptians.

Then, with the inner certainty of all visions, inspiration came.

Why go as a mere Sun *King*? Why not a Sun *God*?

'I've changed my mind,' he said to the weary assistant. 'I'd like to see the Greek costumes, please.'

It was obvious, really. He would go as Apollo.

In the breakfast room at Farne Castle, a great turreted keep set on a wave-lashed shore which the Nettlefords' ancestors, after centuries of bloodshed, had wrested from a doomed Northumbrian king, the Lady Lavinia was eating kedgeree.

She was well satisfied with life. Her bridesmaid's dress had arrived that morning, her costume for the ball was waiting for her in Newcastle. This time, she was certain, all would go well. At the Ritz, Tom Byrne had been charming and attentive, there could be no possible competition from the goitrous Cynthia Smythe and she had been able, by certain feminine gestures, to show the best man that she found him pleasing. Meanwhile, the morning's shopping trip to

Newcastle would provide more immediate delights. Not that one would ever seriously *demean* oneself, but still . . .

Stretching away to her left on either side of the dark oak table, sat the Ladies Hermione, Priscilla, Gwendolyn and Beatrice, all of them sporting, in various combinations, the close-set eyes, haughty expressions and huge, beaked noses which had struck dread into so many subalterns and Lloyd's underwriters in the ballrooms of high society. At the head of the table sat the duke, buried in *The Times*, which he had scarcely put down since he'd discovered that his fifth child, too, was a girl. And opposite him Honoria Nettleford, his duchess, surveying, with some anxiety, her brood.

The season was virtually over and none of the girls had had so much as a matrimonial nibble. In three weeks it would be the twelfth and though they'd got up a good party for the shooting, it was singularly short of eligible young men, all of whom seemed to have previous engagements. Which was a pity, for the girls, though thin, were strong, hardy girls and showed, the duchess considered, to better advantage jodhpured and oil-skinned against the keening winds of a Northumbrian summer than in the tulle and feathers suitable for the overheated ballrooms of London Society.

What a problem it all was, thought the duchess, helping herself to kidneys. Where, oh where, in a world which the war had so cruelly decimated of young men, was she going to find anyone suitable? Because there was going to be no lowering of standards for the Nettlefords. Let other women bestow their daughters on fledgling curates or half-baked university professors. She, Honoria Nettleford, would never lower the flag!

So everything now depended on the wedding at Mersham and the ball at Heslop which preceded it. Lavinia herself seemed confident that Tom Byrne had grasped the advantages of marrying a Nettleford, but the duchess had seen too many best men scratch at the starting post to be certain. Should she give young Byrne a hint, perhaps? Mention Lavinia's certificate for the 250-yards breast stroke? Or tell him what the vet had said about her when she delivered the Jack Russell of six puppies and one of them a breech? Lavinia was not only the eldest but – it had to be admitted – the bossiest and the plainest: once Lavinia was off her hands, the duchess was certain the others would quickly follow. Surely, at the ball, waltzing with Lavvy (but here the duchess closed her eyes, for the waltz was not quite Lavinia's forte) Tom Byrne would see her worth? He had a younger brother too – perhaps he would do for Beatrice?

She was glad, really, that Lady Byrne had decided on fancy dress. It would give the girls more scope. Priscilla was going as Cleopatra, Beatrice as a Daffodil, Gwendolyn as Grace Darling, the local heroine. With Hermione (who had made rather a jolly severed head out of papier mâché) as Salome, and Lavinia as the water sprite, Undine, they should make quite an entrance. Once Lavinia's costume had been altered that is, because those tight-fitting, glittering scales had suggested something quite different when Lavinia had first tried them on. It was to add a gauze overskirt and some gauze veiling that she was taking her eldest daughter to Newcastle. This done, she was sure the effect would be all they hoped for: mysterious, subtle and marine.

'Don't forget to be ready on time, Lavvy,' she said now. 'I told Sergei to bring the car round at ten.'

The Ladies Hermione, Priscilla, Gwendolyn and Beatrice stopped chewing in unison, and in unison put down their forks. Four pairs of pale eyes fixed themselves on Lady Lavinia. Here was treachery: naked and unashamed.

'You said *Hudson* was driving you,' hissed Hermione to her eldest sister.

'I really can't see that it matters which of the chauffeurs drives us,' replied Lavinia, tossing her head.

'Oh, can't you just!' muttered Gwendolyn under her breath.

'Mother, can I come in with you?' asked Beatrice, quickest off the mark. 'I've completely run out of wool for my tapestry cushion.'

'Me, too,' said Gwendolyn. 'I want to go to the library.'

'Well, I'm not staying by myself,' said Priscilla. 'Can I sit in the front, Mother? I always feel so sick in the back.'

'You never feel sick when Hudson's driving,' hissed Lavinia.

'Girls! Girls!' The duchess held up her hand.

'Silence, *please*! If you all want to come we'll have to take two cars. Gwendolyn and Beatrice can go with Hudson in the Daimler and—'

'*No*, Mother, why *should* we? It isn't *fair*, just because we're the *youngest*!'

It was at this point that the duke, though he had trained himself never to listen to a word spoken by his family, subliminally heard the warning bell which caused him to fold his newspaper and quietly steal away.

Anna had not given up her plan to cut her hair. She had received the earl's message, duly delivered by Proom, and she had set it aside. She was leaving Mersham three days after the wedding and it was unlikely that she would see the Earl of Westerholme again. Nor did she believe that so busy and august a personage would have time seriously to concern himself with the length of a housemaid's hair. Pinny was a more serious matter, but Pinny would be convinced when Anna swept into the little house in West Paddington, dazzling all who beheld her with her modernity and chic. And even had she felt inclined to hang back, she would have found it hard to do so in view of the support and encouragement she had received from the staff. For, one and all, the domestics of Mersham were convinced that Anna, with her dark hair cut softly to curve like a raven's wing into her cheek, would provide a much-needed touch of below stairs glamour for the coming nuptials. It would also be one in the eye for the servants at

Heslop when Anna, going over to help out at the ball, turned up with bobbed hair.

'Because they're a right snooty lot, I can tell you,' said Peggy. 'Give themselves all sorts of airs.'

It was quite a deputation, therefore, that saw Anna off on her free afternoon just a week before the wedding, clutching a whole half crown and bound for Maidens Over and the salon of René, *Coiffeur des Dames*, a young man who was reported to have trained in Paris and to be wholly conversant with the new techniques of shingling, bobbing and the rest.

René's shop, painted a garish orange, was situated in the Market Square between a chemist and a fishmonger. Ignoring the churning of her stomach, which seemed not to have caught up with the New Thinking about hair, Anna pushed open the door. Inside, the shop was small and distinctly scruffy. Pieces of hair of all colours lay about as if dropped by confused and nesting birds, the washbasins were stained, the material covering the chairs was shiny and worn. It looked as though René's Parisian days might be some considerable time behind him. Anna waited, examining pictures of Irene Castle with her shining bob, of Princess Marie of Roumania with her cropped fringe, trying to avert her attention from the trolley with its jumble of dirty combs and curling tongs.

'Good morr-ninck, mademoiselle. May I assist you?'

René's French accent was so strong that Anna,

225

polite as always, felt compelled to address him in his native tongue.

'Bonjour, monsieur. Je voudrais que vous me coupiez les cheveux, s'il vous plaît. Très court!'

René's button eyes popped. Consternation spread over his florid face. Too late, Anna perceived her gaffe.

'I would like my hair cut short, please,' she translated hastily. 'Bobbed.'

René's eyes lit up. This new fashion for short hair was going to make him rich. Not only were frequent visits necessary to have the hair restyled and trimmed, but nine out of ten girls who came to have their long tresses cut had no idea of the value of their discarded hair, which he sold, at a most gratifying profit, to a wigmaker in London.

'Certainly, mademoiselle. Perhaps mademoiselle would care to be seated? Elsie, come here!'

Elsie came from the back of the shop, a vacant-looking girl of about fourteen, who took Anna's straw boater and jacket and helped her into a far from clean flowered overall.

'Comb, Elsie,' ordered René.

Elsie loped over to the trolley, rootled in the debris, and produced a comb.

'Not that one, you foolish girl! The big one. How often do I have to tell you?'

More rootling, accompanied by nervous sniffing, and Elsie produced the big one. René began to loosen Anna's pins and his eyes glistened. Amazing that such a slim young girl could have such masses of hair. It was soft yet heavy, with beguiling threads of chestnut and bronze highlighting the inky darkness. He should get ten shillings a pound for it if she didn't know its value and he was sure she didn't. Painstakingly, greedily, René combed out Anna's hair and set it free in a mantle which covered the back of the chair, flowed down her arms, fell in rich coils on to her lap.

'You have beautiful hair, mademoiselle. It is excellently suited to the new styles.'

Anna, watching in the mirror, was fighting a growing panic. 'It's only hair,' she told herself, 'dead stuff. No blood vessels, no nerves.' Yet it was as if in the falling cascade that surrounded her she again read her past.

Memories crowded in on her. Herself, aged four, sitting in the huge bath in the nursery wing in Petersburg while Old Niannka rubbed her scalp with some devilish concoction which she swore would strengthen the roots and turn the fine, dusky down that covered Anna's head into thick and abundant tresses. Any compliment to Anna's hair in later years was always taken by Niannka as a tribute to herself and followed by a detailed account of the magic recipe, which had included wolfsbane and (she swore) the blood of bats. Niannka, who had later betrayed them, stolen their jewels, and vanished . . . Petya, strap-hanging on her pigtails as he took the first, tottering steps across the limitless ocean of the bearskin rug beside his cot. And her father . . . Thinking of him she made a small, characteristic movement of the head, as if to shake away the pain, and René paused and said, 'Am I hurting you?'

'No . . . no.'

Her father, who had come in from a day of frustration, trying to make the tsar listen to reason over some matter of policy, and gone up to say goodnight to her, plunging his hands into her hair where it lay spread on the pillow as into a cooling stream. 'And yet it isn't cold, your hair; it's as warm as the rest of you. Fire water you've grown there, my silly Little Candle.'

More and more memories came. Sergei, pulling her out of the river by her hair when she fell out of the rowing boat at Grazbaya. The Princess Norvorad, her godmother, that formidable *grande dame* whom the Bolsheviks had gunned down in the cellar of her house, loosening her braids as she came with Pinny into the drawing room and saying in her exquisite, archaic French: 'After all, *ma chère*, we need not despair. Something can be done with her, I think. Yes, something can certainly be done.' And Pinny, who, every night, ignoring the grumbles of the nursery maid, had herself administered the three hundred strokes with the Mason Pearson hairbrush from the English shop in the Nevsky . . .

Am I mad? Anna now thought, as René, with a flourish, put down his comb. Am I completely mad to cut my hair?

One last memory rose before her: not of Russia, not of her childhood. A recent one . . . by the lake at Mer-

228

sham . . . of herself standing in the water desperately shaking out her damp locks so as to cover her naked shoulders, her breasts . . .

And with this image came courage and determination. She lifted her head.

'I am ready, monsieur,' said Anna. 'Please begin.'

Anna was not the only person from Mersham visiting Maidens Over on the Wednesday before the wedding. Rupert, who had business with his solicitor, had driven his mother over so that she could visit Mrs Bassenthwaite in hospital and purchase some trimmings for the wedding outfit which Mrs Bunford was excitedly savaging in honour of The Day. Now, her tasks completed, she sat in the comfortable, chintzy lounge of the Blue Boar Hotel taking tea with her great friend, Minna Byrne.

'So everything's going splendidly, Mary?' asked Minna Byrne, wondering why the Dowager Countess of Westerholme, with her fine bones and inherent elegance, should so resemble, a scant week before her son's wedding, the hungrier kind of alley cat.

'Oh, yes; quite, quite splendidly,' said the dowager brightly. She closed her eyes for a moment as though to banish the spectre of Uncle Sebastien, sitting caged and shamed in the east wing with that unspeakable nurse; of Rupert, who had returned from Cambridge only to ride off at daybreak to the furthest corner of his estate; of Cynthia Smythe, who had arrived the previous day and whose idea of making herself useful

229

was to follow Muriel from room to room, obsequiously repeating her remarks. The servants, too, all seemed to be going mad, knocking on her door one by one and begging her to take them to the Mill House at half their wages to do work that was grossly beneath them. James asking to be a handyman, Mrs Park offering to be a cook general and to *scrub*! Only she couldn't take them, how could she? There wasn't the money or the room. And Mrs Bassenthwaite really *had* lost her memory; she'd remembered nothing, just now, about the arrangements made for Win. 'Yes, everything's fine,' the dowager repeated – and launched into a description of the menu for the wedding breakfast, an inventory of the presents received, an account of the trousseau for the honeymoon, which was to be short and spent in Switzerland. 'And Muriel has been marvellously efficient. She's dealt with everything. You can imagine what a comfort I have found it.'

'She seems to be a most capable girl,' said Minna.

'Oh, she is, she is! Muriel never *dithers* like some girls. She knows her own mind.'

'And she's so very beautiful,' said Minna.

'Yes, indeed. That creamy skin.'

'And her eyes. So very blue.'

'She carries herself well, too,' said the dowager. 'It's so unusual these days to see a girl that doesn't slouch.'

A silence fell. Minna, about to embark on a sentence in praise of Muriel's good health, abandoned it,

230

aware that she was beginning to sound distinctly agri-cultural. Both women were light eaters, but they paused now to order crumpets.

'How's Ollie?' asked the dowager. 'We haven't seen her for a while.'

'She's fine.' It was Minna's turn, now, to push away her anxieties. The bridesmaid's dress had arrived and Ollie had *seemed* pleased. It was going to be all right, surely? 'She's looking forward very much to Hugh coming home. He gets back tomorrow with this new friend who seems to be a paragon of all the virtues. Just as well, with Honoria Nettleford and her brood as house guests!'

The dowager smiled. 'I can't thank you enough for that. Honoria and the Herrings under one roof really wouldn't have done!'

'I'd have had Lavinia too, but she'll want to be with Muriel,' said Minna. 'And everything's settled for the ball. I've got Bartorolli to play, did I tell you? Snatched him from the Duchess of Norton with an hour to spare! Quite a *coup*! Oh, and you won't forget to let me have Anna, will you. I've an absolute spate of foreigners coming.'

'No, indeed.' The dowager's face had softened at Anna's name. 'Proom's arranged for her to get over to Heslop early so that Hawkins can instruct her in her duties. It'll mean someone else will have to dress Muriel and I'm afraid she won't like it but—' The dowager broke off. 'Oh, good, there's Hannah! I haven't seen her for days.'

Hannah Rabinovitch had entered the lounge, loaded with parcels, and was picking her way between the tables, looking for one that was free. The dowager rose, waving one of her chiffon scarves. 'Here, Hannah! We're over here!'

Hannah looked up and saw her. She took a few eager steps forward – and paused, a deep flush covering her face. Then abruptly she turned, walked quickly back to the door, and vanished.

The dowager sank back into her chair, her eyes smarting with sudden tears. There are greater griefs than rejection by a valued friend, but none which wound more instantly.

'She cut me, Minna! Hannah cut me dead! I don't understand it – I've never known Hannah do anything like that before.' She tried to pick up her cup, found that her hands weren't steady, and put it down again. 'Could it be that Muriel hasn't thanked her for the wedding present? They sent an absolutely priceless dinner service. But Muriel swore she'd write and anyway Hannah isn't like that; she's the least stuffy person I know. And I won't see her now till the wedding . . .'

Minna hesitated. Susie had come to see them the day after Muriel's note had reached The Towers. She'd been quiet and resigned on her own behalf, but when she spoke about her mother there had been something in her voice that had sent Tom, later that night, stamping up and down the great hall like a madman, raking his red thatch of hair and spitting fire. 'If it was anyone else in the world but Rupert I'd turn the whole thing in, even now, but I can't do it to him. Oh, God, I could kill her; I could wring her neck in cold blood. How dare she, how *dare* she?'

Minna had made up her mind. 'I don't think Hannah is coming to the wedding, Mary,' she said quietly.

The dowager stared at her friend, suddenly feeling old and stupid and utterly at sea. 'What do you mean? They're not going to be away, are they? Surely Hannah would have told me?'

Minna searched for words that carried no overtones of malice. 'Muriel felt that . . . a Christian ceremony would embarrass them. That they would feel . . . out of place. So she said they should not feel it necessary to come. I'm sure she meant it kindly, but of course . . .'

The dam of breeding and reserve that had sustained the dowager now broke with a devastating suddenness, leaving her shaking with misery and despair.

'She means nothing kindly, Minna. *Nothing!* She is a hateful, spiteful, dreadful girl. And Rupert will never jilt her. From the age of three I've never known him break his word.' Over the congealed crumpets she stretched a hand out to her friend. 'Oh, God, he's going to be so unhappy! What am I going to do, Minna? What am I going to *do*?'

Rupert had been closeted for nearly an hour with Mr Frisby, the senior partner of Frisby, Frisby and Blenkinsop, who had handled the affairs of his family for generations. The business was long and involved, for the documents relating to Rupert's marriage needed expert and detailed scrutiny. There were the settlements drawn up by Muriel's advisers to examine, there was a new will to be made and, in between, Mr Frisby's congratulations and happy enquiries to receive. For of course Rupert's marriage to an heiress could not fail to delight his solicitor, who for years had coupled deep respect and admiration for the Fraynes with anxiety about the state of their finances.

'And how is Miss Hardwicke liking this part of the world?' Mr Frisby asked now, while they waited for the clerk to bring in another box of documents.

'Oh, very much,' Rupert answered with his friendly smile.

He got up and moved over to the window, irked by the hours spent indoors on such a lovely day. The square was quiet in the early afternoon. An old woman sat on a seat sunning herself; a handful of children played hopscotch on the cobbles . . .

Suddenly, Rupert stiffened. A girl in a dark coat and skirt was hurrying in a purposeful manner across the far side: a girl whose quick, light walk as of an accidentally earthbound angel was appallingly familiar. Now she was slowing down, hesitating, standing looking upwards at the windows of a shop. He narrowed his eyes, making out the lettering.

The clerk came back with a box file, which he set down on the desk. Mr Frisby opened it, began to search among the documents . . .

Anna had gone into the shop. The door had closed behind her. The minutes passed.

'Ah, this is the one we want, I think,' said the solicitor, taking out a sheet of foolscap. 'Now if you would just look at paragraph three, my lord. In my view—'

He broke off, utterly amazed. The Earl of Westerholme, always so polite, so meticulous, had gained the door and, without a word of apology or explanation, run out into the street.

René had finished his combing.

'To here?' he enquired, indicating a place level with Anna's throat.

'Shorter,' said Anna, placing two fingers on her jaw, just below the lobe of her ear. 'To here.'

René nodded. 'Scissors, Elsie!' he commanded.

Elsie resumed her scuffling and produced the required article.

'Not those, you half-wit,' said René, his French accent slipping badly. 'The big ones.'

Elsie returned to the trolley, circled it, pounced, and eventually produced the big ones. At which moment the door of the shop was thrown violently open, a peremptory voice said: 'Stop! Stop that at *once*!' – and a man, apparently in the last stages of lunacy, took two strides across the room and jerked René's arm away, sending the scissors clattering on to the floor.

René stopped. It had taken him some moments to recognize in the wild-eyed, breathless and clearly insane young man, the handsome Earl of Westerholme

235

back from the war. Having done so, he had no desire to cross him and retreated to the far side of the shop, his sharp nose twitching with curiosity and the hope of scandal.

'I told Proom – I made it absolutely clear – *that I will not allow you to cut your hair.*'

Anna, sitting captive and encircled by her tresses, had turned to see whether the crazed image in the mirror could be real. Now, her tobacco-coloured eyes wide with amazement, she addressed her employer.

'Oh? Really? You forbid it?' The last lingering traces of Selina Strickland vanished. Her face had grown pale with what Pinny would unhesitatingly have labelled as temper. 'It will no doubt amuse you to tell me why?'

'You are in my employ,' said Rupert, who was aware that he had taken leave of his senses and did not, at that moment, greatly care. 'None of the servants at Mersham are permitted to have short hair. It is against the regulations.'

'What regulations?' said Anna sweetly.

'The regulations I have drawn up. They will be issued tomorrow.'

'Very well,' said Anna. 'I resign. I will forfeit a week's wages and leave tomorrow.'

'Oh, God.' The madness began to drain from Rupert. He suddenly looked like a man at the end of his endurance; the skin tight over his cheekbones, the eyes shadowed. When he spoke again it was in a voice so low that Anna thought she had misheard him.

'I must have *something*, Anna,' said the Earl of Westerholme.

She felt the ground open beneath her feet. Desperately she groped for her former rage, trying to claw her way back to normality. 'Short hair is very modern. One must move with the times.' The banal sentences lay where they had fallen. 'I wish to be attractive for your wedding,' she went on pleadingly, lifting her face to his. 'Is that a crime?'

'Ah, yes; my wedding.' The word reared up to meet him, banishing the last traces of lunacy. He became aware of René staring at him salaciously, of Elsie, with her mouth open, clutching a towel . . . 'You will be very attractive for my wedding,' he said lightly. 'For my funeral also, *je vous assure*.' He lifted a hand, laid it for a moment on the rich, dark tresses where they mantled her shoulders, then turned it, letting the backs of his fingers run upwards against the shining waves. For an instant she felt his touch on her cheek; then he stepped back. 'There, that was my ration for all eternity. People have died for less, I dare say.' He turned and walked over to René. 'I must apologize for having interrupted you,' he said, taking out a sovereign. 'Perhaps you will be kind enough to accept this as compensation for any inconvenience I have caused you.'

'Thank you, your lordship. Thank you very much.' René, greatly pleased, was all bows and obsequiousness.

'You will now cut mademoiselle's hair exactly as she

instructs,' said the Earl of Westerholme – and was gone.

Anna, left alone, sat mute and trembling, staring into the mirror at a girl she did not know, while René picked up the scissors, flourished them, advanced . . .

It was Potter who found Anna on her return from Maidens Over. He came across her in the stables, one arm flung round the white mare's neck, her head pressed against the horse's shoulder. Anna's hat lay where it had fallen and she was still as stone.

Potter looked at the girl and proceeded to remove her. Had she been suffering from spavins or a slipped stifle, he would have been happy to deal with her himself. Anna, however, did not have spavins and whatever ailed the girl was clearly a matter for Mrs Park or Louise. And retrieving her hat from the straw, he led the dazed and aquiescent girl back to the house.

The head groom's lack of interest in current hairstyles was absolute. It was therefore with surprise and irritation that he saw Anna, on entering the kitchen, become surrounded by a bevy of excited and chattering girls. However, he soon put a stop to this fuss and clatter.

'She's had a bit of a shock, I'd say,' he said aside to Mrs Park.

But the kind cook had already seen. 'Now that's enough noise, everyone,' she admonished them. 'Mildred, get the kettle on.' She pulled out a chair. 'Come along, dear, and sit down. What you need is a nice cup of tea.'

Supper in the servants' hall was a silent meal that night. Everyone was behaving very well: not a reproach, not a question had crossed their lips – and indeed only a professional sadist would have found it possible to reproach Anna in the state she was in. Still, it was a disappointment, no good pretending that it wasn't. As for Anna, she sat between Peggy and Louise, very carefully chewing up pieces of roast beef and equally carefully swallowing them because Pinny had said that no food must be left uneaten on the plate and making, in the intervals of this arduous task, conversation of a quite devastating politeness. Even Proom, sitting magisterially at the head of the table, was unnerved by his housemaid's reversal to her early upbringing. It had never been necessary for Anna to 'make' conversation before, it had bubbled from her in a never-ending spring. To silence Anna had been Proom's problem, and he now sat frowning and exchanging glances with Mrs Park, whose concerned and caring gaze had hardly left Anna's face since the girl's return.

Painstakingly, Anna exhausted the topic of the peace celebrations in London, the question of Home Rule for Ireland – and embarked on a discussion of the weather. Occasional convulsive movements of her narrow throat indicated the end point of another piece of successful mastication.

'It will rain tomorrow, I think?' said Anna.

And Louise, curbing for once her acerbic tongue, agreed that most probably, tomorrow, it would.

While the servants were at supper, Muriel was preparing to address her fiancé on a topic of considerable importance.

For some time, Muriel had been wondering when best to disclose to Rupert certain things of an intimate nature which Dr Lightbody, during their recent lunch at Fortman's, had most tactfully explained to her. And it had occurred to her that on his return from Maidens Over, reminded by his solicitor of her financial generosity, he would be in a suitably receptive mood.

Rupert, however, had not yet come in and it was to an empty chair that Muriel, determined to be word-perfect before his arrival, addressed her opening remarks.

'Dearest,' she began, 'I have something . . . a little personal to say to you.' Pausing for the imagined look of eager interest directed at her by Rupert, she resumed the rehearsal. 'It is about our intimate life together,' she continued. 'I want—' She broke off. 'We *both* want, do we not . . . to have perfect children? Children who will be worthy of their great inheritance?'

Another pause for Rupert's enthusiastic concurrence.

'Well, it so happens,' Muriel's lips curved into a beguiling smile, 'that Dr Lightbody has studied the matter in *great* detail and he has explained to me that it would be wrong – indeed *disastrous* – if you were to approach me at any time. Like an animal.'

As if on cue, Baskerville, patiently awaiting his master in the corridor, gave a loud and desperate moan. Muriel frowned. Where *was* Rupert? Surely he must be back by now?

She cleared her thoat. 'There are times, you see, connected with the waxing of the moon which are . . . favourable. And it's during those times alone that one may expect to conceive a totally unflawed human being. Whereas—'

Another moan from Baskerville. Muriel, her irritation mounting, tried once more. If that wretched animal would shut up she'd get it right.

'Whereas at other times . . . merely, I mean, to gratify the lower instincts and—'

But Baskerville's loneliness and frustration had become uncontainable. Raising his head, he shattered the silence with a howl of such pain and anguish as would have done credit to King Lear. And suddenly unable to control her fury, Muriel opened the door and, as the dog turned his entreating, bloodshot eyes towards her, she kicked out at him hard with the heel of her spiky shoe.

Anna had finished with the rain, its possible effects on the begonias of Mr Cameron, the likelihood of subsequent flooding. Looking down at her plate she perceived that the unfocused splodges she had been devouring were, in fact, vegetables and meat. Another whole course to go, then . . .

'Soon it will be time to begin the grouse shooting, will it not?'

A sudden, violent thump against the door of the servants' hall interrupted her. A second and louder thump achieved its objective. The door burst open and, in concerted amazement, the staff looked up at the figure thus revealed.

'That I should live to see the day!' said James. 'That great, drooling snob showing his face down 'ere!'

Torn between despair and embarrassment, between loneliness and shame, the earl's dog stood before them, his great head raking the room. He had done it, the unspeakable thing. The degradation, the horror of it, was behind him – and now where was she? Had it all been in vain; the debasement, the agony, the *choice*?

But no, it was all right. He'd seen her. She was there. She would make whole what was broken, console him for his master's absence, would understand his imperative need to be scratched *now*, this minute, and for a long time in that special place behind his ear. To show too much joy in a place such as this would be unseemly but, as he padded towards her, his tail was extended in a manner which would make wagging possible should all go as expected. Anna just had time to pull back her chair before he was upon her, butting and blowing, letting his head sink, at last, with a moan of relief on to her lap.

She put up a hand to scratch him, and as she bent

forward the pins, jabbed ill-temperedly back on her head by the frustrated René, loosened, sending a strand of her uncut hair forward across her shoulders.

'Oh, Baskerville,' said Anna – and only then began to cry.

12

Inner peace now descended on Baskerville, who found his new life of abasement below stairs a beguiling and hitherto undiscovered world of the senses. It did not, however, descend on the focus of his adoration, Anna Grazinsky.

Anna had not caught so much as a glimpse of the earl since he'd walked out of René's shop in Maidens Over, which made her suppose that he, too, was avoiding any place where they might meet. Worked off her feet, as were all the maids, Anna had in addition to act as handmaiden to the incessant bodily horticulture with which Muriel prepared for her Great Day. Packs of oatmeal and buttermilk had to be poured over Muriel's white limbs, purées of soft fruit to be smeared on her face. Pummice-stoning Muriel's elbows, massaging egg-white into her scalp, applying an amazing quantity of sliced cucumber to her eyelids as she floated in the bath kept Anna in a state of bemused exhaustion from dawn to dusk. For the rest, she kept silence. Only her eyes betrayed her wonderment that love, when it came at last, should be so physical, so exhausting and so sad.

The fatigue below stairs, the anxiety above, as the dowager wondered whether Uncle Sebastien, aged by five years in the last weeks, would get to the church to give away the bride, were not echoed by Muriel herself. Muriel felt fine. With five days to go she was certain that her decision to have a quiet wedding at Mersham had paid off. Not one of her father's disreputable relatives had shown any sign of life and soon, now, Dr Lightbody would arrive to see the completion of her journey into the aristocracy.

Yet at the very moment that Muriel was anticipating his arrival with such pleasure, the doctor was sitting in an ante-room in the Samaritan Hospital in the Edgware Road, in a state of bewilderment and shock.

'I can't believe it,' he said, shaking his blond and handsome head. 'It isn't possible. Not Doreen.'

'We've expected it for some time, Dr Lightbody,' said the matron, who had indeed tried several times to give the obstinate man an idea of his wife's condition. 'She was very ill when she was admitted, as you know. It was only a matter of time.'

Alone in his lodgings that night, the doctor sank wearily into his chair. He was a widower. Doreen had done the unbelievable thing and without a word to him, without, so to speak, his permission, she had died. Really, it was quite appalling, quite unbearable.

And not only that. In two days' time he was supposed

to go to Mersham, to Miss Hardwicke's wedding and the ball which preceded it.

He would have to cancel it, of course. But how dreadfully disappointed Miss Hardwicke would be. She had been so interested when he had hinted that he might be willing to come and work at Mersham. And how agonizing it was for him to break his word.

But would he in fact *have* to break it? The doctor rose and walked over to the mirror. Considering the shock he had just sustained he was looking wonderfully well. Supposing he went very quietly to the wedding? In a black armband to signify bereavement, emitting a restrained sadness which could not fail to touch Miss Hardwicke's heart. Yes, in a sense it was his duty to go. One could, after all, be a little vague about exactly *when* Doreen had died.

Yes, he would go to the wedding. It was, when all was said and done, a religious ceremony. But not to the ball. People might really think it was odd if he came to the ball in a black armband. And in any case a black armband would not go at all well with the white tunic, the golden circlet of laurel leaves and the lyre of Apollo. Sighing, the doctor moved over to the wardrobe and opened it. Nathaniel and Gumsbody had done him proud – the outfit was extremely becoming, simple yet regal, and they had thrown in, at half price, a bottle of liquid make-up for his arms and legs. He had tried a little on his knees last night and the effect was excellent: sportive yet glowing. But of course a black armband would kill that. It was impossible.

For a while he stood looking at the white folds of the chiton, the finely wrought sandals. Was he perhaps being rather *selfish*, obtruding his grief like that? Why wear a black armband at all? Why, in fact, *tell* anyone that Doreen had died? To go, keeping to himself this bereavement, to pretend to laugh and dance and be merry when his heart was breaking – was not that the noble thing? Was that not what Apollo himself would have counselled? To dance with Miss Hardwicke, to hold in his arms her full-breasted, white skinned loveliness, to remind her, under cover of the music, of her procreative duties, was that not a worthier task than to sit here mourning and grieving, a victim of self-pity and despair?

Of course there was the funeral. But Doreen's parents, with whom she had never quite cut off relations though he had begged her to often enough, would be only too happy to organize all that without interference. And a thoroughly lower-class business it would be – but that was their affair. The actual interment, after all, wouldn't be for at least a week and he'd be back by then.

Yes, it was a hard choice, a task that would take all his self-control but he would do it. He would go to the wedding and the ball – and somehow contrive to enjoy himself. In which case, as he was going to see the florist anyway about a suitable wreath, he'd better enquire about a white carnation to go with the morning clothes he'd hired. Or would a gardenia be better? That is, if

gardenias were worn at country weddings before
lunch . . . ?

The Herrings, meanwhile, had perfected their plan for
getting to Mersham with a minimum of financial
outlay. It was a complicated plan and though Melvyn
had explained it several times to Myrtle, she was
having trouble with it, her physical endowment,
though generous, not being of the kind that extended
to the grey matter of the brain.

'Look, it's like this,' Melvyn explained patiently. 'I
buy one ticket for the two of us, see?'

'What with?' asked Myrtle, unhooking her corsets,
for they were preparing for bed.

'Just leave that to me, will you? I buy a return ticket,
see? Then you wait till there's a good crowd pushing
round the barrier an' you go through and give up your
half of the ticket all properly like, and as soon as you're
through you push the return bit of the ticket back in
my hand. Then I come along and the inspector says,
"Tickets, please" and I say, "I've already given it to
you".'

'But you haven't,' said Myrtle, rubbing the weals
the whalebone had left in her burgeoning flesh.

'No, Myrtle; I know I haven't. Because *you* have. So
then I say, all innocent like, "But I gave it to you" an'
he says, "No, you didn't" and I say "Yes I did an' if
you look you'll see I have because 'ere's the return half
with the number on it and if you look you'll find the

248

same number on one of the tickets in your hand." And then 'e looks and sure enough, there it is.'

'What about the twins?' asked Myrtle, slipping back into the black *crêpe de Chine* petticoat that did double duty for a nightdress. That was what she liked about black undies; there wasn't all that bother about washing them.

'We'll do the same with the twins. Buy one ticket between the two of them.'

'All right. Only *you* go and explain to them what they've got to do.'

Melvyn rose and opened the door of the adjoining room. Owing to an unfortunate spot of bother with the bailiffs, the twins were sleeping on a mattress on the floor. Dennis was lying on his back; his full-lipped mouth hung open and, as he breathed, the mucous in his nose bubbled softly like soup. Beside him lay Donald, apparently overcome by sleep in the act of eating a dripping sandwich, the dismembered remains of which lay smeared across his face.

Melvyn stood looking down at the swollen cheeks, the pendulous chins and bulging arms of his offspring and his fatherhood, never a sturdy plant, wilted and died.

'Meat,' he said wearily to himself. 'That's all they are. Just blobs of meat.'

He went out and closed the door. 'They're asleep,' he said to Myrtle. 'I'll tell them in the morning. But it'll work, you'll see. It wouldn't have done if we were going all the way to Mersham, but they're sending the car to Maidens Over. There'll be enough of a crowd there.'

Myrtle got into bed and reached for the cold cream. 'I suppose it's better than being locked in the lav,' she said. 'But your Aunt Mary'd better come up with something good once we're there.'

'She will. She's got a soft spot for me on account of I look like her Rupert. I've got the Templeton eyes, see.'

Melvyn, for once, was not boasting. Both his own features and the twins' dough-like countenances, were unexpectedly pierced by the wide, grey eyes, with their gold-flecked irises, which the dowager had bequeathed to her son.

'Mind you, I'll have to get past that old sod of a butler,' said Melvyn, remembering Proom's unequivocal stand over the gold sovereigns and the Meissen figurine. 'He hasn't half got it in for me.'

'Oh, leave 'im to me,' said Myrtle. 'If 'e's a man I'll 'andle 'im,' and began to giggle, delighted at her *double entendre*.

Melvyn was less sanguine. From what he remembered of Cyril Proom, Myrtle was on a losing wicket there.

Prince Sergei Chirkovsky, sitting in his neat, grey uniform at the wheel of the huge, plum coloured Daimler with the Nettleford Arms (a serpent extended in fess, the head raised . . .) embossed on the door, steered his way expertly between the carters' drays, the buggies and dawdling delivery vans of the interminable stretch

250

of road between Darlington and York and wondered how long he could endure his present post.

He was the most easy-going of men, his incredible good looks reinforced by a serene and undemanding acceptance of what life brought. 'God was in a good mood when he made Sergei', the matrons of Petersburg used to say, looking fondly at the charming, handsome, unassuming boy. But Sergei, who had accepted without complaint the hardship of exile from the land he deeply loved, was fast meeting his Waterloo at the hands of Honoria Nettleford and her 'gals'.

The duchess's snobbery and meanness, her rudeness to him as an underling, were deeply unpleasant but not unexpected. It was what he had to put up with from Hermione and Priscilla, from Gwendolyn and Beatrice and the equine and haughty Lady Lavinia, all of whom he was now conveying southwards to the Earl of Westerholme's wedding, that made Sergei wonder how much longer he could hold out.

All his life, Sergei had been pursued by women. He was six years old when the tiny, dimpled Kira Satayev, eluding the vigilance of his Miss King, had ambushed him behind the Krylov Monument in the Summer Gardens and informed him that he found favour in her eyes. The peasant girls on his parents' estates, the gypsy dancers on the islands, the *ingénues* in the ballrooms of Petersburg and their worldly mothers in its salons – all had made it clear to him, in their different ways, that they were his for the asking. He had learned very early to accept with gratitude and pleasure where

251

acceptance was appropriate, to refuse with tact and gentleness where acquiescence might involve impropriety or pain. But never in all his life had he encountered anything as crude and displeasing as the advances of these snobbish and lascivious girls.

He accelerated to pass a Model T Ford and though his skilled driving had effected the manoeuvre with perfect smoothness, the Lady Lavinia managed to hurl herself, as if impelled, against his side. She was the worst by far. When it was her turn to sit in front there was nothing to which this high-born lady would not stoop, yet when there was anyone looking on she spoke to him as his reactionary old grandfather would never in his life have spoken to the humblest of his serfs. And in the back of the car he could hear her four sisters snickering and bickering and awaiting their turn. How had Hudson wangled it, Sergei wondered, so that he went ahead conveying only the duke and duchess and the trunks? True, Hudson was the senior chauffeur, but he might have distributed the load a little less unevenly.

Sergei sighed, assisted the Lady Lavinia to right herself and apologized for the non-existent jolt. If only, he thought, any of the girls had had just *one* redeeming feature: pretty hair, nice eyes, a fondness for little children – it might have been possible to snub them even if, as seemed likely, they would retaliate by seeing that he lost his job. But how could one rebuff girls of such unredeemed ugliness, girls who had only to appear at any social gathering to send every young man in the room running for cover?

'*Boch ti moy,*' sighed Sergei, calling on his Maker. And at Heslop, where he was to spend three nights, there would be the lady's maids, the upper house-maids . . . And another complication. For one of his duties there would be to drive the Lady Lavinia to and from Mersham where she was staying. And Mersham was the place where Anna, so Pinny had told him, was also staying as a guest. He'd have to be very careful not to be seen by her in his role of chauffeur. Anna was quite incapable of acting sensibly and cutting him dead.

Anna . . . As he thought of her, Sergei smiled – that dazzling, tender smile of his – and the Lady Lavinia, seeing it, edged closer. But Sergei was far away now . . . In the birch woods round Grazbaya as Anna ran towards him cupping fresh-picked wild strawberries for him in her hands . . . Anna, whose cry of 'Look, Seriosha, oh, *look*!' had been the thread running through their childhood as she shared with him her delight in a ring of white and crimson toadstools, a new foal, a skein of wild geese flying south to the Urals. If only he could find a job that would make it possible for him to look after her, and Petya too. She'd looked so tired when he saw her last at the club, so thin. Or should he, after all, marry Larissa Rakov like the grand duchess wanted? He'd fled from the baroness's pallid plainness, her boring conversation, but compared to the Nettleford girls, the grand duchess's dumpy lady-in-waiting seemed a miracle of propriety and intelligence and she was certainly very rich. Her banker father had seen the catastrophe coming long before anyone else and transferred all his assets to London. If he married Larissa, he could make a home for his parents and the Grazinskys too.

Beside him, the Lady Lavinia, watching the tender lines of his mouth as he thought of Anna, felt her heart miss a beat. There was no question, of course, of her losing her head. She was travelling towards her destiny in the person of the Honourable Tom Byrne, in whose arms, as Undine the Water Sprite, she would, in less than twenty-four hours, circle the ballroom of Heslop Hall. But really this foreigner was shatteringly attractive. Would a small pinch on the thigh be going too far?

They had reached York and, following instructions, Sergei drew into the courtyard of the King's Hotel where Hudson was already parked. He opened the doors and the girls swept haughtily past him into the restaurant.

'We're to wait here by the cars, her grace says,' said Hudson. 'No gallivanting off.'

Sergei nodded. He had been less than six weeks in the service of the Nettlefords, but long enough to know that their chauffeurs need not expect anything as vulgar and mundane as lunch.

'You're late,' said Hawkins, Heslop's awe-inspiring butler, staring disapprovingly from his great height at Anna.

It was the evening of the ball. Anna had been conveyed to Heslop by the carter, an uncle of Peggy and

Pearl, and now stood nervously before Hawkins, her eyes cast down. She had not thought of Selina Strickland for some days, but now she felt a pang of longing for the *Domestic Compendium*. For Heslop, with its labyrinthine corridors, its vast staff and rigid protocol, was a different world from Mersham.

And she *was* late. Furious at being deprived of Anna's services, Muriel had kept her to the last second, finding a dozen unnecessary jobs for her to do, so that if it hadn't been for the dowager's Alice almost pushing Anna out of the door, she could not have come at all.

'I'm very sorry, sir,' she said – and immediately came under fire from the other half of Heslop's Dual Monarchy: the formidable housekeeper, Miss Peel.

'Pull your hair back, girl. We don't allow *waves*!'

Anna pulled dutifully at her hair. Louise, consulting with Mrs Bassenthwaite in hospital, had put Anna into the uniform the maids had been issued for Lord George's Twenty-first: a black silk dress to the instep, a white fichu, a short apron of snowy lawn finely tuckered and edged with lace. A frilled cap of the same lawn was set demurely back on Anna's dark head.

'It's old-fashioned but it'll be right for Heslop,' Mrs Bassenthwaite had said, 'with Miss Peel being such a stickler.'

Unable to find fault with Anna's appearance, yet aware that the girl somehow did not look as she wanted her to look, Miss Peel said, 'Let me see your fingernails.'

Anna extended her hands. The obvious antagonism she had felt the moment she set foot in Heslop hurt and puzzled her. She was too inexperienced to realize what an affront her arrival was to servants jealous of their privileges and rights. As though they couldn't provide all that was necessary for the ball without an upstart and a foreigner being wished on them! Not only that, but she was to be employed *upstairs*, in a position of prominence, serving drinks in the great hall when the guests arrived and showing the ladies to the cloak-rooms. Unable to take their resentment out on Lady Byrne, who had given these instructions, they prepared to give no quarter to the foreign girl, who by all accounts had been thoroughly spoilt at Mersham.

'I'll take her along to get started,' said Hawkins now. 'She's too late for tea, the girls are just coming out.'

Anna, who due to Muriel's bullying had had no lunch, repressed a sigh, curtsied to the housekeeper and followed Mr Hawkins down a short flight of steps, along a winding corridor and through an enfilade of sculleries and store rooms to the pantries. Minna had done everything she could to provide her servants with comfort: the floors were carpeted, there were electric lights, new boilers, glass-fronted cupboards – but the tone of an establishment is set by those who run it and Anna was not surprised, passing the kitchens, to hear a scream and see the door burst open to eject a hyster-ically weeping kitchen maid, who gave a gasp of terror at the sight of Hawkins, threw her apron over her head and scuttled blindly away.

Mr Hawkins stopped at the door of a large pantry where three girls, under a barrage of admonitions from the first footman, were laying out trays of glasses and cutlery.

'Here's the Russian girl, Charles,' said Mr Hawkins, pushing Anna into the room. 'She's to go upstairs at eight, but there's plenty of time for her to make herself useful before then.'

'There is indeed,' said the first footman with a sour smile. He turned to Anna. 'You can start by rinsing all those knives through hot water and polishing them. *Hot* water, mind, and no fuss about it hurting your hands. The sink's over there.'

Watched by the hostile eyes of the other girls, Anna went to work.

Upstairs, Heslop was *en grande tenue*. The great hall blazed with lights, tubs of poinsettias and camellias glowed like captive fireworks against the rich darkness of the tapestries. In the ballroom with its triple row of chandeliers, Minna, remembering that she was welcoming a bride, had kept the flowers to white: delphiniums, madonna lilies, roses and the quivering, dancing Mexican poppies that she loved so much. Garlands of white ribbons and acanthus leaves wreathed the long mirrors, and the end windows, on this lovely summer evening, stood open to the terrace with its fountains of rampaging gods, its lily ponds . . .

Minna had dressed early and now walked quietly from room to room checking details; the French chalk spread evenly over the dance floor; the clustered grapes arranged in a suitably dying fall over the chased silver bowls; velvet cushions placed on the chairs put out for Mr Bartorolli's orchestra . . . She wore the dress her Puritan great-grandmother had worn for her Quaker wedding: dove grey silk with a wide, white collar. Like her husband, Minna did not care for fancy dress, but she was glad now of the dignity lent by the old-fashioned dress. If she was to welcome Muriel Hardwicke as she should be welcomed, she had need of every aid to mannerliness and poise. Now, pausing for a moment at the door of the state dining room, where two whispering footmen were putting the finishing touches to a dazzling cold collation on the sideboard, she nodded, well pleased. There had been disasters and clashes below stairs, the chef had given notice no less than seven times, but now, like a prima donna who forgets her rehearsal tantrums, Heslop was ready to go on stage.

Minna went upstairs, smiling as she passed her husband's dressing room and heard the choleric expletives which attended the efforts of his lordship's valet to button him into the dress uniform of an eighteenth-century hussar, and hurrying quickly past the suite she had allocated to the Nettlefords, she entered Ollie's room.

'Look, Mummy, look at Hugh and Peter, aren't they *smart*!' Ollie's eyes shone with pride as she pointed to

258

her brother and the schoolfriend he had brought down from Craigston – and indeed the two boys sitting side by side on the window-sill in their cadet uniforms were quite spectacularly scrubbed and brushed. 'Peter says he'll stay up in the minstrel's gallery with me at the beginning to watch the guests arrive and afterwards he's going to creep up and bring me things to eat. I can stay up long enough for that, can't I?'

Minna nodded and smiled affectionately at Hugh's new friend who, in the space of two days, had become the object of Ollie's hero worship. Not only the boy's nationality but his temperament had been a surprise and delight to Minna. Peter was a first class boxer, Hugh said, and had won the Junior Fencing Cup within a few weeks of arriving at school. And yesterday, when the boys had gone out riding, Tom, with whom horses were almost a religion, had offered Peter his own hunter to ride whenever he wished. Yet he was interested in matters which most English boys would have considered effete or embarrassing: textures and fabrics, even flowers. It was to Peter that Ollie, slowly recovering from the wound that Muriel had inflicted, showed her bridesmaid's dress and his unfeigned interest, his support during the wedding rehearsal on the previous day, had enabled Ollie to hold her head high and to aquit herself with distinction. If Ollie was once again looking forward to Muriel's wedding, it was largely due to the Russian boy.

Back in her room, Minna sat for a few moments, absently dabbing scent behind her ears. If only things had been different she might have hoped, in years to come, of a marriage between Ollie and just such a boy as Hugh's new friend. Whereas the way things were . . .

Then there was a knock at the door and Peter's blond head appeared round it. 'There has been a disaster with the head of John the Baptist,' he said, grinning. 'Lady Hermione has sat on it and wishes to know if—' He broke off, came into the room. 'You are sad?'

'No . . .' Minna shook her head, then remembered that the 'nothing-is-the-matter' technique had never gone down well with the Russians of her acquaintance. 'But it won't be easy for Ollie later . . . at dances . . . at balls . . .'

The boy closed the door and came to stand beside her chair. 'We have a proverb in Russia,' he said. 'It goes: "The fox knows many things but the hedgehog only knows one thing". Ollie, I think, is a hedgehog – like her Alexander.'

'And what is the one thing that she knows?'

'How to make people love her,' said Peter quietly.

Minna looked up, tears in her eyes. She had never known a boy of thirteen who could speak like that – who could use, so unaffectedly, a word which even her own boys shied away from – and the suspicion she had entertained from the moment she met him hardened into near certainty. But she only brushed his cheek lightly with her fingers and said: 'You know, Peter, I think I shall change my plans and get *you* to take Honoria Nettleford into supper!'

*

260

Anna had been in the pantry for an hour, bent over a sink of near-boiling water. After an exchange of giggles, the spiteful girls who worked with her had made a point of tipping a treble load of soda into the water every time she changed it and her hands, already chapped and raw, hurt so much that it was all she could do not to cry out. But she kept on and at last even Hawkins could not postpone her journey upstairs any longer.

The main entrance at Heslop led into a domed vestibule from which the grand staircase swept upwards and the original Elizabethan hall, raftered and galleried, opened on the right. It was in the hall that the guests would be greeted and assemble for conversation and light refreshment before ascending to the ballroom, a later addition reached by a flight of shallow stairs at the far end.

Anna, following Hawkins up the service stair, received a spate of instructions over his shoulder. 'There'll be two footmen at the entrance and two at the foot of the stairs and I'll be doing the announcing. You're to stand out of the way in the great hall beside the service table. Mr Briggs is in charge there,' he said, referring to the tyrannical and sour-faced Charles. 'He'll tell you when you're to take up a tray and offer drinks. There's to be no putting yourself forward – and no slacking either. And remember, the ballroom's out of bounds – you've no call whatever to—'

He stopped with an exclamation of annoyance, aware that Anna was no longer following closely. She

261

had suddenly stumbled, had put out a hand to the wall of the corridor, trying to steady herself.

'What on earth are you doing?' he asked sharply, but he was anxious too. What if the wretched girl should faint on him? Perhaps he should have let her have some tea?

But it was no longer hunger or exhaustion that had made Anna stumble, though she was tired enough. It was a fragment, a haunting, insidious snatch of melody carried across the well of the servants' court-yard by a suddenly opened door. A tune known and loved from childhood which came, now, as only music can, to break down her defences and flood her with such longing, such an agony of homesickness for the world that was lost to her for ever, that she thought she would die of it.

'What on earth did you bring that for?' said the first violinist, putting down his bow. 'It's as old as the hills, that.'

'Oh, I dunno,' said Mr Bartorolli, alias Bert Phipps of Bermondsey. 'I just put it in at the last minute.' He shrugged and put the yellowing sheets of the 'Valse des Fleurs' back on the piano. Then he continued to hand out freshly bound copies of the latest hits: two-steps and tangos, to the musicians now arranging their places on the dais.

'The Earl of Westerholme, The Lady Lavinia Nettle-ford, The Dowager Countess of Westerholme, Miss Muriel Hardwicke, Miss Cynthia Smythe, Dr Ronald

Lightbody,' announced Hawkins, and the party from Mersham moved through into the hall and towards the great fireplace, where Lord and Lady Byrne, with Tom, were waiting to greet their guests.

Minna embraced the dowager, who was becomingly and, she herself considered, aptly dressed as Mary Queen of Scots Ascending the Scaffold, and turned to welcome what appeared to be an outsize codfish or perhaps a trout.

'You've met Lavinia, of course,' prompted the dowager. 'And this is Cynthia Smythe, Muriel's other bridesmaid.'

Cynthia, who to no one's surprise was dressed as Little Bo Peep, gushed her way towards her hostess and was followed by a man with knees like carriage lamps, who bent obsequiously over Minna's hand, clouting her as he did so with his lyre.

But now the Earl of Westerholme came forward, escorting his fiancée. Rupert's instructions to his butler to 'for heaven's sake find him something to wear' had yielded a perfect replica, used in theatricals years ago, of the costume that his disreputable ancestor, Sir Montague Frayne, had worn to be painted in by Romney. The velvet breeches, the ruffled shirt and high stock suited him to perfection and Minna, seeing him approach, thought she had never seen him look as handsome – or as tired.

But it was Muriel, the guest of honour, who rightly drew all eyes. Muriel's dress was of blue and silver, the colours that the Sun King used above all others for the glory of Versailles. A myriad bows glittered on the satin bodice; the elaborately flounced overskirt was sewn with tiny bunches of gauze roses and forget-me-nots. Priceless lace edged the sleeves and the low *décolleté*, diamonds sparkled on the high, white wig and in the heels of her silver slippers – and round her throat, perfectly matching the blue of the dress and of her eyes, she wore the sapphires that were the bride-groom's present to the bride. If Muriel looked pleased with herself she had every right to do so, for here was a Pompadour to silence all beholders.

'My dear, what an unbelievable dress!' said Minna, genuinely impressed. 'You'll set everybody by the ears.' She turned to Rupert. 'You'll have to surrender her for the first dance, I'm afraid. Harry will want to open the ball with her, but after that . . .'

Meanwhile, obedient to her instructions, Anna had remained quietly out of sight behind a potted palm which flanked the serving table over which Charles, the first footman, was presiding.

'What the dickens are you doing, wool-gathering there,' he hissed now. 'Can't you see the party from Mersham's arrived? Why aren't you out there offering them drinks?'

Anna took a tray, stepped out into the hall.

'Ah, here's Anna come to offer us some refresh-ment,' said Minna. 'That's orange juice in the tall glasses, Muriel.'

Rupert had been standing a little apart from the others in the shadow of a high, carved screen. Now,

264

hearing Anna's name, he looked up sharply – and was flooded, suddenly, by a joy as violent as it was absurd.

She had not cut her hair.

He had had time to wince a thousand times at his behaviour in Maidens Over. He had been arrogant and mad and mistaken on all counts, for Anna would, as he had since realized, have looked enchanting with her hair cut short. He had deserved only to be snubbed and disregarded. Instead, she had given him this gift, this undeserved benison. And standing there, bound by the iron fetters of duty to a marriage he knew would bring him nothing but pain, he was nevertheless consumed by happiness because his under-housemaid had not cut her hair.

'Rupert! Hello!' The earl turned to see Hugh come down the last of the steps from the minstrel's gallery with a handsome, fair-haired boy a little taller than himself. A boy who suddenly stood stock-still and then, with a whoop of delight, rushed towards them.

'Annoushka! It *is* you! Oh, how lovely! I hoped and hoped you would come. Pinny said you were staying near here and I was going to ask if I could ride over.' Ignoring the dismay in Anna's eyes, the gasp of indrawn breath, he leant over the tray to kiss her, then circled her admiringly. 'You look so *good*! That dress is most becoming! It's clever of you to wear something so simple. Do you remember that ball that Mama told us about at the Anchikovs where the Princess Saritsin went as a nun and suddenly everyone else looked over-dressed?'

There was a titter from Little Bo Peep, and involuntarily the eyes of all the women went to Muriel Hardwicke. But Petya, unaware of any implications, rushed happily on. 'Only you're silly to have a *tray*, 'Noushka. How can you dance with a tray?'

'How indeed?' said an amused voice at Petya's elbow. 'I think you'd better introduce your sister,' continued the Earl of Westerholme. 'She is not known to everyone present.'

'No, Petya, *please*.' Anna's hands, with their cracked knuckles, had tightened in desperation around the silver handles of the tray.

But Petya was concerned only at his breach of manners. 'I'm so sorry.' He turned with a charming bow to his host and hostess. 'Permit me to introduce my sister, the Countess Anna Petrovna Grazinsky.'

There was a hiss from Muriel; the codfish mouth of Undine the Water Sprite fell open and Lord Byrne, who had not expected to enjoy himself, beamed on the company.

'But I thought she was—' began Cynthia Smythe, and found that the Dowager Countess of Westerholme had stepped heavily on her foot.

'Petya, I *beg* of you,' whispered Anna, and added a few words of entreaty in Russian, imploring him to leave her.

The certainty, the joy, drained visibly from the boy's face. He looked at the hostile woman in the silver dress, at Anna's desperate eyes . . . Had he made a mistake? Was it possible . . . but it couldn't be! Uncle

266

Kolya, he knew, was a doorman at the Ritz. But *Anna*! Half-remembered fragments of conversation at West Paddington came now to plague him. If she was working as a servant while he was lording it here . . . If . . .

'Your *hands*,' he said, his collar suddenly choking him. 'They're *bleeding*.'

Minna, who had seen the boy's face, moved to his side. But the Earl of Westerholme had stepped out of the shadows. 'You must blame your Stanislavsky and his Method Acting for that. Anna spent the whole afternoon at Mersham dipping her hands into soda so as to get the feel of the part! I told her it was unfair to her partners but she wouldn't listen!'

The light voice, the amused tenderness with which he looked at Anna, partly reassured the boy. But Hawkins, waiting to announce the next guests by the double doors, had sent an irate signal to Charles. Now, the first footman approached, his face as purple as his livery. What was the wretched girl doing? She'd been hours serving drinks and now she was actually *talking* to the guests.

Lord Byrne, with his bluff kindness, prepared to intervene. It was unnecessary. Anna, too, had seen her brother's face. Her head went up, she turned – and as the bullying footman approached she said with a serene and charming smile: 'Ah, Charles. How kind! You have come to relieve me of my burden.'

And before he knew what was happening, the footman, responding instinctively to the practised authority in her voice, found himself holding the loaded tray.

'Well, what are you hanging round for?' said Lord Byrne to the goggling Charles. 'You heard what the countess said. Take the thing away.'

'Ah, that's better!' Anna had shaken out her skirt, straightened her apron, tilted her cap – and suddenly it was obvious that she was in fancy dress; no real uniform ever had such grace, such gossamer lightness. 'How good it will be to dance again!'

'With me?' said Petya excitedly. 'Will you dance with me?'

'Of course, *galubchik*.'

'No,' said Tom Byrne. 'First with me.'

'I'm sorry to disillusion you both,' said the earl, 'but as Anna's host at Mersham I undoubtedly have first claim.'

Petya's face blazed with pride and happiness. This was like the old days, with men fighting to dance with Anna. What an idiot he'd been! For a moment he'd really thought . . .

'She's a marvellous dancer,' he told the earl, of whom, as a partner for his sister, he thoroughly approved. 'Especially when she waltzes. Fokine said when you play Anna a waltz you can see her *eat* the music. She goes round and round and she never gets giddy!'

Rupert smiled enquiringly at his hostess. 'A waltz could perhaps be arranged?'

'Very easily, I think,' said Minna, to whom nothing that had happened had come as a surprise.

Rupert turned to Anna. 'May I have the pleasure of the first dance, Countess?'

She lifted her face to his, not even trying to hide her blazing joy. 'You may, my lord.'

And so they went together into the ballroom to dance for the first and last time in their lives, the 'Valse des Fleurs'.

13

A great deal had happened to Tchaikovsky's sumptu-
ously orchestrated showpiece to turn it into a suitable
waltz for the ballroom, but Mr Bartorolli was not
dismayed.

'Told you,' he said to his first violinist when Minna
came with her request, 'I had a sort of hunch,' – and
lifted his baton.

It begins slowly, this well-loved, well-remembered
waltz. The preluding is gentle, the phrases soft and
pleading, the dancers have time to smile in each other's
arms, to catch their breath. But not for long. Soon the
familiar phrases try out their plumes, begin to preen,
to gather themselves up until reality is swept away in
an intoxicating, irresistible swirl of sound.

To this waltz, born in a distant, snowbound country out of longing for just such a flower-scented
summer night as this, Rupert and Anna danced. They
were under no illusions. The glittering chandeliers,
the gold mirrors with their draped acanthus leaves, the

plangent violins might be the stuff of romance, but this was no romance. It was a moment in a lifeboat before it sank beneath the waves; a walk across the sunlit courtyard towards the firing squad. This waltz was all they had.

So they danced and neither of them spoke. As the music began and his arms closed round her, he had felt her shiver. Then the melody caught her and she moved with him, so light, so completely one with him that he could guide her with a finger. Yet as he held her he had no thought of thistledown or snowflake. Here, beneath his hands, was tempered steel, was flame . . .

He checked, reversed, and she followed him perfectly. It seemed to him that she could fold her very bones to lie against his own. And tightening his arms, drinking in the smell of green soap, of cleanliness personified, which emanated from this changeling countess, he allowed his mind, soaring with the music, to encompass their imagined life together.

He had not wanted Mersham – had returned to it reluctantly as to a burden he must face. In the few weeks she had been there, Anna had changed all this. Her feeling for his home was unerring, as inborn as perfect pitch in music. Bending to arrange a bowl of roses, standing rapt, with her feather duster, before the Titian in the morning room, bringing in the mare at daybreak, each time she seemed to be making him a gift of his inheritance. Like those dark Madonnas on the icons whose patient hands curve up towards their infants' heads, Anna's every gesture said: 'Behold!'

271

Anna, in his arms, was without thoughts, without dreams. Rupert had imagined her folding her bones to shape them against his. She had done more. She had folded her very soul, given it into his keeping – and danced.

'Oh, God!' said the dowager softly. And then to Minna, standing beside her. 'Did you know?'

'That Peter was her brother? I guessed almost as soon as he came. Or did you mean . . . ?'

She did not finish. There had been no scandal yet – only a drama of the kind that any hostess must delight in. Her Harry had led Muriel first on to the floor; Tom, good soul that he was, was dancing with Lavinia; other couples had quickly joined in and were swaying and swirling beneath the glittering chandeliers. Yet it seemed to Minna and the dowager that there was no one in the ballroom except those two.

'If only they would *talk*,' said the dowager.

And indeed the silence in which those two danced was as terrible as an army with banners. Only Muriel, armoured by her outrage at Anna's presumption as she gyrated heavily in the arms of her host, entirely failed to see what had happened.

'What an extraordinary business,' said the Lady Lavinia, lurching in her skirted codfish costume against the long-suffering Tom. 'Is she really a countess?'

'Yes.'

Tom had seen Susie come in. She was dressed as a gypsy and accompanied by her mother in the costume of a Noble Spanish Lady – and by that stout bullfighter,

Leo Rabinovitch. If only he could get to Susie it would be easier to bear what he had seen in Rupert's face.

'Muriel doesn't like it, does she?' continued Lavinia with satisfaction. 'She looks as though she's swallowed a porcupine.'

Tom glanced at Rupert's fiancée. Muriel certainly looked angry, but he could see no sign on her face of distress or pain.

But now the music was gathering itself up, manoeuvring for the climax. Mr Bartorolli had done all he could. With his fine social antennae he had understood exactly what was happening. The ball might be *for* the stiff, white-wigged lady in silver, but it was *about* the young girl with her ardour and her Byzantine eyes who seemed to be one flesh with the young Earl of Westerholme. So he had played the first repeat, the second, demanded – to the surprise of his orchestra – a reprise. But now there was nothing more to be done. For the last time, the melody soared towards its fulfilment, the dancers turned faster, faster . . . and with a last, dazzling crescendo, the music ceased.

It was over.

They drew apart and for a moment Anna stood looking up at him, dazed by the silence.

Then, for the last time, she curtsied.

If it hadn't been for that curtsy, Rupert would have left her then and there. He expected no more miracles. But what she made of that gesture, combining her former respect and humility with the elegance, the lightness of the ballroom – yet all of it, somehow, heartbreakingly on a dying fall – was more than he could bear.

'Come outside for a moment. You must be hot.'

She shook her head. 'No, Rupert.'

He did not hear the denial, only that she had used his Christian name – and followed by every pair of eyes in the room he led her out, still protesting, through the French windows and on to the terrace. Nor did he stop there but, as familiar with Heslop as with Mersham, led her down a flight of shallow stone steps to an arbour with a lily pond and a stone bench, protected by a high, yew hedge.

'Anna,' he said, guiding her to the seat, 'I shall do what is right. I shall not jilt Muriel. The mistake is my mistake and I will live by it. But if you have any mercy tell me just once that you feel as I do? That if things had been different . . .' He drew breath, tried again. 'That you love me, Anna. Is it possible for you to tell me that?'

She was silent, and suddenly he was more frightened than he had ever been. Then she turned towards him and gave him both her hands to hold and said very quietly: 'I have no right to tell you, you belong to someone else. But I *will* tell you. Only I will tell you in my own language so that you will not understand. Or so that you will understand completely. Listen, then, *mylienki*, and listen well,' said Anna – and began to speak.

It was already dusk. The ancient yews which sheltered them stood black against a sky of amethyst and fading rose; close by the fountains splashed and from the ballroom came the sound of a mournful, syncopated melody filched from the negro slaves.

And Anna spoke. In the wonderful, damnable language that separated yet joined them, with its caressing rhythm, its wildness and searing tenderness. He was never to know what she said, but it seemed to him that the great love speeches of the world – Dido's lament at Carthage, Juliet's awakening passion on the balcony, Heloise's paean to Abelard – must pale before the ardour, the strange, solemn integrity of Anna's words. And allowing himself only to fold and unfold her pliant fingers as she spoke, he saw before him her whole life: the small child, shining like a candle in the rich darkness of her father's palace, the awakening girl, wide-eyed at the horrors of war . . . He saw her as a bride, faltering at the church door, dazzled by joy, and as a mother, cupping her slender, votive hands round the head of her newborn child . . . He saw her greying and rueful at the passing of youth and steadfast in old age, her eyes, her fine bones triumphant over the complaining flesh. And he understood that she was offering him this, her life, for all eternity and understood, too, where she belonged because her sisters are everywhere in Russian literature: Natasha, who left her ballroom and shining youth to nurse her mortally wounded prince . . . Sonia, the street girl who followed Raskalnikov into exile in Siberia and gave that poor, tormented devil the only peace he ever knew.

'Have you understood?' she asked when she had finished.

'I have understood,' said Rupert when he could trust himself to speak.

Then he bent to kiss her once very lightly on the lips and went back to the house to find his bride.

Muriel, however, was nowhere to be found. She was not in the ballroom, nor in the great hall and Tom, the most recent of her partners, said that she had excused herself to go upstairs.

The sudden elevation of her lady's maid to the status of a guest had infuriated Muriel, but she had suffered no personal anxieties. The thought that anyone could be preferred to herself was not one that had ever crossed her mind. And when she had danced with the admiring Dr Lightbody and the dutiful Tom, it seemed to her, Rupert being temporarily absent, a perfect moment to carry out her plan.

First, the cloakroom, where she had left a large parcel which she now retrieved, opening the cellophane-covered box and looking at its contents with a satisfied smile. Yes, the doll was a triumph! White porcelain eyelids with thick, blonde lashes closed with a click over round, china-blue eyes; golden curls clustered under a muslin bonnet and when up-ended she clearly and genteely pronounced the word: 'Mama'. No, Muriel did not grudge the expense though it had been considerable. Ollie would love a doll like that and, after all, Dr Lightbody had been right that day at

Fortman's. Diplomacy was needed in a case like this – it wasn't as though she was dealing with servants. Whereas if she carefully explained to Ollie how exhausting the ceremony would be, how harmful it would be for her to stand for a long time on her bad leg, how much better to rest quietly at home with this lovely doll, Ollie would surely cooperate.

Ollie's marigold head had been absent for a while now from the minstrel's gallery. The child would certainly be in bed by this time. Muriel had found out where she slept. The problem now was seeing that she got to her alone.

Tom had been assiduous so far in the performance of his duties. He detested dressing up but he was wearing the navy sweater and bell-bottoms of a sailor in His Majesty's Navy. He was indifferent to dancing, but he had waltzed with the detestable Lady Lavinia and snatched Muriel Hardwicke from Dr Lightbody's arms when the music ceased, so as to give Rupert a few last minutes of happiness.

Now, however, he felt entitled to some solace and by this Tom meant – and had meant for the past two years – the company of the plump and bespectacled Susie Rabinovitch.

He found her, as he might have expected, with her mother, making easier by her uncomplicated presence the first emotional meeting between Hannah and the dowager since the day at Maidens Over.

'I should have known,' Hannah was saying. 'I

should have known that Miss Hardwicke's note had nothing to do with you. It was so foolish – but this particular thing . . . we make jokes about it but for us it is like a deep, black hole, always there. Sometimes we don't wait to be pushed, we jump.'

'Oh, my dear.' The dowager, already deeply shaken by what she had just learned about her son, pressed her friend's hand. 'What a wretched tangle it all is. I suppose you couldn't come to the wedding just the same? It would make it all a little more bearable—' She broke off. 'Ah, here comes Tom! Have you come to claim Susie for a dance?'

'To claim her at all events. I thought she might like some lemonade.'

Susie smiled and followed him. But she was destined to get no lemonade that night. Tom led her out of the ballroom, through the great hall, and into an ante-room where they could be alone.

'Susie,' said Tom, and she saw that he was in an unusually grim and serious mood. 'How many times have I asked you to marry me?'

'I *think*, seventeen,' said Susie in her quiet, pedantic voice, looking up at him and wishing yet again that he wasn't *quite* so handsome. 'But it may only be sixteen; I'm not completely sure.'

Tom had found a silver ashtray and was picking it up, putting it down again . . .

'You saw Rupert and Anna just now?'

'Yes, I saw them. Can nothing be done? They are so completely right for one another.'

'Nothing,' said Tom savagely. 'Muriel will never let him go. She's after that title like a stampeding buffalo. And Rupert'll never jilt her because he's a gentleman and because of some idiot promise about Mersham that he made to George before he died.'

Susie was silent and Tom stood looking down at her. Since the day he'd first seen her in her parents' over-furnished drawing room, blinking like a plump owl through her spectacles and marking the pages of her book with a determined finger, he'd wanted ceaselessly to be with her. Hitherto, he'd been prepared to wait. Now, seeing what had happened to Rupert, he was prepared to wait no longer.

'Susie, are you really going to ruin our happiness because of your parents' wretched religious prejudices? Even though I've told you a hundred times that you can bring up our children in any way you like?'

Susie hesitated. She, too, had been badly shaken by seeing Rupert and Anna dance. 'It's not that. My parents aren't so orthodox any more. They'd moan a little, but there's no question of them disowning me or saying a *kaddish* over me. They're far too kind and too concerned for my happiness.'

Tom stared at her, amazed. 'But *why*, then, Susie? Why do you keep on saying no?'

Susie studied him carefully. 'Tom, have you ever *looked* at me? At *me*? Not someone you've made up inside your head.'

She stepped forward so that the overhead light shone full on her face. The gypsy dress, as she well

279

knew, was extremely unbecoming to her and she was flushed and mottled from the heat.

'I'm plump now,' she continued in her level, unemotional voice. 'In ten years I'll be fat, however much I diet. I have a hooked nose; most of the time I need glasses. My hair is frizzy and my ears—'

'How *dare* you!' Tom had seized her shoulders; he was shaking her, hurting her. The famous Byrne temper, scourge of his red-haired ancestors since Doomsday, blazed in his eyes. 'How *dare* you talk to me like that! You are *insulting* me!'

'What do you mean?'

'How *dare* you suppose that I don't know who you are or what you are? That I don't understand what I see? Do you take me for some kind of besotted schoolboy? It is *unspeakable*! You could weigh as much as a hippopotamus and shave your head and wear a wig and it wouldn't make any difference to me. I never *said* you were beautiful. I never *thought* it. I said that you were *you*.'

Susie loosened his hands. Then she smiled, that tender, wise smile that made nonsense of her ugliness and said, 'Well, in that case we must just hope that our children don't inherit your awful temper. Or my nose.'

'*Oi, Gewalt!*' said the Noble Spanish Lady, seeing their faces as they returned to the ballroom. 'Look, Leo! It has happened! What shall I tell Moyshe and Rachel? And Cousin Steffi? You know she wanted Susie for her Isaac!'

'To mind their own business,' said that stout bullfighter, Leo Rabinovitch, hitching up his cummerbund. 'That is what you shall tell Rachel and Moyshe, and Cousin Steffi also,' – and went forward resignedly to greet his new son-in-law.

The Duchess of Nettleford, helmeted and lightly daubed with woad, for she was nothing if not thorough, surveyed the dancers with an unusually benevolent eye. Things, it seemed, were going well for the girls. Like the Ancient British Queen she represented, she had led her troops into battle and she had conquered. Tom had opened the ball with Lavvy and was quite clearly interested. Beatrice (an undoubted and very yellow daffodil) was dancing with a young subaltern whom Minna had led up to them. And Gwendolyn, too, was on the floor – almost literally, for the poor girl could never master the tango and the wooden clogs of that staunch Northumbrian heroine, Grace Darling, did not really help. Fortunately the good-looking sunburned gentleman dressed as some kind of Greek who partnered her had seemed to be perfectly aware of the honour of standing up with the daughter of a duke. True, Hermione and Priscilla, clutching respectively the head of John the Baptist and an asp, were still sitting unclaimed beside her and there had been a disappointment about Tom Byrne's younger brother. At thirteen he *was* too young, even for Beatrice, though in the old days when marriages had been sensibly arranged, no one would have bothered about nonsense like that. Still, on the whole, things were going well. As for that scandal at the beginning when some serving maid had turned out to be a countess or the other way round, the duchess had scarcely heeded it except to notice with pleasure how furious it had made the grocer's daughter who had ensnared young Westerholme.

'Ah, Lavvy,' said the duchess as Lavinia, looking complacent and freshly caught, came up to her. 'How's it going, eh?'

'Very well, Mother,' said Lavinia, smirking. 'Tom says he knows he can trust *me* to look after Ollie at the church.'

'Ah, knows he can trust *you*, does he!' The duchess was delighted. 'Did you . . . you know, give him a bit of a hint?'

Lavinia dropped her eyes. 'Well, Mother . . . you know . . .'

'Look, there's Tom now,' said Priscilla, pointing with her asp. 'What's he doing with that dumpy Jewish girl, do you suppose?'

'He took her out just now,' said Lavinia. 'I expect she was feeling ill.'

The music stopped. With an alacrity that was proper but not quite pleasing, the Ladies Beatrice and Gwendolyn were returned by their partners to Boadicea's side, and on the dais, Mr Bartorolli wiped his brow.

'The Byrnes are very *democratic*, aren't they,' drawled Hermione. 'Lady Byrne's *kissing* that Jewish girl now.'

Lavinia, perfectly confident, waited. And her confidence was justified. Tom, his deep happiness assured, moved by his stepmother's unforced pleasure on his behalf, had determined to do everything that was needed to make the ball a success. And what was needed, as Minna had just assured him, was for someone – anyone – to dance with the Nettleford girls.

So Tom, radiant with happiness, approached the Boadicean Camp and aware that he had already danced with the eldest and the worst of them, bowed before one who seemed to be dressed in a great many muslin nappies and to be nursing a papier mâché head dipped in tomato juice.

But Hermione's triumph was short-lived. They had scarcely circled the ballroom half a dozen times when the music stopped abruptly and was succeeded by a fanfare. And looking up at the dais, the dancers saw Lord Byrne standing beside Mr Bartorolli and holding up his hands.

'Ladies and gentlemen,' he said. 'I have an announcement to make. An announcement which I know will give great pleasure to everybody present . . .'

Anna stayed for a while in the garden, standing with her back to a great cedar as though thereby she could draw in some of its strength. She was as cold, as still, as stone.

Rupert had gone. She must live without him. It was done.

There were just a few things to do before she slipped

away. Explain to the dowager that she was leaving, thank the Byrnes, say goodbye to Ollie . . . And after that, Mersham, to pick up her things and wait for the milk train to London. It was ten miles by road from Heslop to Mersham, but from her dawn rides on the mare she knew of a short cut across the fields which she would find even in the dark. By the time the other servants woke, she would be gone.

But first, Petya. She had promised him a dance. Back to the ballroom, then, whatever it cost . . .

He had been searching for her. 'Ah, there you are, Annoushka,' he said, beginning to talk excitedly in Russian. 'You've missed such an exciting thing! Tom is engaged to marry Susie Rabinovitch and they stopped the orchestra and announced it and everyone clapped. And you know that girl dressed like a fish – only she's not meant to be a fish, Hugh says – well, I was standing next to her and she sort of *whooped* when Lord Byrne announced it and went purple, just like in a book, and then she rushed out! Tom's very happy and Susie's really nice and there's going to be lots and lots of champagne. And Lady Byrne's going to ask you to stay here instead of Mersham – she says you've been there long enough as a guest and it's her turn to have you, so do come, 'Noushka, because they're so nice and their horses are *fabulous*!'

'Petya, I must go back to town,' said Anna. 'I've been away so long and it isn't fair on Mama.'

'Oh, no! We'd have such fun! There's the wedding, too – you must stay for that!'

284

'I can't, love. Maybe I'll come back,' she lied, 'but it's Pinny's birthday next week and you know I like to be there for that: she's done so much for us. So now let's have our dance and then I'll slip away quietly. Listen, it's a polka! We'll show them!'

And they did. But when it was over and Anna, under cover of the supper break, tried to gain the double doors, she was suddenly arrested – for sweeping into the ballroom, still laughing at Hawkins' efforts at pronouncing their names – there came the Ballets Russes!

They came in costumes borrowed from *Firebird* and *Sheherezade* and all the other costumes immediately looked drab and uninteresting. They came as guests, not performers, but all eyes were instantly fixed on them, such was their vitality, their 'otherness'. There was La Slavina, darling of the Maryinsky for two decades and still, in her forties, a woman from whom it was almost impossible to avert one's eyes. There was the ineffably stylish designer, Lapin, with drooping eyes and a white streak in his jet-black hair. There was the silent and beautiful Vladimir on whom the mantle of Nijinsky seemed likely to fall, a choreographer with a bald and yellow skull, a pale, tragic-looking girl straight out of a 'blue' Picasso . . .

They surged forward to greet their host and hostess, embracing everybody in their path, seizing glasses of champagne from the passing footmen – and the temperature of the party soared. Then La Slavina paused, threw out an arm, and let out a high and enchantingly modulated scream.

'*Mon Dieu! C'est la petite Grazinsky!*'

'You look charming, Countess,' said Lapin approvingly. 'But *not*, I think, the cap. One wishes only to *suggest* a costume.' He unpinned Anna's cap, tossed it away, plucked a white poppy from an urn and tucked it unerringly into her hair.

'Ah, but it is *magnificent* to see you, *ma chère*,' said La Slavina, hugging Anna. 'And look, there is the little brother also!' She turned to Lady Byrne. 'You have no idea how *good* the Grazinskys have been to us in Petersburg! Such benefactors, such hospitality! Of course they always loved the ballet. Do you remember, Countess, when you ran away? You were seven years old and all the police in Petersburg were searching – such a scandal! And where was she?' she enquired of the bystanders. 'In Theatre Street, in the ballet school, trying to audition for a place!'

'And when she tried to sell her rubies to pay for Diaghilev's first tour of Europe?' said the choreographer. 'Do you remember? All by herself she went to see old Oppenheim in the Morskaya! Often and often he has told the story: how there comes this little girl whose head is not over his desk and brings up her arm with in it her shoe bag and out falls this necklace which has been insured for fifty thousand roubles!'

'You have lost everything, I have heard?' said La Slavina in a low, sympathetic voice.

Anna shrugged. 'We're all right.'

'Ah, you have courage. And a fine brother!' She pinched Petya's cheek. 'But tell me,' her voice, this time, dropped half an octave, her splendid boudoir eyes became veiled in a profound and personal nostalgia. 'What has happened to your so beautiful Cousin Sergei? I have heard that he was safe, but no one has seen him in London and the Baroness Rakov is *désolée*.'

'He is working in the north, somewhere,' said Anna cautiously.

'As a chauffeur, I have heard! *Est-ce-que c'est possible?*'

They had collected, inevitably, a crowd – and among its members were the Nettlefords, who had closed ranks after the dreadful news of Tom's engagement and were conveying a stunned Lavinia to the supper room.

La Slavina threw out an arm to include the company. 'Ah, if you could see the prince! Never, never have I seen a man so 'andsome. And fearless, too. Do you remember, Lapin, when he won the St Catherine Cup on that unbroken horse of Dolgoruky's? But all the Chirkovskys were like that. It was Sergei's father who gave me my first diamonds. I was still in Cechetti's class at—' She broke off to say with her enchanting smile: 'I beg your pardon, mademoiselle.'

But the fault had not been the ballerina's. A tall and avid-looking girl covered in scales had cannoned into her, *en route* for the open French window through which she now vanished. There was a short pause, then with assorted exclamations of fury, four more girls in an extraordinary collection of clothes raced after her, one of them dropping, as she did so, a rubber asp.

'*Drôle!*' said La Slavina, raising her eyebrows. Then she tucked her arm through Anna's and led her entourage towards the supper room.

Anxious to avoid the servants' hall, with its backbiting and gossip, Sergei had spent the evening in The King's Head down in the village. Now he was smoking a quiet cigarette in the paddock which adjoined the stableyard until he should be summoned to take the Lady Lavinia and her fellow bridesmaid back to Mersham.

'Sergei! Sergei! Where are you?'

'Here, my lady.'

The Lady Lavinia, in full tilt, careered round the corner of the stables and panted up to him. Her scales caught the moonlight; an even fiercer glitter lit up her eyes.

'Do you wish to leave early, my lady? The car is ready.'

'No, no, Sergei! The night is young!' She came closer. 'But I'm very cross with you, Sergei! Very, very cross,' said Lavinia, waggling a bony finger in his face.

'I'm sorry to hear this, my lady.'

'Very cross indeed! You've been a naughty boy, Sergei! A *very* naughty boy.'

Sergei looked round for a way of escape, but short

of simply leaping the fence and racing away across the paddock there was nothing he could do.

'Why didn't you tell us your *real* name?' said Lavinia, now fixing his arm in a vice-like grip.

'But I did, my lady.'

'No, you didn't! Not *all* of it!'

'I'm afraid I don't understand.'

'Oh, naughty, *naughty*!' said Lavinia, entranced by her proximity to this devastating man. 'What about the prince, hey? *Prince* Sergei Chirkovsky. You didn't tell us that!'

'I did not think it was important, my lady.'

'Not important! Ooh, you *are* a funny man!' She edged even closer, her shoulder digging into his side. 'Don't you see, it means you can take your place in society if you wish? That is if . . .' She glanced up at him, her thin eyelashes fibrillating in the silver light, 'if you had someone to support you and—'

'Lavvy! Lavvy! Where are you?'

The pack was closing in. Furious at Lavinia's head-on start, her sisters had rushed off down the terrace steps in hot pursuit. Unfortunately, Salome's ankle bangle had caught in the turned-up spike of Cleopatra's golden sandal, eliminating the Ladies Hermione and Priscilla, who rolled down the remaining steps in a vituperative and flaying tangle. But Gwendolyn, and the headless daffodil that now was Beatrice, had reached the stableyard.

'Ah, there you are! You've found him. You're a crafty one, Lavvy! Just as soon as you found out he was a prince you came running after him. Don't take any notice, Sergei; it's just cupboard love.'

'It's because Tom got away,' said Beatrice who had perfected spite to a degree remarkable even for a Nettleford.

'So now she wants to be a princess, don't you, Lavvy?'

But Sergei had now had enough. His accent very pronounced, he bowed and said: 'Ladies, I have two things to say to you. Firstly, as from this moment I resign absolutely my post as chauffeur to your family and you may tell the duke and duchess this. Secondly, I am engaged to be married.'

And before the girls could recover themselves, he had vaulted over the five-bar gate and vanished into the trees at the far side of the paddock.

After the arrival of the Russians, no one could doubt that the ball was a triumph. But at its heart was not Muriel Hardwicke, stiff and disapproving in her elaborate dress: at its heart, her escape cut off, was Anna. Anna dancing a tango with Lapin, Anna drinking champagne with Mr Bartorolli, Anna and Vladimir demonstrating a polonaise . . . Anna besieged by partners and never, not for one minute, looking at Rupert, who never, for one minute, looked at her.

'That girl seems determined to make an exhibition of herself,' said Muriel, frigidly executing a two-step in the arms of her fiancé. 'I hope you don't expect me to have her back at Mersham after this?'

Rupert did not answer. Anna had paused at the end of her dance to thank her partner and straighten the flower in her tumbled hair. Caught off his guard for an instant, Rupert gazed at her just as her control, too, snapped and she raised her eyes, brilliant with fatigue and excitement, to his.

And at that moment it became clear to him with an absolute and blinding certainty that he could not live without her and that he must break his engagement even if it meant disgrace and ruin – and that he must break it that very night.

Sergei had taken refuge in the Italian garden, the statues and arbours of which gave shelter even in the bright moonlight. Here he would wait quietly till the Nettleford girls returned to the ballroom and then pick up his things from the coachhouse and make his way to the station. Thank heaven he had not spent his last week's wages; at least he had money for the fare.

He was just beginning to make his way back when he heard a sound: forlorn and small and infinitely sad; the sound of someone resolutely *not* crying. And turning aside he saw, framed by a trellis of jasmine, a girl sitting on the rim of a fountain, her head in her hands. A girl whose pose, whose slender outline, seemed heart-rendingly familiar.

Rupert's glance had cut through Anna's mood like a sword, and excusing herself from her latest partner, she had slipped away, wanting now only that this long night should end at last.

'Annoushka! Mylienkaya! Eto ti?'

The voice, known and loved since childhood, the tender Russian words, brought her to her feet – and into the arms of the tall man coming towards her.

'Seriosha!'

For a moment they stood locked together in an embrace of homesickness and love. If there was one person in the world that Anna needed at this hour it was the cousin who was now brother and father, protector and friend. If there was one person who could make him think well again of women, it was this girl with her steadfastness and courage, her spiritual grace.

'I didn't know you were here, Sergei. Why didn't you come into the house?'

'I'm not a guest, little idiot; I'm the Nettlefords' chauffeur. Or I was.' And he quickly told her what had happened, making her smile through her tears. 'And you?' he pursued, looking down at her. 'You are in fancy dress? Or . . .' his voice sharpened, 'or have you been working also? Tell me the truth, Annoushka.'

There no longer seemed any point in concealment. 'But Petya must *never* know, Sergei,' she said when she had recounted the events of the evening. 'He'd leave school at once if he knew we were penniless. So please just help me to get away quickly now. Then when I have seen Mama and Pinny I can begin to look for another job.'

'No! You shall not work again like this! I forbid it absolutely!' And as he spoke, Sergei knew exactly what he would do and that the lie he had told the Nettleford girls had been a prophetic one. 'I'm going to marry Larissa Rakov,' he went on. 'She's a kind, understanding person; it will be all right, you'll see. And you and Petya and your mother shall live with us, and Pinny too. And if you're good,' he continued, gently flicking away a tear, 'I shall find you a rich husband – one who will beat you only twice a week.'

She tried hard to smile. 'No, Seriosha . . . I don't want a rich husband. Or any husband except . . .'

Sergei took out his handkerchief. He had dried the eyes of countless weeping women, but none more tenderly than those of this girl. 'Poor *coucoushka*,' he said, settling her head against his shoulder. 'Now, tell me everything, please. Of course if he has harmed you I shall kill him, whoever he is,' he added matter of factly. 'But otherwise, perhaps something can be done.' He gave a last dab at her face. 'Blow your nose, *dousha*,' he commanded, 'and begin.'

So she told him everything, always blaming herself for not seeing in time what was happening, and as he held her and stroked her hair, he caught from her voice the immensity of her love, her inexhaustible tenderness and the total lack of hope that came from the sense of another person's honour. And it seemed to him that she had grown up and surpassed him, this girl who had always been to him a younger sister, such was her committal and her certainty.

It was thus that Rupert, looking for Anna in the garden, found them. Leaning against each other as if

293

they were one substance, the man bending over her, holding her close, while she turned to him in total trust – and her hair, loosened by the dance, streamed across them both.

14

It took one hour and twenty minutes for news of Anna's sudden elevation at the ball to reach the servants' hall at Mersham. One of the Heslop chauffeurs, going to fetch late arrivals from Mersham Halt, had mentioned it to the station master, who thought it of sufficient interest to merit a telephone call to his old friend Mr Proom.

Though it was late, only the bossy Mildred who had replaced Mrs Park's beloved Win, and the two new, enormous and asinine footmen imported for the wedding had gone to bed. Mrs Park was patiently icing the exquisite *petits fours* and *mille-feuilles* with which she proposed to supplement the five-tiered perfection of the wedding cake. James and Sid, cobwebbed from a long session in the cellar, were polishing the Venetian decanters; Peggy and Pearl, resting their aching feet on the slumbering Baskerville, were folding damask table napkins into intricate flower shapes; Mr Cameron, on a rare visit indoors, was giving Louise instructions about the disposition of his orange trees.

Mr Proom's entry put a stop to all these activities.

'A *countess*!' said Mrs Park, putting down her forcing bag and sitting down suddenly. 'Well, I never!'

'The Russian aristocracy is more numerous than its British counterpart,' said Mr Proom judiciously. 'For example, all the offspring of a prince or a count will carry the title.' But he was considerably shaken all the same.

'It's that Charles's face I'd like to have seen,' said James, who had suffered at the hands of Heslop's first footman.

'Fancy her dancing with his lordship,' said Peggy. 'It's like that film . . . you know, the one with Lillian Gish, where she comes up from the country all innocent like . . .'

Mr Proom and Mrs Park exchanged glances. Certain things about Anna's recent behaviour were becoming clear to them.

'A countess, eh?' Mr Cameron, into whose ear-trumpet the news had duly been shouted, had begun to wheeze with unaccustomed and silent laughter. He knew, now, what to call his new rose, and the joke – obscure, private, pointless – was just the kind he particularly enjoyed.

'Remember that day she first came,' said Pearl, 'when she went and sat down right at the bottom of the table, below Win, even?'

'Aye.'

For a moment they were silent, all in their different ways remembering Anna.

'It just shows about that dratted dog, doesn't it,' said Sid. 'Bloomin' snob. 'e must have known.'

But sharp Louise had seen another aspect. 'She won't be coming back, not for a minute. We've seen the last of Anna.'

'Anna's not like that,' said Peggy hotly. 'She'd never—'

'It's nowt to do with Anna,' interrupted Louise. 'It's that Miss Hardwicke. She won't have Anna in the house, not after his lordship's made such a fuss of her. Not for a minute.'

Proom inclined his domed head in acknowledgement that Louise spoke the truth.

'Mrs Proom will miss her,' he said heavily.

'She's not the only one,' said Mrs Park, brushing away a tear.

In the small hours, after the ball, the weather broke. A niggling wind shuffled the leaves, clouds scudded in from the west, it began to rain.

To the girl stumbling in her torn sacking dress up the grassy path that led from Mersham woods to the kitchen gardens, the rain meant nothing. She was in the last stages of exhaustion; her hair filthy and matted, her bare feet bleeding, a frayed tape with a number stamped on to it still clinging to her wrist. Every so often she would stop for breath and turn her bruised, vacant face towards the woods, listening for pursuit, before she was off again and as she ran she sobbed continuously like a child.

She had reached the kitchen gardens, passed through the door in the wall, crossed the orchard. In her clouded brain there was only one bright image: one room, one person to whom she could no longer give a name.

Nearly spent now, she stumbled across the servants' courtyard, dragging herself along the damp stone walls of the kitchen quarters, groping, putting up a hand with its torn fingernails to feel for the window, the one window behind which was sanctuary.

She had found it. With a last desperate effort she leant across the water butt and tapped once on the pane of glass behind which Mrs Park lay sleeping, before she slithered, unconscious, on to the cobbles.

Win had returned.

'There'll have to be an enquiry, Rupert,' the distraught dowager said to her son. 'Dr Marsh says there's no doubt Win's been seriously ill-treated. It must be an absolutely diabolical place – she was dressed in sacking, literally. She's half-starved, too, and terrified. If you go up to her, even though she's barely conscious she puts up her arms as though she expects to be hit. I'm going to get it closed down if it's the last thing I do. And Rupert, you must speak to Muriel – the servants are dreadfully upset! Mrs Park's given in her notice – she's going to take Win to her sister's when she's well enough. I can't think how Muriel came to find such a place. It's miles away, thank heavens, and notorious, I understand.'

'Surely Muriel must have made enquiries?' said the earl, dragging himself out of his private hell to attend to his mother.

'Well, she should have gone herself to see it, Rupert. You can't imagine how much harm this will do below stairs. They're upset enough about Anna's going, and though it's noble of her it's quite unnecessary because Minna asked her to stay and the Rabinovitches also—'

'Noble?' Rupert's voice tore at the dowager's raw nerves like sandpaper. 'That's rich! That's very rich! Anna hasn't gone alone, I assure you. She's eloped. I found her in the garden carrying on like a guttersnipe with one of the chauffeurs.'

'The chauffeurs?' The dowager's brow cleared. She smiled. 'Oh, yes, I forgot you weren't there when that came out. It seems that the Nettlefords' chauffeur was her Cousin Sergei, the one she's so fond of! You can imagine how Honoria carried on when she found she'd let a perfectly good prince get away.'

'I see. That explains it.' Rupert's voice was grimmer than ever. 'Well, they should make a very handsome couple – and at least we're spared the strain of having our coals carried upstairs by a princess.'

'No dear, I'm sure Anna—'

Rupert swung round and the dowager stepped back a pace. Never in all her life had she seen him look like that.

'You will not mention Anna to me again, please,' he said. 'Not *ever*.'

By the time Rupert came to find her, Muriel was in a very nasty temper. Louise, sent for to replace Anna, had refused to wait on her and Muriel had been compelled, on a morning on which she particularly wished to dazzle, to dress herself.

'She'll have to be sent away, Rupert,' she said now, angrily recounting her tale of woe.

'There is not the slightest question of Louise being sent away,' said Rupert levelly. He had just spent half an hour cross-examining his butler. Proom's attempts at honourable evasion had withered before the tactics that Rupert had perfected in four years of dealing with his men. The earl was now fully informed of the situation below stairs and his anger, though perfectly contained, far outstripped Muriel's own. 'Louise was upset because of your treatment of Win, which, I don't scruple to tell you, Muriel, was monstrous! As far as I can see, you virtually had the girl kidnapped on her day off.'

'How *dare* you, Rupert. How dare you speak to me like that!'

'I won't humiliate you by countermanding the orders you have already given,' continued Rupert as though she had not spoken, 'but there must be no further interference with Proom's arrangements. As for Mrs Proom, Mersham is her home and will be until the day she dies.'

'Mersham!' hissed Muriel. 'Don't talk to me about Mersham. Your precious Mersham would be under the hammer now if it wasn't for me.'

'Yes,' said Rupert quietly. 'And better it should be than that it should be destroyed by the kind of ideas perpetrated by your friend Dr Lightbody. If George were alive he'd think that too.'

'Oh? What's wrong with Dr Lightbody's ideas? I happen to be about to invite him to come and work down here.'

Rupert looked at her in amazement. 'You can't imagine I would allow that?' he said.

'Allow?' shouted Muriel, her chest heaving with operatic rage. 'Allow! Who do you think you are?'

Rupert's next words were spoken very softly.

'The owner of Mersham, Muriel,' he said.

And in the stunned silence which followed he went on more gently: 'Surely you didn't imagine that your wealth would allow you to bully me? As for Dr Lightbody, you are, of course, perfectly free to choose your own friends, but that I should allow a man whose ideas are wholly repugnant to me to set up shop at Mersham is quite ridiculous.' His face creased into a smile. 'On the other hand your *relations* are quite another matter.'

'My . . . relations,' faltered Muriel.

Rupert nodded. 'Your grandmother, for example, would be perfectly welcome to make her home with us,' he went on silkily, 'or your Uncle Nat. I've always wanted to meet a rat-catcher – especially one with such original ideas about what to do with the skins.'

'You . . . wouldn't,' said Muriel, who had turned quite white.

'Not if you don't wish it. But remember what I have said.' Suddenly he reached out, took her hand: 'Look, Muriel, you don't love me, do you? You're beautiful and capable and rich; you could marry anyone. It's not too late to free yourself. Think hard, my dear – there are a lot of years ahead of us. Could you really be happy with a man who dislikes everything you hold most dear?'

Panic overwhelmed Muriel. Two days to go: literally the day after tomorrow she would be a countess! Was it possible that this glittering prize could still be snatched from her? On this very morning she had meant to tell Rupert at what times he might physically approach her. That he might find it in himself not to approach her at all had never even crossed her mind. And, squeezing her eyelids together, she managed a perfectly authentic tear.

'Please don't talk like that, dearest,' she said, and for the first time he saw her genuinely afraid. 'I'm extremely . . . devoted to you.' And as he remained silent, 'You wouldn't . . . jilt me?'

Rupert shook his head.

'No, Muriel,' he said, trying to keep the weariness out of his voice: 'I wouldn't do that.'

Crossing the hall on his way out with his dog, the earl came upon a cluster of servants grouped round the

302

library door, which had been left slightly ajar. Peggy with a feather duster, James with his stepladder . . . Sid.

Moving closer, he heard a voice issuing forth: high-pitched, well-modulated, self-assured . . .

'. . . Can anyone seriously doubt, ladies and gentlemen, that the elimination of all that is sick and maimed and displeasing in our society can – and indeed *must* – be the aim of every thinking . . .'

The servants, seeing his lordship, scuttled for cover. Rupert pushed open the door. On the dais at the far end of the empty library, one hand resting on the bust of Hercules which had given Anna so much trouble, stood Dr Lightbody, testing the acoustics of his new home.

Rupert entered, Baskerville at his heels. The door shut behind him. The servants crept slowly forward again. Till the door flew open and a dishevelled, blond-haired man shot out into the hallway and collapsed in a heap on to the mosaic tiles . . .

Very late that night, Proom, on his last rounds, found a light still burning in the gold salon and went to investigate.

Lying sprawled on a sofa, his head thrown back against the cushions, one arm flung out – was his lordship. His breathing was stertorous; the decanter of whisky on the low table beside him was empty.

For a long moment, Proom stood looking down at his master. Something about the pose of the body, both taut and abandoned and the weariness of the slightly parted lips, half-recalled an entry he had seen in one of his encyclopaedias . . . Something about 'Early Christian Martyrs', he thought. Then suddenly it came to him: Botticelli's altarpiece of St Barnabas in the Uffizi.

He leant forward to shake his lordship by the shoulder. Whereupon the earl opened an unfocused eye, pronounced, with perfect clarity, a single word – and at once passed out again.

'Tut,' said the butler, expressing in the only way he knew, his deep compassion.

Then he went downstairs to order James to come and help him carry his lordship to his bed.

On the following day, the last before the wedding, Mr Proom received a telephone call. It was from the station master at Maidens Over and informed him that a family by the name of Herring had been apprehended while trying to cheat the Great Western Railway of two fares.

'Where are they now?' asked Proom when he had digested this piece of information.

'They are locked in my office, Mr Proom, pending further investigations. What would you wish me to do with them?'

'If you would be so kind as to keep them there, Mr Fernby,' said Mr Proom. 'Just keep them there. On no account let them out till I arrive.'

'It will be a pleasure, Mr Proom,' said the station master.

But when he had replaced the receiver, Proom did

not go to find the earl or the dowager. Instead he stood for a long time lost in thought. Mr Proom remembered Melvyn Herring. He remembered him very well . . .

'It is impossible,' said Mr Proom to himself after a while. And then: 'It is absurd. I must be losing my reason even to think of such a thing.'

He continued to stand by the telephone, the light reflecting off his high, domed forehead. 'Quite absurd,' he repeated, 'and in the worst possible taste. Yet could anything be worse than things as they are now?'

They could not. And presently Proom went first to find James to tell him that he would have to deputize for a few hours, and then to Mr Potter to ask if he could spare one of the cars.

Leo Rabinovitch was working in his study. He had retired from the rag trade, but his business sense was inborn and since he and Hannah had come to the country their wealth, due to his astute investments, had trebled. Now it seemed as though his fortune would go, not as he had hoped, to further the interests of the Cohens or the Fleishmanns or the Kussevitskys, all of whom had sons whose mothers had watched Susie reach marriageable age with unconcealed interest, but to the Byrnes, whose record in matters like the burning of the synagogues in medieval York, for example, was far from impressive. Still, there it was. Tom was a nice lad and Susie's very spectacle frames, since the ball, seemed to have turned to gold.

It was at this point that the parlourmaid, round-eyed

with wonder, announced Cyril Proom. Proom had come to the front door, a gesture which had brought beads of perspiration out on his forehead, and the maid had nearly fainted. Not because she had expected him to come by the back door either. She had simply expected him to be for ever at Mersham; immaculate, planted, *there*.

Rabinovitch looked up – and was at once attacked by a deep, an almost ungovernable lust.

Hannah was a good housekeeper. The Towers ran well, the food was excellent, the rooms clean and cared for. But Hannah, sensibly knowing her limitations, stuck to women servants, and these she treated in the traditions that prevailed in the village homesteads of her youth. In the servants' quarters of The Towers nothing was secret, nothing, felt Leo Rabinovitch, was *spared*. The Rabinovitches' maids got the shingles and the piles and were nursed by Hannah. They were crossed in love and their sobs floated up to the study where Rabinovitch was trying to read his company reports. They dreamt about nesting crows and royal babies and fire engines and told him so while serving breakfast. They walked in their sleep, their aunts fell off bicycles, poltergeists infested their cousins' cottages – and every disaster, minutely chronicled, reverberated through the rooms and corridors of his house.

But if Proom had come to offer his services . . . If Proom were to take over the running of The Towers . . . Leo's eyes momentarily closed and a series of dizzying vignettes flashed through his mind. Himself sitting at dinner while a totally silent footman, an *English* footman, inscrutable and powdered, approached with the *lebernockerl* and *sauerkraut*. Himself arriving after a day in the city, handing his hat and coat to Proom himself and receiving only a pleasant: 'I trust you had a successful day, sir?'

But as he looked at Proom, standing respectfully before him in his unaccustomed lounge suit, Leo knew that all this could not – should not, even – be. For Proom belonged to Mersham. Proom *was* Mersham.

'You will sit down, Mr Proom?'

'No, thank you, sir.' The mere idea had made Proom flinch. He was extremely embarrassed now, wondering why he had come, and putting off the moment when he would have to make his request, he said, 'May I be permitted to felicitate you on the news of Miss Rabinovitch's engagement? The event gave great satisfaction below stairs.'

'Thank you. How *are* things at Mersham?' enquired Rabinovitch.

Proom, in pursuit of his plan, made no attempt at polite evasion.

'Bad, sir,' he said with finality.

Rabinovitch nodded. 'You know we shall not be visiting any longer?'

'I had heard, sir. There will be a number of changes – and none of them for the better.'

Rabinovitch waited. 'I can help you, perhaps?'

Proom cleared his throat. 'A long time ago, sir, you

said that if I ever needed help, I had only to come to you.'

Leo nodded. 'I said it and it is true. Never shall I forget what you did for Susie.'

The incident to which Rabinovitch referred had taken place shortly after they came to The Towers. They had all gone in a party to a local race meeting, taking along the twelve-year-old Susie. Susie had patiently watched three races, after which she had drawn a book out of her pocket and settled herself on a folding stool to read. She was deep in her story when a Bugatti coupé, incompetently parked on a slope, began to roll towards her and it was Proom, standing guard over the picnic hampers, who had seen what was happening and pulled her to safety.

Proom plunged. 'I need a considerable sum of money, sir. Immediately. And in cash.'

He mentioned it and Rabinovitch's bushy eyebrows shot up in surprise. The sum was one which would keep a man and his family in comfort for a year.

'You shall have it, Mr Proom. But I wonder whether you are wise to take it in this way. If you are considering the purchase of a cottage for Mrs Proom, for example, it might be wiser—'

'It's not for me, sir,' said Proom, shocked. 'I'd never ask it for myself, sir. I can take care of myself; I've a bit saved.'

'For what, then?' asked Leo, surprised. 'Or do you not wish to tell me?'

'It isn't that I don't want to, sir. But . . . well, I have

this plan and I don't really want to involve anyone else. It's a very . . . peculiar plan.'

'You are trying to help someone else?'

'You could say that.' There was a pause. 'Things couldn't be worse at Mersham, sir. Lady Westerholme, well she's at her wits' end and Mr Rupert – his lordship, I mean – I saw him in hospital when they first brought him over from France and he looked better than he does this morning. And Anna's gone—'

Leo smiled. 'You heard what happened at the ball?'

Proom inclined his head. 'Yes, sir. The account gave great pleasure to all the staff. But it was what was done to Win,' he continued, 'that made me think *anything* was worth trying.'

'Win? Who is Win?' enquired Leo.

Proom told him the story, while Leo made Central European noises of sympathy.

'If I tell you what I mean to do, sir,' said Proom, realizing how unfair it was to ask for help without giving his confidence, 'I'm afraid you'll think I've taken leave of my senses.'

Carefully, much embarrassed by its theatricality, he explained his plan. When he had finished, Leo looked at him incredulously.

'Your plan will not succeed, I think; there are too many people who will fail to act as you hope. But if it does, don't you see, you are destroying also yourself? The financial consequences to Mersham would be disastrous.'

'I know, sir. But . . . well, I taught Mr Rupert to ride

a bicycle. There wasn't the fuss made of him there was of Lord George, but there's no doubt who was the finer gentleman. And seeing him like this . . .'

There was a pause. Then Leo nodded. 'You shall have the money, Mr Proom. Immediately. And in cash.'

Anna, meanwhile, was fine. She was very well. She had, as she frequently informed Pinny, never felt better in her life.

'I don't doubt it, dear,' said Pinny. 'All I said was that I wish you'd eat something. You've been home twenty-four hours and you haven't touched a thing.'

Anna gazed obediently at the breakfast table set out in the little parlour, took hold of a piece of toast and conveyed it to her mouth.

'It doesn't go down,' she said in a puzzled voice, exactly as she had done when she was five years old and sickening for quinsy.

Pinny's heart contracted with pity and helplessness. From Anna's account of Mersham, which seemed to be inhabited by absolutely everyone except its owner, she had drawn her own conclusions.

'I have been thinking,' said Anna, 'and I believe it would be best if I went to Paris. Kira has said she can find work for me in her salon – selling perfumes and such things. It would,' she added bleakly, 'be very interesting.'

Since none of them had the fare to Pimlico, let alone to Paris, Pinny felt free to agree that it did indeed sound a fascinating way of life.

'Ah, no, my little flea,' said the countess, patting her daughter's hand. 'Paris is so far! Something will come along soon, you see. Dounia has a new plan,' she continued, referring to her irrepressible sister-in-law, the Princess Chirkovsky. 'We are to make very much *kvass* in Miss King's kitchen – she has permitted it – and sell it to the teashops of the Lyons because nobody in England knows at all about *kvass*—'

'Luckily for them,' said Pinny under her breath.

Anna tried to smile. But added to the ceaseless, searing pain about Rupert, there was another anxiety now about Sergei. If she could not find suitable work soon and help her family, Sergei might well sacrifice himself and marry Larissa Rakov and a loveless marriage seemed to Anna, in her present state, to be a hell like no other.

'There are always good things happening,' said the countess, determined to divert her daughter. 'For example, have you heard about Pupsik?'

'No?' This time Anna's smile was not assumed. The troubles of the Baroness de Wodzka were very close to her heart. 'Has he . . . ?'

'No,' said the countess. 'He has not. But the daughter of Colonel Terek has married a very rich man with many factories, and of course the Colonel has always had a *tendresse* for the baroness ever since she came from the Smolny, so he has sent Pupsik to a very expensive clinic in 'arley Street and they have made Röntgen rays and found absolutely clear the Rastrelli diamond in some part of him that begins, I think, with a "c".'

311

'That's marvellous! So now they will be able to operate?'

'They will be *able*,' admitted the countess. 'But they *will* not, because the baroness does not permit that Pupsik should suffer and has taken instead a job where she receives the washing parcels in a laundry in, I think, Clapham. But you see how there are always wonderful things.'

'Yes, Mama,' said Anna tenderly, getting up to kiss her.

She wandered over to the window. In three hours, Rupert and Muriel would be man and wife. 'Help me to endure it,' she prayed. 'Oh, help me, please.'

'There are many wonderful things,' her mother had said. Well, she would have to find them somehow. Even in this wedding, perhaps. And suddenly, unbidden, she *did* find something. Ollie's pride and joy as she walked down the aisle in her pink dress, holding up Muriel's train. For Ollie would be all right now. Anna, slipping upstairs, meaning to say goodbye to Ollie, had seen Muriel go into the child's room carrying a most beautiful doll. Clearly Muriel was sorry for what she had said and had come to make sure that nothing spoilt the little girl's joy on her big day.

Lost in reverie, Anna did not at first pay any attention to the huge, black car which had drawn up in front of the house. A car with a pennant on the bonnet and two serious-looking men in dark suits in the back. Men who now descended to allow the chauffeur to hand out

312

a figure wrapped in innumerable shawls . . . an old woman in a kerchief . . .

Anna gave a gasp. 'Mama! Pinny!'

But when they reached her she could not speak and it was the countess, tears running down her cheek, who cried:

'It's Niannka! Dear God, it's Niannka come back!'

The men from the Foreign Office had left, pointing out sternly that while they were delivering this old woman she was in fact stateless, without papers or permits, and that the authorities would be in touch. Nor was their departure attended by any expressions of gratitude on the part of Old Niannka herself, who clearly felt that in collecting her from the Orient Express and whisking her through customs, they had done no more than their duty. Now she sat on the sofa, emitting the familiar smell of camphor and oiled wool; toothless, emaciated, fierce as an eagle – and in her hoarse, Georgian dialect, told them her story.

She had been arrested on the way to their rendezvous in one of those pointless raids that were so much a feature of the times. For three weeks she and a haphazard collection of unfortunates scooped off the streets had been kept behind barbed wire in a detainment camp near Chudvo. From there, some wretches were marched off to permanent imprisonment or death, others, arbitrarily, were released, given back their ragged bundles and sent on their way.

Niannka was released, but when she reached Chudvo

Station to meet her employers, the Grazinskys had gone. Since they themselves had not been certain of their destination, she thought the only thing to do was to go back to the palace in Petersburg and wait for news.

The Grazinsky Palace, however, had been taken over by the Metal Plate Workers' Union – an organization which made it clear that she had better remove herself, and fast. When she wouldn't leave, they sent for the Red Guard. The first time the soldiers escorted her over the Anchikov Bridge they were friendly, cracking jokes with the old woman. The second time they were not amused. The third time they told her that if she attempted to return to the palace she would be shot.

'So I went home, *Baryna*,' said Niannka now, shrugging aside the ten day journey in an unspeakable train across a war-torn country, the trek across the mountains without food.

Her relatives were not overjoyed to see her, but Niannka commandeered an adjoining cave, stowed her bundles and prepared to wait till the Little Father should be back on his throne and the Grazinskys return.

It was a hard time, she said, but she had done what she could to make herself useful, requisitioning the new babies as soon as they were born and preventing her pig of a brother-in-law from putting dead cats in the *shashlik*.

Then one day, a party of English with mules and

porters had come to the village. Leading them was a tall man like a stork, who had begun to question her. At first she had laughed so much at his extraordinary Russian that she couldn't hear what he said, but when she gathered that he knew where the Grazinskys were she stopped laughing very soon.

'Even so, I was not stupid,' she said, tapping the side of her nose. '"How do I know you are telling me the truth?" I said to him.'

But then, continued the old woman, he had described the Grazinskys – but most particularly Annoushka – in such amazing detail that her doubts were soon stilled. 'For he knew *everything, doushenka*,' she said, turning to Anna. 'The way your hair jumps out from behind your ears and the way there are freckles only on the top of your nose and even the place where the chicken made a hole in your thumb, do you remember?'

So as soon as she had gone to the monastery to thank St Nino, she packed her belongings and prepared for the mule journey across the valley to where she could catch a train to England. And here, said Niannka, shaking her head, the Englishman had proved himself very slow in the uptake, not realizing that of course it was necessary for her to set off at *once*, that there was no question of her waiting till the expedition was ready to return. She had had to sit for several days actually *on* the bag of tools he was using for his digging to make this clear. But at last he had got the message and taken her down to Batumi and sent many telegrams and put her on the boat to Constantinople . . .

'So now I am here,' she finished, 'and ready to work.' Her fierce eyes swept the tiny room, looking for the missing icon. 'But first, *Baryna*, I must ask for your forgiveness.'

And with tears springing to her eyes again, she began to apologize. She had not, she said, been able to bring the Crown of Kazan. It was so cumbersome and heavy that it would certainly have attracted suspicion, so she had buried it under some rocks just before she reached her village. She could remember the exact spot and would take them there as soon as the Little Father returned, if only the *baryna* would not be angry. Everything else, of course, she had brought.

'Everything else?' said the countess faintly.

Niannka bent down to the malodorous, mudstained carpetbag which had been lying like a sick animal against her skirts. Then she rose, carried it over to the green baize card table and, watched in a silence that even embraced Miss Pinfold's sister's budgerigar, began to unpack. She drew out a pair of woollen stockings, a flannel petticoat, a crucifix . . . There followed a wooden comb, a rolled up daguerrotype of St Xavier the Bleeding Heart . . . Then a large, flat piece of felting, stiffened with cardboard, the false bottom of the case. Then crumpled up newspaper, a great deal of it. Once more her hand came out, this time cradling a lake, a dazzling pool of blue . . .

'My sapphires,' cried the countess. 'Oh, Niannka, my sapphires!'

Niannka nodded and turned back to her rooting. Then, with a grunt of satisfaction, she let fall on the green baize table the translucent, shimmering snake that was the famous triple row of pearls. Quite impervious to their exclamations and the countess's tears, she unpacked the Potemkin pendant, a diamond tiara, a butterfly brooch, three pairs of earrings . . . There followed the Empress Sophia's pectoral cross and the rubies that had been Anna's christening present from her godmother. And lastly, laying the stones down respectfully but without undue excitement, as one completing delivery of a useful batch of groceries, what was arguably the most valuable set of jewellery in Christendom: the emerald *parure*.

15

Baskerville woke first on the morning of the wedding. Woke, stretched and yawned in the small room in the bachelor's wing which Rupert still occupied for this last night. Woke and padded over to the two suitcases, strapped and labelled for Switzerland and howled as dogs have howled at their master's luggage for centuries.

And after Baskerville, came Proom.

Proom had seen to the arrangement of the trestle tables for the tenantry and the timing of the cars to go to church. He had supervised the setting out of the striped awning and the strip of red carpet that led from the front door down the steps. He had seen that the telegrams were laid out on a silver salver by the best man's chair and that the Damascus steel knife from the Topkapi Palace was in place next to the wedding cake. He had even procured five pounds of rice from Mrs Park and ordered it to be parcelled out and delivered to the villagers, who, in the matter of spontaneous festive gestures, could not, where this particular wedding was concerned, be relied upon.

No one seeing him would believe how heavy his heart was, for his plan had not succeeded. He had wasted Rabinovitch's money. He had failed.

It had been necessary to take the old-established servants into his confidence and they had played their parts to a man. By the time Proom, the previous night, had gone to Dr Lightbody's room and requested a private interview with that eminent eugenicist, everything was ready. But though Proom had been able to substantiate his disclosures, though the doctor had been violently agitated and upset, he had not acted. 'He hasn't slept a wink,' Sid, who had brought up his shaving water, had just reported, 'but he hasn't done a thing.'

And now it was too late.

'No luck, then?' enquired Mr Potter, fetching the white ribbons to tie on the Daimler – a query echoed with increasing hopelessness by Louise, directing the extra village women hired to carry the jellies and syllabubs, the patés and terrines upstairs, by James, busy with the wine coolers, by Mr Cameron, bringing in the corsage for the dowager and the buttonholes for the bridegroom and the guests . . .

By eleven o'clock no one even asked any more, and on the instructions of Mr Proom they went upstairs to change for church. But when the maids came down in their polka dot muslins and cherry trimmed hats, they found Mrs Park still in her overalls.

'I'm not going to the church,' she said with finality. 'I can't leave Win.' The little kitchen maid whom Mrs Park had put in her own bed was slowly recovering, but she was still very weak.

'Oh, Mrs Park,' wailed Peggy. 'And your new foulard and all!'

'I don't mind,' said Mrs Park. 'I'm not keen. It's just Miss Ollie I'd like to have seen.'

Upstairs, the dowager's Alice was lowering Mrs Bunford's powder blue silk over her employer's head. 'It's not too bad,' she said. 'Except for the sleeves, of course.' She sighed, noticing the dowager's shadowed eyes, the lines of strain round her mouth. Well, there was nothing to be done. They were packed and ready to go to the Mill House on the following day and a damp, dark hole it seemed to Alice *and* the worst place you could think of for her rheumatism, but where Lady Westerholme went there Alice Spinks would follow. 'Mr Cameron's waiting, my lady, with your corsage. He wanted to give it to you himself.'

'Oh, Mr Cameron, how *beautiful*! It's got your new rose in it!' The dowager's eyes misted. The garden at the Mill House was small and overshadowed, and she and this dour old Scotsman had shared thirty years of delight in flowers. 'Have you found a name for it yet?' she asked into his ear-trumpet which had proved staunchly Muriel-proof. 'Anna said you were thinking of naming it for Miss Hardwicke?'

The old man's face broke into a crafty smile. 'Aye,' he said, 'I'm calling it "Countess".'

'Just "Countess"?' said the dowager, puzzled.

The gardener nodded and began to wheeze with his special brand of private laughter. 'Just "Countess",' he said – and took his leave.

'It's time to go, my lady,' said Alice gently.

'Yes.'

Well, at least, thought the dowager, letting Alice adjust her hat, I've been spared the Herrings.

For Proom, sent to settle the Herrings' outstanding fares and bring them back to Mersham, had returned empty-handed. The Herrings, it seemed, had taken umbrage and returned to Birmingham. God did that sometimes, the dowager had observed. Pushed you to the limit and then gave you just one little bonus: in this case, a wedding without Melvyn, Myrtle and the twins.

In the east wing, James, offering to valet Uncle Sebastien, had been repulsed by the sour-faced nurse, who was now helping the old man to get ready, talking to him like a child, with a dreadful, arch coyness. 'We're going to be very important today, aren't we? We're going to give the bride away, aren't we? So we don't want any nasty cigarette ash on our nice clean clothes, do we?'

And in her bedroom the baulked and furious Lady Lavinia snapped the gold bracelet that had been the bridegroom's present to the bridesmaids on to her scraggy wrist and went along to Queen Caroline's bedchamber.

But at the sight of the bride even Lavinia's ill-temper subsided and she gave an involuntary gasp of admiration. Flanked by the obsequious Cynthia and the new Swiss maid who had providentially arrived the day before, standing erect and without a trace of nervousness in her glorious ivory dress, the future Countess of Westerholme was quite simply breathtaking.

'My prayerbook and my gloves, please,' she ordered. 'Cynthia, pick up my train. I'm ready.'

Mr Morland, robed and waiting in the vestry, came forward with outstretched hands to greet the bridegroom. If the medieval saints had gone to their deaths as to a wedding, the Earl of Westerholme, thought the kind and scholarly vicar, looked as if he was preparing to invert the trend.

'I'm afraid Mr Byrne's not here yet,' he said, concealing his surprise, for the best man had hitherto been most punctilious in the performance of his duties.

He moved over to the door and stood looking out at the congregation. Sad that the bride had no relatives at all. In the packed church only her erstwhile chaperone represented her side of the family. At the organ, Miss Frensham was peering with her half-blind eyes at the keys, anxiously memorizing the strange piece that Miss Hardwicke had ordered instead of 'Lohengrin'. The formal urns of lilies, the gardenias and carnations stiffly wired to the pew ends by the London florists who had replaced Miss Tonks and Miss Mortimer gave off an almost overpowering scent.

Mr Morland frowned. What was it that struck him as so unusual?

And then he realized. Absolutely no one was crying! Strange, thought Mr Morland, who could not remember such a thing. Exceedingly strange.

But if no one was crying there was one member of the congregation who was clearly *in extremis*. Dr Lightbody, sitting beside old Lady Templeton in the pew behind the dowager, was in a piteous state. Sweat had broken out on his forehead, his hands were shaking and once he rose in his seat and threw out an arm as if he were about to break into anguished speech.

'Are you ill?' whispered Lady Templeton, who could not approve such conduct in the House of God. 'Do you wish to go out?'

The doctor managed to shake his head, but the phantoms that had haunted him since the Mersham butler, nursing a grievance against the family as these old retainers were apt to do, had been to see him, ran riot in his brain. For the fate awaiting Muriel Hardwicke was too terrible to contemplate. This white goddess, this vessel of perfection was going – and on this very night – to be most hideously defiled by the satanic brute that she had chosen to espouse. And he had been too weak to save her. Well, it was too late now. He closed his eyes, buried his head in his hands. Let him at least not *see* . . .

Five minutes passed, ten . . . The congregation was growing a little restive. Miss Frensham's store of introductory music was running dangerously low. But it was not the bride who was causing the delay. It was the best man, who should have been here hours ago to help and succour the bridegroom.

'Of course his presence is not essential to the ceremony,' said Mr Morland. 'Even if he has the ring.'

But now Tom came striding into the vestry. His apologies were perfunctory, his expression grim and it was almost with hostility that he led Rupert – whose sense of being caught in a nightmare from which he could not wake was growing stronger by the minute – to the chancel steps.

And now it was beginning. With her old mouth nervously puckered, Miss Frensham began to play the strange piece demanded by Miss Hardwicke – and on the arm of Mr Sebastien Frayne, the bride entered.

A gasp of sheer admiration greeted her. A slightly different gasp followed the entry of the two adult bridesmaids in their pink ruffles and petalled caps.

Then a rustling, whispers of surprise, of indignation, murmurs of disappointment, puzzled looks . . .

The bride reached the altar rails, handed her prayer-book to the Lady Lavinia; Mr Morland cleared his throat, when the voice of the bridegroom was heard saying clearly and imperiously, 'Wait! Where is the third bridesmaid? Where is Ollie Byrne?'

Tom turned to his friend. Everything in him longed to blurt out what Muriel had done. Longed to show him Ollie as he had left her, lying white and despairing in her bed because there was nothing, now, to get up for and nowhere, now, to go. Ollie, who had seen so totally and searingly through Muriel's concern for her health, her unctuous bribery . . . who had told the nursemaid coming to brush her marigold curls that there was no point because cripples didn't need to be tidy, and now lay with her face to the wall beyond reach of comfort or of hope.

But Muriel, shocked at a voice raised in church, whispered, 'Hush, dear. Ollie isn't well, it seems,' – and Mr Morland bent his head and began to repeat what are surely the best-loved words in the world:

Dearly beloved, we are gathered here in the sight of God and in the face of this congregation, to join together this Man and this Woman in Holy Matrimony . . .

But Tom's disclosure would have been superfluous. Rupert had understood, and as clearly as if he were again present he remembered Ollie's sad little question in the taxi on the way from Fortman's and his own answer: 'If you are not a bridesmaid at my wedding then there will *be* no wedding, and that I swear.'

Only there was a wedding. He was in the midst of it. He was marrying Muriel Hardwicke.

. . . but reverently, discreetly, advisedly, soberly and in the fear of God, duly considering the causes for which Matrimony was ordained.

First it was ordained for the procreation of children . . .

In his pew, Dr Lightbody groaned. The procreation of children yes . . . But what children? What monsters, what fiends in human form would that lewd and treacherous earl beget on the unsullied body of his bride? Oh, God, was there no one to warn her, no one to whom she could turn?

. . . for the mutual society, help and comfort that the one ought to have of the other, both in prosperity and adversity. Into which holy estate these two persons present come now to be joined. Therefore if any man can show any just cause why they may not lawfully be joined together . . .

I gave my word to Ollie, thought Rupert – and lifted his head. But it was not his own voice which suddenly tore through the church: the frenzied voice of a human soul in torment, crying: 'Stop! Oh, stop! This marriage must not be!'

Mr Morland looked up. The startled silence which followed was broken only by the small exclamation which escaped Lady Templeton as the doctor, stumbling from his pew, stepped heavily on her bunion.

'It must not be!' repeated Dr Lightbody, his pale eyes glittering now with a Messianic fervour. He brushed aside the Lady Lavinia, reached the altar rails: 'This lovely woman has been most hideously deceived!'

The vicar blinked. In her pew, the dowager, who had read *Jane Eyre* no less than seven times, shook her head in disbelief. And Muriel, within minutes of her goal, turned furiously on the doctor.

'You seem to have taken leave of your senses, Dr Lightbody.' And to the vicar, 'Pray, proceed.'

'No, no!' The doctor was now quite beside himself. 'You must listen, Miss Hardwicke. You are in danger

326

'– terrible danger! There is tainted blood in the Wester-holmes!'

'Nonsense!' But Muriel's pansy-blue eyes had dilated in sudden fear. 'It isn't true, Rupert?'

'Of course it isn't true,' said Rupert contemptuously.

'It *is* true, it *is* true!' screamed Lightbody. He pointed with a shaking finger at the earl. 'Ask him what is hidden in the folly in the woods. Ask him, Miss Hardwicke. Ask him!'

The whispers and murmurs among the congregation were growing to a climax.

'Ask him,' yelled Dr Lightbody. 'And if you don't believe me, ask *him*!' And he swivelled round to point at Mersham's butler, sitting composed and immaculate in the back pew. 'Go on! Ask Proom!'

The name, with its overtones of high respectability, rang through the church. Mr Morland, who had been about to order the doctor from the church, laid down his prayerbook. And Mr Cyril Proom rose slowly and majestically to his feet.

'Please come forward, Mr Proom,' said the vicar. 'I'm sure there is a perfectly respectable explanation for this gentleman's remarks.'

Steadily, with his usual measured tread, Mr Proom advanced up the aisle. As he drew level with her pew, the dowager threw him a glance of total puzzlement and he held her eye for a long moment before he moved up to the altar rails and, bending his head respectfully, addressed the vicar.

'I'm afraid Dr Lightbody is perfectly correct, sir. I felt it advisable to make certain disclosures to him in view of his well-known interest in eugenics. And in any case,' he said, 'I am owed several months' wages by the family.'

The lie, in its pointless blatancy, momentarily pierced Rupert's sense of nightmare and he narrowed his eyes.

'*What is in the folly?*' demanded Muriel, who was no longer calm. 'Tell me at *once*!'

'Imbeciles!' cried Dr Lightbody. 'I've seen them! Dreadful, dribbling imbeciles. And they're his *cousins*! His *first* cousins. By blood.'

'It isn't true! Rupert, tell me it isn't true!'

'He won't tell you – he won't admit it, he wants your money. But I tell you, I've seen them! I saw them last night. He keeps them locked up in that tower and they're like animals – worse than animals.'

Mr Morland's bewilderment was total. He'd been Vicar of Mersham for twenty years and never heard a whisper of scandal. But could *Proom* be lying?

'Is it really so?' he asked the butler, above the growing uproar in the church.

'I'm afraid so, sir. The family's given it about that the folly's haunted by the ghost of Sir Montague Frayne, so nobody goes near it. But the screams – well, they're not the screams of ghosts, sir; they're the screams of his lordship's relatives.'

Rupert had been listening to this farrago of nonsense in silence. Now he turned and raised enquiring eyes at his mother.

The dowager rose and slipped from her pew. There was the sound of tearing silk as she threw up her arms to embrace her son. Then:

'Oh, Rupert, darling,' she exclaimed in tones of theatrical despair, 'don't you see? The game's up!'

Proom had been against Myrtle Herring pretending to be a chicken laying an egg. It was his opinion that people asked to simulate mental derangement always picked on chickens and the routine, wing flapping, squawking performance was invariably hackneyed and unsatisfactory.

Myrtle, however, had convinced him. Myrtle had been in vaudeville and during their run-through in the folly, sitting atop a pile of straw, brought to her frenzied cluckings such an extreme of gynaecological anguish rising – as she examined the imagined egg – to such awed and ecstatic triumph, that Proom had been deeply impressed.

He had expected to encounter some difficulty in persuading the Herrings, as he conveyed them by a roundabout route to the back gates of Mersham, to follow his plan. True, they were lucky not to be in prison. Still, they had expected to come to a wedding. Instead, he proposed that they should give a full performance in the folly tower for the benefit of Dr Lightbody, spend the night there (albeit surrounded by oil stoves, mattresses and a hamper of food sent up

329

by Mrs Park) and then – all traces of these comforts having been removed – give a repeat performance should the doctor decide to speak.

No persuasion had been needed. The sight of one hundred pounds in notes with the promise of another three hundred to come, should they succeed in convincing Miss Hardwicke that they really were deranged, had stilled all doubts. Not only that, but in setting the deception up they had proved to be cooperative and creative. The scruples that had troubled Proom and Mrs Park, the accusation they had levelled at themselves of appearing to make light of the mentally afflicted, did not trouble the Herrings. Nothing troubled the Herrings faced with four hundred pounds.

Towards the folly, then, in its setting of deep woodland, came the wedding party. Proom was at its head, his expression grave, his bearing deferential. Dr Lightbody followed, the bearer of terrible news, the man who had taken fate into his own hands and felt the decision pressing on him almost unbearably. Then came Muriel, holding up the train of her dress, still stately but no longer composed, and beside her, Rupert, convinced that his grasp on reality had finally slipped away. The dowager, the old Templetons, and Mr Morland, escorted by Tom Byrne, brought up the rear. Everyone else had been persuaded to stay behind.

The padlock on the door yielded to Proom's fingers, the door creaked back. A smell of damp and decay met them, cobwebs brushed their faces . . .

'But this is disgusting,' said Muriel. 'What—'

330

She was arrested by a scream. A truly horrible scream, followed by a burst of cackling laughter.

'This way, miss,' said Proom – and led the way up the round, dank stairs to the first of the tower rooms.

The thing that lay on the floor must once have been human, but it did not seem human now. Its face was livid and distorted, it had burrowed into the straw like an animal, its filthy fingers tore and clawed at its ragged clothes.

'Good heavens!' Old Lady Templeton was deeply shocked. 'It can't be . . . surely that's poor dear Melvyn, isn't it?'

'Quite so, my lady.' Proom turned to Miss Hardwicke. 'This . . . er, gentleman, is his lordship's first cousin, Mr Melvyn Herring.'

'Oh my God!' Muriel's poise was shattered at last. She was as pale as her wedding dress. 'No, I don't believe it. His *first* cousin!'

'Yes, miss. You will see he has the Templeton eyes and – oh, careful, miss.'

For the thing had arched its back, blobs of spittle came from its mouth – and suddenly it sprang.

It was Dr Lightbody who saved Muriel, dragging her back before the demented creature could sink its teeth into her hand.

'He's been like this for a while, miss, and I'm afraid he's getting worse.'

'But there are others,' cried Dr Lightbody. 'Dearest Miss Hardwicke, there are others! This monster has been allowed to marry, to beget other tainted beings.'

Proom inclined his head. 'Dr Lightbody is correct. If you would care to follow me.'

They ascended another dark and curving staircase to the next room. On the floor lay two enormous boys, to all outward appearance, boys of fourteen or fifteen. But they wore nappies, their fingers were in their mouths; one drooled, the other hiccupped . . .

'Master Dennis and Master Donald Herring,' announced Proom. 'As you see, they have remained in an infantile stage. The doctor gives no hope of improvement.'

'It isn't possible!'

But even as she spoke, Muriel saw that it *was* possible. Like the mad thing that was their father, these boys had the grey, gold-flecked eyes, the short nose of the Templetons.

A last flight of steps and they reached the top of the tower.

Myrtle had made a splendid nest. There were feathers in her hair, a deep and committed broodiness lit up her features and, even as they watched, she emitted a loud and fulfilling squawk . . .

'And this is *Mrs* Herring,' said Proom. 'She, of course,' he added conscientiously, 'is no blood relation.'

But Myrtle Herring had been too much for Rupert. And collapsing against a wall, he began to laugh.

It was this laugh which finished Muriel. Hysteria, another dangerous mental aberration, began in just this unbridled way – and stepping forward she slapped him hard across the cheek.

'You swine! You unmitigated, vile, scheming swine! Trying to get my money out of me! Trying to trap me into a marriage so that I could bear you some more deformed and squirming . . . *things*. I'll have you for this, Rupert! You'll pay me back every penny I put into that estate – every brass farthing, *and* the damages I'll sue you for!'

'Oh, Miss Hardwicke, if you would only take my protection!' cried the doctor. 'We could go to America! I could make you the priestess of the New Eugenics. You would be a goddess to me all my life!'

'And your wife?' said Muriel coldly.

'She is dead.'

Muriel registered this information with a flicker of her pansy eyes. Then she began to remove her engagement ring. The doctor's pale, beautifully manicured hand, closing over the solitaire diamond like a vice, prevented her.

'I'm sure his lordship would want you to keep it as a memento.'

Rupert, still weak from laughter, nodded.

'Yes, indeed! Do please keep it, Muriel.'

'Very well.' She replaced the ring, gathered up her train. 'Come, Dr Lightbody.'

'Ronald,' he begged.

'Come, Ronald,' said Muriel Hardwicke, and with a last look of disgust and loathing, swept down the stairs.

16

'I can't write a letter like that, Mr Proom,' said Mrs Bassenthwaite weakly. 'Not to a countess, I can't.'

Ten days had passed since the interrupted wedding and Mrs Bassenthwaite, released from hospital, was convalescing on the sofa in the housekeeper's room.

'I'd write it myself,' said Proom, 'but it would be better coming from you. More correct, you being in charge of the maids.'

Mr Proom had emerged as a local hero, sharing with Leo Rabinovitch and the Herrings, the acclaim of the entire district during the merrymaking which had followed the departure of Miss Hardwicke. Even the knowledge that Mersham would almost certainly have to be sold in order to meet the demands of Miss Hardwicke's solicitors had not diminished the delight of the villagers, the tenants and the gentry in being rid of a woman so universally detested. To the general happiness, however, there was one exception – the earl himself, who had put Mersham's affairs into the hands of his agent and was about to depart for the Hindu Kush.

'I'll tell you what to say,' persisted Proom – and went to fetch the inkwell and the paper.

'There's a letter for you, Anna!' said Pinny, looking at the postmark and trying not to let the relief show in her voice.

It was Petya, coming to London to greet Niannka and discuss the sale of the jewels, who had told them about the interrupted wedding. Pinny, watching Anna, had seen her turn almost in an instant from the kind of thing one expected to find under a pile of sacking after an earthquake or a famine into a radiant and enchanting girl. Anna, discussing with the delighted Mr Stewart at Aspell's, the jewellers, what he assured them would be 'the sale of the century'; Anna, helping her mother buy presents for the other emigrés, treasuring the conviction that it was through Rupert's good offices that Niannka had been found, was the Anna of the old St Petersburg days with a new glow, a new maturity.

But that had been more than a week ago. Since then, Pinny had watched, day by day, the glow lessen, the joy ebb as the postman still brought no letter, the doorbell still failed to herald the longed-for visitor.

Anna had opened her letter, begun to read – and as she did so the eagerness and expectation in her face was replaced by puzzlement.

'It is from the housekeeper at Mersham,' she said, her voice bleak. 'She says that I have broken my contract. I was engaged till the end of July so I have five more days of work owing to them. She refuses to send the rest of my clothes or Selina Strickland until I make up the time.'

'Well, really!' Pinny was outraged. 'I've never heard anything so ridiculous.'

'No, they are correct. I thought as I had not been paid for the last week it would be all right but she says not. Rup . . . the earl . . . has already left for India and the house must be made ready to go up for sale so there is a great deal to do.'

'You aren't *going*, Anna?'

'I must, Pinny. Petya will be at his school camp in Scotland so it will be all right. If there is work owing,' said Anna, lifting her chin, 'it must be paid.'

'You're to treat her exactly as before,' Proom had instructed his staff. 'She may be a countess, but while she's here she's still a maid.'

'I can't!' wailed Pearl. 'I'll curtsy to her, see if I don't.'

'You will do nothing of the kind,' said Mr Proom – but he was not as relaxed as he pretended, and secretly felt outraged by what he was about to do.

The outrage, the embarrassment, lasted exactly as long as it took Anna, in a blue cotton dress, carrying a straw basket, to cross the kitchen floor and be enveloped in Mrs Park's motherly arms. But the instructions she received from Mr Proom when the greetings and gossip were over and she had changed into her uniform made her for a moment doubt her ears.

'You wish me to *wait at table*? In the *dining room*?'

For the butler's view on women actually waiting at table, with its middle-class overtones, were well known.

'One must move with the times,' said Mr Proom portentously. 'It is only a small dinner: Lady Westerholme, Mr Frayne, Lord and Lady Byrne and a Mr and Mrs Clarke-Binningfold who are considering the purchase of Mersham. His lordship, as you know, has already left.'

'Yes,' said Anna, managing to keep her voice steady. 'I had heard.'

For she knew, now, that Rupert had not cared, had not meant what he'd said in the garden, wanted only to be free of her and all entanglements.

'The meal is a simple one,' Proom continued. 'Grapefruit, *Consommé Beauharnais, Sole Marie Louise*, carbonnade of beef, macaroon *soufflé* and the dessert. James'll be at the sideboard, Sid'll be handing the main dishes. All you have to do is follow him with the vegetables and the sauces and help clear. Can you manage that?'

'Yes, sir,' said Anna, rallying. 'Because it is all in the *Domestic Compendium*. How I must approach from the left to serve but from the right to remove the plates, and how I must clear the crumbs with a napkin because

337

a crumb brush is *déclassé* and how I must not breathe 'eavily and not address the guests.'

'You must certainly not do *that*,' said Proom.

The dinner party, whose dénouement was subsequently reported in detail by Sid and James to a spellbound audience below stairs, began quietly with the consumption of grapefruit and some rather desultory conversation. The dowager was discussing the launching of the new airship with Lord Byrne, Mrs Clarke-Binningfold was giving Uncle Sebastien her views on The Fecklessness of the Poor – when the door opened to admit Anna, her head bent in profound concentration over a *famille rose* tureen of Mrs Park's incomparable chicken soup.

Gravely, aware of the honour that Proom had done her, she began to move towards the sideboard.

'*You!*'

Anna jumped, clung desperately to her tureen – and looked up to find that the Earl of Westerholme, supposedly absent in the Hindu Kush, was glaring at her from the head of the table like an assassin out of *Boris Godunov*.

'What the devil are you doing here?' continued the earl, his customary good manners quite banished by the shock of seeing this girl whose treachery had not prevented her from haunting his dreams, sleeping and waking, ever since she had gone.

Anna, resolutely maintaining silence, had reached the sanctuary of the sideboard and put down her tureen. Rupert was mad, he no longer loved her, but he was *here* and there was nothing she could do to still the pounding of her heart.

'Rupert, you really must not speak to the maids like that,' said the dowager, suddenly looking extremely happy and aware that she had been less than just to dear, departed Hatty Dalrymple.

'Who *is* this person?' said Mrs Clarke-Binningfold, greatly displeased.

'An excellent question,' said Rupert. He turned to Anna, who was now clearing the finger bowls, totally concentrated on her task. 'You don't seem to be wearing a wedding ring, so may we assume that we are not yet addressing the Princess Chirkovsky?'

James had served the soup, Sid had begun to hand it round. Anna, still resolutely maintaining silence, picked up the silver filigree basket of bread rolls and followed him.

'I asked you a question, Anna.'

She had reached Lady Byrne on Rupert's left. 'I am not permitted to address the guests,' she said under her breath.

Rupert's hand came up and fastened round her wrist. 'This guest, however, you *will* address. Please answer my question. When are you getting married? Where is your fiancé?'

But Anna had now had enough. Disengaging her wrist, holding with both hands on to her basket, she drew breath.

'Very well. You have, of course, ruined this dinner

party in which I wished to wait perfectly at table so as to help with the giving of more responsibility to women. So I will tell you, first that I think you are mad, and second, that I am not going to marry Sergei because that is not how I love him and in any case I do not wish to have children who will have breast blisters – only, I must say chest blisters, I think, because this is a country of hypocrisy and coldness where breasts are not respectable. And also Sergei has proposed to the Baroness Rakov, although I have told him it is not necessary because we are now rich and will of course share everything, but he says she is *tranquille* and will keep away from him the other women. And last, if I had not been *assured*,' she said, glaring at Sid and James, 'that you were already in the Kush, where you absolutely belong because it is full of stones and ice, I would never have come back,' she finished – and burst into tears.

'Don't, Anna! Ah, don't, my darling,' said Rupert. He pushed back his chair, removed, with ineffable tenderness, her basket of rolls and, quite impervious to the assembled company, gathered her into his arms. 'Only, you see, I saw you in the garden with the prince. You were hanging from his arms like . . .' He broke off, even now racked by the memory.

'A dishcloth?' suggested Anna.

'*What?*'

Anna, her career abandoned, was now ready to converse. 'In *La Fille Mal Gardée*, which is a most *beautiful* ballet, she hangs exactly in this way from the shoulder of the hero, very soft and . . . limp, you know, like a cloth and at the same time she does little *battements* with her feet. It is in Act Three and *very* moving; you will like it very much.'

'Shall I, my love?' said Rupert, dabbing gently at her eyes and nose.

The door opened. Proom stood on the threshold.

'Ah, Proom,' said the earl. 'Just the man! We want some champagne. The Veuve Cliquot '83 that you've been guarding with your life.'

'I have it here, my lord,' said Proom, advancing. 'Thinking you might be requiring it, I took the liberty of putting it on ice earlier in the day. I think you will find it to your satisfaction.'

The wedding of Anna and Rupert the following June was not a quiet wedding. For one thing, absolutely everybody cried. Miss Frensham, preparing to thump her way lustily through 'Lohengrin', cried, as did Miss Tonks and Miss Mortimer, who had framed the altar steps in an entrancing riot of delphiniums, larkspur and phlox. The Ballets Russes cried, the dowager soaked three handkerchiefs before the bride even set foot in the church, Kira, who had come from Paris with her banker fiancé, wept elegantly into her muff. Susie Byrne did not actually cry, but she seemed to find it necessary to polish her spectacles a great many times and Hannah Rabinovitch, sitting beside her daughter, was quite simply awash.

Nor were the servants at the back of the church any

more restrained. Mrs Park, next to her devoted Win, was already blotched and swollen; Peggy and Pearl, Louise and Florence and the two pretty housemaids engaged with an eye on Uncle Sebastien had completely ruined, with their sniffs and gulps, the effect of their morning ablutions in the new attic bathrooms. Mrs Proom, in her wheelchair, had howled herself into hiccups and outside, Baskerville, shut into the gigantic limousine which had been the Baroness Rakov's engagement present to Sergei, enduring both social exclusion and the company of the dachshund Pupsik, threw back his head and bayed in agony.

To this outburst of emotion there was one notable exception: Heslop's formidable butler, Hawkins, sitting with disgust beside Old Niannka and listening with loathing to the raucous blubbering of this malodorous foreigner who was now permanently installed at Heslop, trying to set up icons in the billiard room and driving him insane. For it was Niannka who had cut through the gentle persuasions and medical advice which had followed Ollie's despairing collapse on the night of the ball. What exactly had happened when Anna took her ancient nurse to visit Ollie no one knew. But the old woman had banished everyone from the nursery, wax had been asked for, and pins, and in the silence that followed, Ollie's voice had been heard gleefully joining in the utterance of unspeakable Russian curses. Minna, returning to find a silver-wigged and unmistakable effigy of Muriel Hardwicke spreadeagled on the floor, had been shocked and angry – until she saw Ollie's bright face; since when Old Niannka could do no wrong.

But now the bridal car drew up and, on the arms of Petya, almost as tall now as she was herself, Anna walked towards the porch. Her dress was simple and unadorned, she carried only a bouquet of the roses that Mr Cameron had so cunningly named for her, but Countess Grazinsky, waiting to adjust her daughter's veil, had to turn her head away, so overcome was she by what she saw in Anna's face.

'Here are your gloves, dear,' said Pinny, trying – and failing – to achieve some kind of briskness. And then, 'It's time . . .'

But as Anna stepped inside the church, saw the sea of faces, heard the pounding music, she faltered and stopped. It was too much . . . the gods would not permit such joy.

'I'm afraid,' she whispered, the colour draining from her face. 'I'm terribly afraid.'

A small voice, brisk and marvellously motherly, came from behind her.

'That's *silly*, Anna,' said the Honourable Olive. 'Being afraid is *silly*, you know it is.'

Anna turned and met the shining blue eyes of her chief and only bridesmaid. The Honourable Olive's dress, like Anna's, had been made by Mrs Bunford. The child had been given free reign for she was all of nine years old now, her natural taste beginning to form, and the white wreath and muslin dress were as simple as Anna's own. But if ever there was a bridesmaid suffused with the sheer joy of living on such a splendid and dazzling day, that bridesmaid was Ollie Byrne.

And Anna smiled and laid her hand lightly on the bright curls, and turned to walk steadily to where Rupert waited: a man who had passed beyond all doubt and uncertainty — a man who had come home.